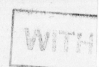

ALSO BY KATHERINE JOHN

Trevor Joseph Mysteries

WITHOUT TRACE
ISBN 9781905170263 £6.99

MIDNIGHT MURDERS
ISBN 9781905170272 £6.99

MURDER OF A DEAD MAN
ISBN 9781905170289 £6.99

THE CORPSE'S TALE (Quick read)
ISBN 9781905170319 £2.99

And, coming out in summer 2008:

A WELL-DESERVED MURDER
ISBN 9781906125141 £6.99

Other Books

THE AMBER KNIGHT
ISBN 9781905170623 £6.99

BY ANY NAME
ISBN 9781905170258 £6.99

www.accentpress.co.uk

For all the Kellys and Alecs in South Wales, especially the Valleys. I hope that one day they will get the help they so desperately need and deserve before we lose any more young lives.

CHAPTER ONE

The night porter who manned the desk in the foyer of the luxury block of flats told everyone who would listen that he was a student. But he rarely opened the text books he carried. Tonight, he'd read the *Sun* that the day porter had left, cover to cover.

He turned back to page 3, studied the topless model girl and wondered what exactly the two 'lady friends' of Mr Jones in Nine were doing to him. Usually they were in and out in an hour. Tonight it had been ... he looked at the clock. Ten past twelve. Three hours and ten minutes .He pictured the scene ... Mr Jones stretched out on his bed, the girls bending over him topless, wearing only stockings and suspenders ... red or black ...

But there might not have been two of them because he thought he had seen the blonde sneaking up the service stairs to a higher floor. He couldn't be sure because the CCTV had blacked out. The cameras on the service stairs and top floor were always blacking out. The day shift porter insisted Miss Smith from the top floor tampered with them so they wouldn't record the 'clients' she entertained in her apartment, although some of them were in and out of the building in a matter of minutes. He didn't believe it, or half the things the day porter said. A fantasist, the man also insisted he'd once enjoyed a threesome with two young actresses who'd been featured in *Doctor Who*, although no one who worked in the building had ever seen him with a woman.

The automated glass front doors slid open. He started guiltily. He was supposed to lock them at midnight to keep out what management called 'riff-raff'. The residents had keys. Not that they had to use them with twenty-four hour porterage and security.

Fortunately the woman who swept in wasn't one of the miseries who complained every time he left the desk to make himself a cup of tea. He suspected that some tuned the security monitors in their apartments to cover reception, in the hope of catching him breaking his rules of employment.

He gave the attractive blonde the full benefit of the toothy smile he practised in front of the mirror every afternoon.

'Good evening, Miss Smith.'

Tall, slender, dressed in a hip-hugging mini-skirt and shoestring-strapped black vest, a tan leather jacket slung over her shoulder, her legs encased in matching thigh-high boots, Amber Smith exuded sex. Tantalizing, exotic, anything goes – pornographic day-and-night-long sex. The blood coursed headily, swiftly through his veins as she approached him. He was grateful the desk was high enough to conceal the bulge in his trousers.

Preoccupied, she walked past him without a look or a muttered, 'Hi.'

No smile. No 'How's it going, George?' Not that his name was George, or he'd ever corrected her. Not even 'Hi.'

Hurt by her indifference, he watched her hit the button for the lift. He could see by the lights it was already on its way down. The door opened and Mr

Jones's 'lady friends' emerged. He could never make up his mind which he preferred, the six-foot redhead or the petite blonde.

'Amber, darling, long time no see.' The blonde kissed the air either side of Amber's face. The redhead followed suit.

'Come for a drink with us?' the redhead invited.

'Some other time, Cyn, Lucy.' Amber entered the lift and pressed the button.

'Hello, ladies.' The porter eyed the enormous bags they carried. Not for the first time he speculated on their contents. He had even drawn up a list after an afternoon spent in a sex shop.

'Hello, gorgeous.' The redhead chucked him under the chin and followed the blonde out of the building. He locked the doors after them.

Disappointed, restless, he returned to his desk and the page three girl. He decided she couldn't hold a candle to Miss Amber Smith from Flat 36 – or the redhead – or the blonde ...

Amber Smith stared blindly at her reflection in the mirrors that walled the lift and mulled over the meeting that had cut her evening short. She knew she'd been stupid to hand over her spare key. There was no predicting what she'd find behind her front door. But what else could she have done? Blood was thicker than water – except in the case of the mother who'd given her and her sisters less thought than a cat did kittens after she'd spawned them.

The lift hit her floor. She walked out into the corridor to her pride and joy – her top floor apartment. In estate agents' terms it was 'compact' but, the way she was making money, it wouldn't be long before she'd be able to move on to bigger and better – her own – not rented.

She inserted her key in the lock and tried to turn it. It seemed reluctant to open. She set her shoulder against the door and pushed.

The explosion shook the building, rocking the foyer ten floors down and activating the fire alarm. The porter forgot his training in emergency procedures and rushed to the lift. He reeled back when black smoke clouded out of the doors, fogging the air and scalding his lungs. He staggered back to his desk, picked up his mobile phone and master keys, left his text books, unlocked the doors and rushed outside. People were hurtling down the staircases. Screams and cries mingled with the wails of sirens in the streets. Within seconds the tranquil marble, steel and mirror-panelled reception area was transformed into smut-filled bedlam.

Emergency vehicles and personnel encircled the building within five minutes. The residents were concerned with preserving themselves and their possessions, the porter with counting the residents, the fire crews and police with saving lives. No one looked at the bank of security monitors above the porter's desk. If they had, they might have spotted a hooded figure running down the service staircase to the basement. There, it lurked in the shadows behind the pillars that flanked the steel doors, designed to keep vagrants out of the underground car park.

When Mr Edwards from Flat 15 ran down to save his beloved Porsche, they might also have seen the figure rolling out, under the barrier, after Mr

Edwards drove out.

Head down, the figure walked quickly – but not too quickly so as to get noticed – up to the street level, wove through the gathering crowd and out onto the pavement skirting the dual carriageway. There was an underpass. Within seconds even the figure's shadow had melted into the night.

Kelly Smith exchanged the sweltering heat and noise of the packed interior of the penthouse for the comparative cool of one of the balconies that encircled the open-plan living area. Closing the patio doors against the ear-shattering music of the live band, she leant against the railings and stared down at the rows of pristine white yachts moored in the marina, fifteen stories below. At ninety-five feet, the largest and most luxurious, *Lucky Star* dwarfed the smaller craft, *Lucky Me* and *Lucky Charm* that were berthed either side of it. *Lucky Star* had three 'state rooms', a Jacuzzi on the fly bridge, and had recently benefited from a no-expense-spared, luxury refit. Kelly had been given a tour but the memory was too recent and raw for her to want to dwell on the experience.

She turned to the concrete shoreline that crusted the Bay. Lights glittered, their reflections dancing in the shimmering waters, illuminating the tides of people that ebbed and flowed in and out of the café bars and restaurants that thronged the water's edge. Snatches of music drifted in the still, warm air as doors opened and closed. She felt a sudden desire to be down there, with nothing more on her mind than which bar to wander into and, how to catch the eye of the first boy she fancied. A blast of music sent her nerves jangling. The living room door opened behind her.

'Hi.' Jake Phillips closed the doors before handing her one of the cans of beer he'd filched from the ice chest built into the Jacuzzi. 'You're one of the Smith girls, aren't you? Keira?'

'Kelly,' she corrected.

'Jake Phillips. I was in school with Marissa and I knew Amber well. I always thought of her as a bright, pretty girl who would go far. I'm sorry about what happened to her.'

'Isn't everyone?' Kelly shrugged. Tears started in her eyes.

'I hadn't seen her in years. How is Marissa?'

'We haven't kept in touch.'

Jake didn't have to ask why. Marissa's nickname in school had been Snow White. It had nothing to do with the fairy tale and everything to do with the amount of white powder she could pack up her nose. 'Last I heard she was living here, on the Bay,' he said.

'That must have been more than two years ago. She lost her job, couldn't make the rent.'

Jake picked up on Kelly's reluctance to talk, but he persisted. 'You look like Amber.'

'It's the hair. Me and Amber used to steal Marissa's hair dye when we were kids. I never bothered to change the colour.' She ripped open her can.

He stood beside her. 'Fabulous view. Every day I wake up in this place, I'm glad I'm alive. Doesn't it make you feel as though you're on top of the world?'

She glanced through the glass doors into the marbled splendour of the open-plan living area. 'You live here?'

'I do.'

'Lucky you. Amber always said you'd do well.'

'Not that well. I'm Damian Darrow's lodger and I pay way below the going rate.' He noted her reaction. 'You know him?'

'Everyone knows Damian.'

'You don't like him?' Jake guessed from her tone.

'I'm not stupid enough to slag him off to his lodger. And everyone knows he's paying for this party to launch his new band.'

Jake watched the band through the glass doors. Dressed in Victorian corsets and white silk stockings they were gyrating their way through a cover of the 1960s hit, *Little Children*, which, given that they were all girls, lent the lyrics about 'kissing your sister' a whole new meaning. 'They're not bad.'

Kelly made a face. 'They're not good either.'

'You know Damian well?'

'What's with the questions?'

'Making conversation.'

'Sounds like a police interview to me.'

'I owe Damian,' he explained. 'Not just because he charges me below the going rate for a room in this place. But I know he can rub people up the wrong way.'

'Damian's all right,' she murmured unconvincingly.

7

'He knows how to have fun and he likes having people around.' He touched his can to hers. 'To us and the steep climb up.'

'You made it, Jake, not me.'

'You're at the best party with the best people.' He flicked a comma of thick black hair from his eyes and preened theatrically, tongue in cheek. 'Not to mention *moi*.'

'You know why I'm here?'

'Because you're invited?'

'Like most of the girls, I'm here because I'm bought and paid for.'

Stung by her bitterness, he said. 'Don't put yourself down. We all sell ourselves to a greater or lesser extent.'

'When did you last let someone fuck you for money?' she snapped.

'Showing your temper again, Kelly.' Mike Knight left the living room and joined them. 'I warned you an hour ago, sour face never won brave knight.'

'I see no bloody knights here.'

Mike pulled a cigarette lighter from his pocket. 'My darling Kelly, you've a body that would stop the traffic on the M4 if only you smiled. As it is, one look from you is enough to make any man reach for the indigestion pills. You're what – eighteen?'

'Sixteen.'

Jake flicked through his memory. 'Amber was eighteen, Marissa twenty-two. You're …'

'Sixteen last month,' she reiterated sharply.

Jake did a quick calculation. The youngest of the three Smith girls would be fourteen, but, as Mike had left the door to the living room open, he kept his thoughts to himself. The band had finished their number and were taking a break. A hubbub of conversation had replaced the throbbing music but they might be overheard and, if whoever had hired the girls – probably Damian, discovered that Kelly was under-age, she'd be blasted for breaking a law that could attract police attention to a party where he'd seen enough minor dealers operating to keep the courts busy for a month.

Mike took a tube of vodka from his well-stocked shirt pocket and upended it into his mouth. 'I told you what to do if you're unhappy in your work, Kelly.'

She turned back to the view of the bay. 'Servicing rugby teams after a match is bloody hard and bruising work.'

'A chef can't pick and choose his customers, darling. Neither can you. As it is, you're vastly overpaid.' Mike was the prop forward for the film-school rugby team.

'You've never paid for my services.'

'Can I help it if people love me enough to cover my expenses?' He looked into the living room. A redhead, Cynara, and Mira, a blonde, were stripping to the accompaniment of wolf whistles and jeers from a crowd of jostling men who were fighting to push bank notes into their G-strings. 'Given the look on your face, it's no wonder you're out here and the other girls are picking up tips in there.'

'I'm taking a break. I work hard for my money.' Kelly lifted her chin defiantly.

Jake attempted to cool the atmosphere. 'Kelly

9

and I come from the same neck of the woods.'

'Backwoods?' Mike mocked.

Jake winked at Kelly. 'Let's say it's a place that fosters ambition.'

'Marissa was stupid. She made good money for a couple of years but she spent every penny, unlike Amber who died in her own place. And like Amber I'll be moving into my own flat right here on the Bay in a couple of years.' Kelly eyed Mike, daring him to contradict her. 'You'll see.'

Jake commented before Mike could. 'I'll be your first visitor.'

Whether Kelly would succeed in her ambition to buy a place on the Bay or not, Jake knew about the desperation that drove people to do whatever it took to get off the estate they had grown up on. Determined to give him a better start in life than his friends, his mother had held down three jobs to pay for tutors to supplement the inadequate education offered by the local comprehensive. He had won a place at university and, unlike Amber, thanks to his mother's foresight, her modest savings and help from his uncle, he'd been able to take it. Now he was earning enough to keep himself and to slip his mother a hundred quid a month; it had enabled her to rent a flat in a quiet street close to the city centre.

Kelly tensed when Damian and Lloyd swaggered out onto the balcony and joined them. They couldn't have been more unlike. Damian was blond with cruel good looks and the over-muscled physique of a personal trainer. Lloyd was short and squat, with nondescript brown eyes and mousy hair that was already thinning even though, like Jake, Mike and

10

Damian, he was in his early twenties.

Damian raised his voice. 'You owe me that paper on special effects …'

'You'll get it tomorrow, Damian,' Lloyd promised, trying to appease him.

'Tonight. I need time to read it before I hand it in …' Damian slurred. He staggered and grabbed the balcony rail.

'I want to go through it one last time. I haven't even printed it off …'

'Darlings, it's party, not work, time.' Jake pulled a couple of vodka tubes and spliffs from Mike's shirt pocket and pushed a spliff into Damian's mouth. Jake wasn't gay but for some peculiar reason Damian found it amusing whenever he adopted a gay persona. Like all Damian's flatmates, Jake had discovered the easiest way of deflecting an argument, before Damian resorted to using his fists, was distracting him.

Annoyed, but too wary of Damian to show it, Mike retrieved the second spliff before Jake could use it. He pushed it into his mouth but was careful to light Damian's before his own.

Damian drew the smoke into his lungs. 'Lucy?' He shouted to one of the girls inside. 'We need a tray of tubes out here, now!'

'Want another of my special presents?' Mike slobbered over Kelly's neck.

'Thanks, but no thanks, Mike. One a night is enough.'

'Your loss, my gain.' Offended by her rebuff, he moved away from her.

'There are friendlier tarts on offer,' Lloyd moved

11

towards Lucy.

'Not for people who are working off a favour to me,' Damian snarled.

'You'll get it first thing in the morning, Damian,' Lloyd pleaded.

'It had better be good …'

'It'll be perfect.'

'Straight A?'

'Guaranteed,' Lloyd said emphatically.

Damian grabbed the well-endowed muscular girl who emerged from the living room with a tray of gleaming blue and red vodka-filled test tubes. He took the tray from her, and handed one to Kelly. 'Drink it,' he ordered when Kelly shook her head. 'This is a party not a bloody funeral.'

Kelly upended it in her mouth and made a face as she swallowed.

'Who said you could go?' Damian thrust the girl who had brought the tubes at Lloyd. 'Lloyd, if you're not straight A grateful in the morning, you'll be out on your arse tomorrow afternoon.'

'I'll be grateful, Damian.'

Damian grabbed Lucy's breast through her transparent blouse and tweaked her nipple before sliding his hand under her mini-skirt and pushing it up to her waist. He slapped her bare buttocks. 'You, Lloyd here, bouncy bouncy. Make it special, but not too special. He's got a hard morning's work ahead of him.'

'For you, Damian darling, anything.'

Jake noted Lucy's subservience and insincere tone. From the deference accorded Damian by all the working girls who frequented his parties, he'd suspected for months that Damian had more than a casual interest in the local parlours. Darrow senior was rumoured to be a billionaire. He certainly didn't deny his only son anything, but, apart from his casinos, Eric Darrow was cagey about his business ventures.

Damian had a big mouth but, whether from ignorance, or fear of offending his father, he never spoke about his father's affairs. The only business Jake had heard Damian discuss was the meteoric film career that awaited him when he graduated from film school and the embryonic agency he had started a few months ago, to 'help' budding musicians and actresses at their school. It wasn't lost on their tutors or fellow students that the only people on Damian's books were female. And he wasn't the only one of Damian's friends who was wary of asking questions. If half the rumours in circulation about the Darrows were true, father and son had the same respect for the law as they had for their enemies; and, according to legend, a few of those had found their way to the bottom of the Bay in concrete boots.

Lloyd pushed Lucy inside. He stopped to watch Cynara and Mira. Stark naked, both were undressing volunteers from the rugby teams.

'What you doing, misery guts?' Damian demanded of Kelly.

'Taking a beer break,' she said, defensively holding up her can.

'You're not here to take a break. You're here to entertain the guests.'

'Which she's just fully and nobly done, my

13

liege.' Jake gave a full Shakespearean bow.

Kelly wished Jake hadn't lied. It was the first she'd seen of him at the party and she sensed Damian knew it.

'Glad you're satisfied, Jake. I'm not.' Damian closed his fist over Kelly's wrist. A 'bang' resounded from the living room. Lloyd and Lucy had disappeared and the tail end of the nude conga Cynara had formed had knocked over a bin of empty wine bottles. The conga dissolved in a heap of naked limbs.

Kelly eyed the prospective dancers. The men were laughing but those whose eyes weren't already glazed by alcohol were hyper, high on testosterone and the chemical cocktails she had seen being handed around. She knew from experience they would take their pleasure viciously – like Damian.

'Do we know how to party, or do we know how to party?' Alec Hodges, Damian's fourth flatmate, danced on to the balcony and threw his arms around Damian's neck.

'Damian certainly does,' Jake steadied Alec when Damian pushed him away.

'And I'm enjoying it, boy.' Alec's eyes rolled alarmingly in their sockets, his entire body was shaking. But not in time to the music that started up again, booming out from the living room.

'What you on?' Mike eyed Alec warily.

'Specials.' Alec lifted his finger to his lips. 'Sssh.' He collapsed in a fit of giggles. 'Wanno box?' He lobbed a punch at Damian that connected with his jaw.

'You stupid bastard!' Damian raised his fist.

'Wimp!' Alec threw another punch but Damian got in first. Alec staggered, lost his balance and would have fallen over the balcony rail if Jake hadn't grabbed him.

'Should have let the stupid bugger go,' Damian growled.

'You want the coppers to come calling?' Jake helped himself to a vodka tube.

'I'd tell them to go to buggery. My father owns the locals.' Damian pushed Kelly at Alec. 'Here. Expend his energy to some purpose.'

Alec peered at Kelly through bloodshot eyes before grabbing her skimpy top and yanking it down over her Lycra mini-skirt. 'Nice boobs.' He lifted her skirt and exposed her naked buttocks. 'Nice arse.' He slapped her hard, raising a welt.

'Give him a good time, Kelly, and I might give you a go myself later.' Damian helped himself to another tube of vodka.

Alec closed his hand around the back of Kelly's neck and squeezed. Kelly winced but didn't attempt to fight him off. He was a foot taller than her and twice her weight.

'Alec's out of it. He could hurt her,' Jake remonstrated.

'Know your trouble,' Damian pushed his face close to Jake's. 'You're bloody soft. Whores are like dogs. They need to be trained to know their place.'

'I want seconds.' Jake prised Alec's arm from Kelly's neck. To his amazement, she shoved him away and used the lie he'd told Damian earlier. 'You've had your share.'

'It wasn't enough.' Jake propped up Alec who

15

was swaying on his feet. Alec fell and Damian kicked him.

'Get the silly bugger to bed, Mike.' Damian clicked his fingers at Cynara. Still naked and very aware of the effect she was having on the men around her, she sauntered, hand on hip, towards him.

Damian wrapped his arm around her and turned to Jake. 'You can have seconds from Kelly, in exchange for that short you're working on.'

'Half the school has seen me filming it,' Jake protested. Living expenses were cheap for Damian's lodgers, but they were expected to supplement their payment in kind. Lloyd wrote Damian's essays and end-of-term thesis. Alec was his 'heavy', chauffeur and gofer.

He had only gained admittance into Damian's inner circle after winning a trophy for producing the best animated short in his first term in film school. And, since moving into Damian's penthouse six months before, he'd put in hours of graphic and modelling studio work that Damian had taken credit for.

'Then you come up with something new. Something as good as 'Long Shots, Short Breaks'.'

The fact that Damian remembered the title of Jake's award-winning animation said it all. Damian wanted a trophy, and he wanted it soon.

'We'll go through some ideas tomorrow.' Jake grabbed Kelly's arm.

Damian dismissed them with a wave of his hand. 'Cynara, it's time you and the girls put on the floor show.'

Cynara beckoned Mira forward and kissed her full on the lips.

'Atta girl, go for it,' Mike shouted.

'Why don't you watch the show?' Kelly said earnestly to Jake.

'If you're free, they'll make you perform.'

'It wouldn't be the first time.'

'We could both do with some peace and quiet.' He pulled her into the corridor that led to the bedrooms. Noises echoed towards them, low soft moans of pleasure, interspersed with hysterical shrieks and a single, blood curdling scream.

'That's Ally, she's a screamer,' Kelly said when she saw Jake staring at the row of doors.

'It sounded as if she was being murdered.'

'You get used to it. I work in the room next to hers in the parlour.' She glanced over her shoulder. 'Let's go back to the party.'

'Why? We could both do with a break.'

'I know you're trying to be kind, but if I'm caught slacking I'll lose my job.'

Jake opened his bedroom door, but, even as he dragged Kelly inside, he sensed her reluctance. He had to physically move her aside to close the door. A light burned on the side table casting shadows. His bed was rumpled and an unpleasant, fishy aroma of sex, expensive cologne and sweat filled the room. Damian's guests never respected his lodgers' privacy. 'Who's going to know if you're slacking or not?'

'People listen,' Kelly said nervously. 'We just did.'

'I can moan but I won't promise to make as

much noise as your friend,' Jake joked.

'Ally's not my friend.' Kelly sat on the bed, kicked off her shoes and pulled off her top.

'Keep your clothes on. I only brought you in here to chill out. You're not sixteen, are you?'

She picked up her top and slipped her shoes back on. 'Yes, I am.' She left the bed and went to the door.

'What you doing?'

'I'm here to work. If you don't want me, you should be out there enjoying yourself.'

He laid his hand on hers on the door handle. 'Kelly, it doesn't have to be this way for you …'

'Don't be nice. I can't stand nice …'

The door slammed back on its hinges with a force that sent Kelly flying across the room. Before Jake had time to turn, hands clamped over his eyes and nose. He tried to shout but when he opened his mouth something coarse, dry and rough was pushed into it, preventing him from breathing. He choked, fought and struggled for breath.

Hands clamped around his waist, lifting him from his feet. His belt was unbuckled; his jeans unzipped and pulled down around his ankles. Terrified of rape, he struggled with every ounce of strength he possessed. Breath hissed from his lungs, loosening the rag in his mouth as he was thrown face down on to the floor. Something hard and bony … a knee? … thrust painfully into the small of his back.

Hands pressed his head face down on to the wooden floor and fumbled at the back of his legs. Kelly's sobs filled the air. They died abruptly after a harsh slap clipped through the air.

A sharp pain penetrated the back of Jake's leg. He felt something wet and warm trickling down his calf. A fuzzy feeling stole upwards through his veins, paralysing his senses. He didn't need to be told what was happening. He knew he'd been injected with something even before the voice hissed in his ear.

'This is on the house.'

The warmth intensified until it flared into a furnace. His head jerked back, his spine cracked.

'I would say we'll contact you before you need more. But this is a one-time special – Mr. Policeman.'

Fire tore through his body, searing, burning, asphyxiating. Hands lifted him up into the air again. A cold breeze cooled his skin and he sensed he'd been carried on to his balcony. He struggled to open his eyes.

Lights wavered far below. He opened his mouth and screamed and didn't stop screaming until he hurtled downwards into darkness.

Kelly was yanked upright in the corner of the room where she'd huddled, head in hands.

Fists propelled her out into the corridor. Alec was stumbling, zig-zagging from one wall to another. He squinted at her.

'Kelly? I'm so – o – o tired ...'

'You need to get your head down somewhere quiet, Alec.'

Ally left one of the rooms and pulled her skirt down over the top of her thighs. 'Give me a hand,

Kelly.'

Kelly stared at the door that had closed behind her.

'Kelly?' Ally repeated.

Slowly, as though she was sleepwalking, Kelly moved to the other side of Alec. Ally opened the door to Jake's room and pushed him in. She closed the door without looking inside.

'Smile, sunshine!' Ally ordered as she walked away. 'That's if you don't want to end up like your sisters. You don't need me to tell you it's a short slide down in this business. And this is a lot easier than being pawed by sweaty old men for hours on end in the parlour.'

CHAPTER TWO

Inspector Trevor Joseph tossed the report Superintendent Bill Mulcahy had given him onto his desk. 'It's a well-known ploy, sir. When a dealer wants to expand his market, to increase profits or cover the escalating cost of a habit, he targets potential punters and offers them freebies. If they refuse they're pinned down and given large enough shots of whatever he's selling to make them want more. A month later the dealer has recovered the cost of the freebie a hundred times over. It's rumoured to have started in prisons ...'

'I don't need a lecture on how it started or why they assaulted Jake Phillips and Alec Hodges and pumped them full of this stuff,' Bill answered shortly. '"Make an addict parties" are a bloody nightmare. Especially in cases like this where scores of people develop amnesia when questioned about the identity of their fellow guests. What I want to know is, was Jake Phillips thrown off that balcony to hide a screw-up, or was it a cold-blooded and deliberate attempt at murder?'

'He was lucky to have landed on that awning ...'

'If you read on, you'll see he's in a coma and not expected to recover.'

Trevor retrieved the file and flicked through it again. 'It's attempted murder or GBH if he does recover. Murder or manslaughter if he doesn't. But devastating as this is for the victim and his family, it's not enough reason for us to dig into our budget to help out a Welsh force. It's their problem, not ours.'

'Ordinarily, I'd agree with you.' Bill sat in the chair in front of Trevor's desk, pressed his fingertips together and gazed thoughtfully at his nails.

Trevor knew what the gesture meant. He had seen his superior do it many times, and always before the superintendent was about to ask him to volunteer for something above and beyond the call of duty.

'There are two reasons why we should make this case our business.' Bill removed a red file marked *Classified* from a folder and handed it to Trevor. 'Professor Robbins's report.'

'Norman Robbins?' Trevor asked in surprise. 'I thought he'd retired.'

'He did – is. But as he knows more about the chemical composition of drugs and their effect on the brain than anyone else we can call on, we sent him the results of the blood tests on our coma victim, Jake Phillips and Phillips's flat-mate Alec Hodges, and also the pills we found in Hodges' pocket.'

'Was Hodges at the party?'

'He was in the penthouse along with 106 others when the locals arrived in response to a call from a passer-by who saw Jake Phillips being thrown from the balcony.'

'Then Hodges is a suspect?'

'He's about the only one there who isn't. He was comatose and incapable of standing upright when the officers arrived within ten minutes of the witness seeing Phillips being thrown. The officers assumed Hodges was drunk. When they tried to wake him, he went crazy. He's been in a psychiatric ward ever since. Look at Hodges' symptoms as listed by his psychiatrist.'

Trevor scanned the report compiled by the psychiatrist who had examined Alec Hodges the morning after he had been admitted to a secure ward. 'Manic behaviour – grandiose delusions – hallucinations – loss of inhibitions – enhanced strength – hyper-activity – loss of all sense of guilt and morality –' he glanced at Bill. 'Some form of hallucinatory. Ecstasy or peyote, possibly combined with crack cocaine, heroin or crystal meth?'

Mulcahy leaned back in the chair. 'Robbins broke down the chemical composition of the pills we found on Hodges. It's our worst nightmare. A synthetic drug that can be created for pence by any teenage chemistry student who has the formula. And all he'd have to do to assemble the ingredients is take a trip to the local supermarket. Every one of them can be found in proprietary brands of cleaning agents.'

'You think Alec Hodges made it and gave it to Jake Phillips?'

'No. Both had been injected in the back of their knees with a fluid in which pills had been dissolved. There were bruises on their backs and residue was found on their skin. Blood tests revealed dangerously high doses in both their bodies. We have to consider the possibility that whoever administered the drug was trying to kill one or both of them.'

'They could have injected one another.'

'It's possible but if they were willing, why the

bruises? Why not just take the pills?'

'Greater and more instant effect,' Trevor closed the report. 'If one of them was the manufacturer ...'

'They are film, not science, students.'

'Alec Hodges has been questioned?' Trevor checked.

'He was out of it when he was taken into the psychiatric ward, and he's still out of it. The doctors came up with the usual, 'the patient is too ill to be interviewed crap' for three days. Never mind that this is a potential murder case and a particularly nasty one that could have repercussions for the community. No one was allowed to go near our man until we got a court order the day before yesterday, and even then there were problems with the hospital authorities. It doesn't help that Daddy Hodges is a judge who knows how to work the system.'

'Did Alec Hodges say anything useful?' Trevor asked.

'No.'

'Is he permanently damaged?'

'When he first came round, he was hyper. The doctors sedated him. According to his consultant and the officers who have tried to interview him he hasn't said one sensible word since. Scans indicate his brain cells are turning to soup.'

'Is the damage permanent?'

'Professor Robbins studied Alec Hodges' medical notes. In his opinion the damage is irreversible. But, until yesterday, Hodges was the only one we knew of who had taken the drug so we had no one to compare him with.'

Trevor dropped the report into his in-tray. 'What

happened yesterday?'

'Disturbance in a tower block flat on a no-go Welsh council estate a few miles from that penthouse on the Bay, and at the opposite end of the economic spectrum. Three dead and four in the same state and on the same psychiatric ward as Alec Hodges. No sign of force being used on any of them. Evidence points to the dead injecting themselves.' Bill pulled a sheet of paper from the front of the file marked *Classified*. 'Pills were found on one of them and blood tests on all seven confirm the same cocktail as Hodges and Phillips, but the pills were of a higher concentration than the ones found in Hodges' pocket.'

'Did the victims die from the effect of the drug?'

'One jumped from an eighth-floor window, shouting he could fly. Another was knifed in the heart. The third – who we think did the knifing – drank two pints of bleach.'

'Any idea where they acquired the pills?' Trevor asked.

'No survivor's in a fit state to give any useful information. But it has to be more than a coincidence that the drug has travelled from a millionaire's penthouse down to the nearest council estate in a few days.'

'What about the other people who were at the party in the penthouse with Phillips and Hodges? Someone must have seen something.'

'You'd think so. But everyone the locals interviewed appear to have been blind and deaf, or engrossed in an orgy in one of the bedrooms.'

'They must have friends, acquaintances. Anyone

hazard a guess as to where Alec got hold of the junk you found in his pocket?'

'Alec Hodges and Jake Phillips share the penthouse with two other film students. They and all of Hodges' and Phillips's friends and acquaintances have been questioned. Some were at that party, some weren't. Locals are checking out their stories. But it will take time.'

'Lucky students,' Trevor mused. 'I was under the impression that all most of them could afford these days was a cardboard box.'

'One of the students, Damian Darrow, owns the penthouse. His father gave it to him. You've come across him, Eric Darrow.'

'The Darrow who owns casinos and nightclubs?' Trevor raised an eyebrow.

Bill smiled grimly. 'Didn't you and Collins investigate him ten years back?'

'We went undercover in his clubs but all we succeeded in doing was arresting a couple of personal users and one small-time dealer.'

'Upstairs is concerned about this one. We've three dead, one in a coma and four walking lunatics. Can you imagine what will happen if one of the gangs gets hold of this formula and starts mass marketing it? That's if they haven't already. Professor Robbins estimates that four dozen pills like the ones we found on Alec Hodges could be produced for under a pound. Trials suggest sniffer dogs would be useless at tracking it down. They're light, easily transportable. Flood the international market and we'd get …'

'Murders, mayhem and a generation of thrill-seekers with pea soup for brains.'

'Exactly,' Bill concurred.

'I understand why the locals cried "Help".'

'They're running the usual investigation, but upstairs want our people out there right away. We need to find out who is manufacturing and marketing this stuff and stop it before it does any more damage.'

'Any ideas?'

'Too many,' Bill complained. 'The Bay is *the* executive and desirable place to live now; but it's an old dock area, you name it, they're there. Chinese Triads, Somalis, Yardies, South Americans, Kurds, Asians, Eastern Europeans, and that's without the Italians. They've had businesses in South Wales for a century and more.'

'Mafia?'

'Most of their businesses are legit these days but we're not ruling out anything,' Bill said tersely. 'We're putting out as many ethnic undercover operatives as manpower will allow.'

'You've forgotten someone.'

'Who?' Bill looked at Trevor through narrowed eyes.

'The Welsh locals.'

'No, we haven't. That's where you and Collins come in.'

'Me? I left the drug squad two years ago. I'm serious crimes.'

'Three dead *is* serious crimes, Joseph,' Bill snapped.

'We're all entitled to a personal life. Lyn is due to give birth in five weeks. I've booked leave …'

'All the more reason to wrap this case up quickly.'

Trevor had been bullied into giving up leave dozens of times by Bill, but this was different. It wasn't just his social life but his family life that would suffer. And there was absolutely no way he was going to miss the birth of his baby, no matter how important the case. 'No. Absolutely not. No! Besides I haven't a Welsh accent. Not even an implausible one.'

'Haven't you heard, boyo, Wales and especially the Bay is the new European international hotspot. They even allow the English in there now. You and Collins are the best undercover operatives I have – or have seen in any force.'

'Flattery won't win me over, and your Welsh accent is the phoniest I've heard.'

Bill became serious. 'What kind of a world do you think your baby is going to come into if this crap hits the streets big time? No one will be safe. Not you. Not me. Not the young mother shopping in the supermarket alongside the chemist buying new supplies. And don't forget the crazed junkie who doesn't know what he's doing and doesn't care as long as he gets his next fix.'

'You sound like a recruiting poster, Bill.'

'I wouldn't be here if I wasn't desperate. How about a compromise? You go undercover for one month? That will give you a week back here before you've booked your leave and, if the baby comes a couple of days early, I won't quibble if you disappear into domesticity.'

'You know as well as I do that undercover – and

babies – can't be timetabled.'

'Operatives can be pulled out. Say the word and I'll do just that,' Bill promised.

Trevor remained unconvinced. 'Try Dan.'

Bill took a deep breath. 'That brings me to the other reason why we should get involved. Jake Phillips wasn't a film student. He's one of us.'

'Undercover drugs?'

Bill shook his head. 'People trafficking and money laundering. The Darrows run a string of massage parlours and brothels as well as casinos. The locals were looking for proof of Damian Darrow's involvement after his father signed over half a dozen companies to him a year ago. Jake Phillips had been undercover for almost a year. He did well, made friends with Damian Darrow and moved into his flat after two months.'

'Did Jake get too close and raise the Darrows' suspicions?'

'Not according to the reports he made. But he could have stumbled onto something that night and attracted the attention of the wrong people.'

'Does Dan Evans know about this case?' Trevor referred to his colleague and immediate superior.

'Jake is Dan's nephew.'

'The one he persuaded to join the force?' The look on Bill's face answered Trevor's question. Dan Evans had engineered Trevor's transfer into the serious crimes squad and, although Dan had never admitted it, Trevor suspected it was Dan's recommendation that had secured his promotion to inspector.

'Will Dan be working on this?'

Bill shook his head. 'You know as well as I do, he can't.'

'That's not what I asked.'

'Upstairs has cleared him to operate on the sidelines and co-ordinate the investigation. He wanted more but, besides the personal aspect, they told him he's too noticeable and well-known for undercover work.'

'People do tend to remember someone his size,' Trevor conceded. Dan was over six feet four and admitted to eighteen stone, although he looked at least four stone heavier to Trevor's practised eye.

'The team's assembling here tomorrow for a briefing. The hope is it's too far from the Bay to get noticed. Back stories and IDs are being created. Including two for you and Collins. He may be an insubordinate bastard but, as I've already said, he's one of the best undercover coppers on this or any other force. You'll work with him again?'

'Do I have a choice?' Trevor resigned himself to the inevitable.

'I can't force anyone on this one. But I'd rather not think about what would happen if we fail to stop this stuff from hitting the streets big time.'

Trevor thought of Jake Phillips and the guilt Dan was undoubtedly feeling. Would he dissuade his own child from joining the Force if the question ever arose?

Bill left his chair. 'Six hundred hours tomorrow. Incident room. You won't be going home afterwards. You'll be heading for the high life. Designer suits, fast cars and five-star hotels.'

'And a couple of bags of confiscated trade

goods?' Trevor guessed.

'You're playing successful dealers.'

'Upstairs must be antsy to put us straight on the job.'

'We can't afford to waste any more lives.' Bill went to the door.

'Because murders create too much paperwork.'

Bill turned and frowned. 'Come again?'

'It's one of Peter's. In appalling taste, but, as I'm going to be living as well as working with him, I'm tuning into his mindset.' Trevor shuffled the reports in his in-tray. 'You have told him about this?'

Bill glanced at his watch. 'I will in the next five minutes.'

'Good luck. You'll need it.'

'I promise I'll be there for the birth.' Trevor had waited until after dinner before breaking the news to Lyn. Thirteen years younger than him, tall, slim and beautiful with long dark hair that fell below her waist when she wore it loose, which wasn't often enough for his liking, she had given him more to live for than he had dreamed possible. Every time he looked at her he couldn't believe his luck.

'You have no idea how long you'll be away?'

He failed to read her expression. 'I'll telephone as often as I can and you'll have a number on which you can contact me any time – day or night.'

'I'll move in with Mum and Dad for a week or two. They're always complaining they don't see enough of me. And, as you insisted I take early maternity leave and Mum's retired, your credit card can look out. We'll go baby shopping.'

He sat back in relief. 'You really don't mind?'

'Of course I mind. And, of course I'm going to miss you, but I knew when I married you that I was taking on you and the job. And, you wouldn't be going if it wasn't important. Just one thing.'

'What?' He grabbed her as she left her seat and began to stack dishes. Taking the plates from her, he set them on the table and pulled her down on to his lap.

'We're too heavy for you.' She patted her bump.

'Combined, you're just the right weight. What's the one thing?'

'Look after yourself. I don't want to have to take our baby into a hospital to meet you for the first time.'

'You won't.'

'Let me go and make coffee.'

'You sit down, I'll make it.' He released her, took the plates and went into the kitchen.

'Is Peter going with you?'

'I shouldn't even tell you that much, but yes.'

'I'm sorry.'

'So am I.' Trevor returned with cups, sugar and milk. 'I'd much rather live with you, and not just because you're prettier.' He dropped a kiss on the back of her neck.

'I mean, I'm sorry for him and Daisy.'

'Trouble?' Trevor asked. Peter Collins and Daisy Sherringham were an ill-matched couple. She was a cultured, elegant and refined doctor. The job – or nature – had honed Peter's cynicism to the point of offensive. He revelled in his reputation as an aggressive and abrasive character and relished winding up his more sensitive colleagues.

Over the years they'd worked together Trevor had occasionally glimpsed a thoughtful, generous and compassionate side to Peter's nature which he took pains to keep concealed from the world. They had met Daisy on a case six years before. Trevor had been one of her many admirers before Lyn had entered his life. But, close as he was to Peter, he simply couldn't understand why Daisy gave Peter the time of day.

'I'm amazed they're still seeing one another,' Lyn said. 'Daisy doesn't say much, but, from the way Peter behaved the last time we went out for a drink with them, a separation might finish off their relationship – that's if they have one that goes further than the odd night out and sleepover.'

'You make them sound like teenagers.' Trevor returned to the kitchen, made the coffee and brought it in. 'It's enough you make me happy without trying to spread peace and harmony throughout the whole world.'

'Not the whole world, just Peter and Daisy. She deserves to be happy but ...'

'Peter doesn't?' He poured the coffee.

'For all his talk, I know Peter would kill or be killed for you if you were in a tight corner and for that I love him. Not that he'd thank me for saying it. But I don't think he is the right one for Daisy.'

'Neither do I. But there's nothing either of us can do about it. They're grown-ups.'

'Peter doesn't often behave like one.'

'I agree with you.' Trevor sat at the table and laid his hand over Lyn's.

'Would you tell me what the case is about if I asked?'

'It's classified.'

'Don't you trust me?'

'It's not a question of trust. If there's a leak, it's easier to say, I never told a soul than explain that I dropped a few crumbs of information to my wife.'

'Is it murder?'

'Sort of.'

'Dangerous?'

'No.' Trevor knew from the expression on Lyn's face that she had seen through his lie.

'You have an early start?'

'I have to be at the station by six and I won't be back. Not for a while.' He spooned sugar into his cup.

'Then we'd better have an early night.'

He smiled. 'Sounds like a good idea.'

'I'll load the dishwasher, you pack. Your undercover clothes are in the plastic bin in the back bedroom.'

'I won't be needing my down-and-out clothes. And, the dishwasher can wait. Love you, Mrs Joseph.'

'Love you too,' she echoed.

'Finished your coffee?'

'Just about.'

'Then let's go upstairs.'

Peter Collins waved to the waiter. 'Two more brandies and coffees, and the bill.'

'I'm operating first thing,' Daisy remonstrated. 'The last thing I need is another brandy – or coffee to keep me awake.'

'I ordered them for me.' Peter emptied his brandy balloon and hunched over it.

'You're not working in the morning.'

'Briefing at six,' he divulged.

'In the morning?'

'Unfortunately.' He lined up the brandies the waiter brought in front of his coffee cups and checked the bill.

'And you're drinking two more brandies?'

'Stop playing the bloody doctor for five minutes, Daisy.'

Daisy fell silent. She'd sensed that Peter was building up to something when they'd met at the restaurant. She suspected he wanted to end their six-month relationship – if dinner three or four evenings a week, drinks with friends, the occasional sleepover in his or her flat and one weekend away could be called a relationship. Much as she disliked Peter in his present mood, she didn't want to end it. Although she couldn't quantify why.

'I won't be able to see you for a while,' he said abruptly.

The moment she had been dreading, had arrived. 'No ties, no commitment, that's what we agreed from the outset.' She succeeded in keeping her voice even.

'Aren't you going to ask why?' he growled.

'That's your business.'

'It's work.'

'Fine.'

'It shouldn't be bloody fine, Daisy.'

'Keep your voice down,' she reprimanded when

the diners around them looked towards their table.

'It's all right, we're practising for the divorce court,' Peter said loudly, addressing their fellow diners.

Daisy picked up her handbag and left her chair.

'Don't you care?' Peter downed one of the brandies in one.

'I'm busy – you're busy – we knew that when we started spending time together.'

'Time together,' he sneered. 'Bloody hell, Daisy, is that all we're doing – "spending time together"?'

The waiter approached their table. Peter pulled out his wallet, tossed his credit card on top of the bill and fumbled in his pocket for a tip. He flung a ten pound note on top of the card.

Daisy walked outside. The restaurant was housed in an old mill. She leaned on the railings that fenced off the river and looked down into the swirling waters.

Peter emerged. 'The waiter's calling us a taxi. You can get out first, unless you want to spend the night at my place.'

'Is that a roundabout way of asking if you can spend the night at mine?'

'No, it's a straightforward way of asking if you want to stop at my place.'

'I'd rather not when you're in this mood.'

'What mood?' he barked.

'The mood you always get into whenever work – or someone – makes you do things you don't want to.'

'I bought fresh ground coffee this morning from the Italian delicatessen.'

36

'There'll be nothing for breakfast.'

'I keep a box of muesli.'

'You never have milk.'

'Eat it with water, it's better for you.'

'I've had better offers.'

He finally unbent enough to tell her what he had been trying to get out all evening. 'Trevor and I are going undercover. It could be a while.'

'And you'd like a going-away present from me?' she challenged.

'Something to remember you by.'

She couldn't swear to it, but she thought his voice had softened. 'You can stay at my place if you want.'

'I'll have to leave by five.'

'It wouldn't be the first time.'

'No it wouldn't, would it?' He saw headlights approaching and clasped her elbow.

CHAPTER THREE

'Some of you know one another, some of you don't. But whatever you do know, you forget right now. That's an order.' Superintendent Bill Mulcahy lectured the officers assembled in front of him. 'I'll introduce everyone by their covers. Take a good look at their faces. It isn't an exaggeration to say that your lives, and theirs, might depend on your reaction the next time you meet.'

Trevor glanced around the room. It could have been a meeting of a sub-committee of the United Nations. He recognised about half the people. Two keen and eager young constables from his station, Chris Brookes and Sarah Merchant, both recent recruits to plain clothes, were there, as was Andrew Jones, an experienced uniformed constable close to retirement.

Trevor wondered why Andrew had been seconded to the operation. He was the least ambitious copper he knew. Andrew had joined fifteen years before him and Peter. Uninterested in promotion, all his energy had been expended on the golf course. He had a cupboard full of trophies that had earned him the nickname of 'T off'. He'd heard that Andrew's second wife had recently divorced him, citing her husband's obsession with the sport as the reason why she had kicked him out of the house.

A fourth generation UK Chinese, Sergeant Lee Tschung from the Met who had worked with him on a past case, was talking to a tiny, dark Hispanic-looking woman, and a brawny fair-haired stocky man. Judging from their accents they were American. Alfred McAlister, a second-generation West Indian recruit to his force was there, as was Tom Naz, an Asian who had only just left police college. But there were another half a dozen he had never seen before.

'Ladies and gentlemen,' Dan Evans's Welsh lilt filled the room. He spoke slowly, enunciating each word carefully. It had taken Trevor a few months of working closely with Dan to work out that it was deliberate ploy to make people think his wits were as slow as his speech. 'You have folders in front of you. They are not to leave this room. Study one another and the information on the sheets. If you know the name of anyone in this room, as the superintendent said; forget it and memorise their cover.'

They all opened the folders and flicked through the papers.

'Use your covers to infiltrate the gangs who control the dealers operating on the Bay. We're looking for whoever is manufacturing and marketing this drug. It could be any one of the gangs, or an individual. As soon as you have information, contact Andy Horton.' Dan pointed to Andrew Jones. 'Every day from nine until five he will be in the Bay office of Jones, Jones and Watkins, Estate Agents. It's legit but serious-crimes have an office there. They're not using it at the moment, so they've allowed us to borrow it. As acting area manager for the firm I have an excuse to make an occasional visit. The rest of the staff believe Andy and I work for the firm. When you go in, ask to see the plans for the penthouses in the highest rise development in the Bay. You will be directed to Andy's office.

'If you need to contact him out of hours, use one of the Sim cards you will be issued with in your pay as you go cell phone. Keep the conversation relevant to property sales. Whenever you phone in your undercover guise, assume the other side are listening in. They could well be.

'Try not to use a card outside of your undercover persona. If you absolutely have to – don't mention any names, including your own. All Sim cards to be destroyed after a single use. If you contact Andy to arrange a meet, make it a public place. Andy blends in nicely with a crowd. Average looks, middle-aged, thinning brown hair, the sort you bump into in a supermarket or newsagent every day and never look twice at. Andy is your only line to me and the locals.'

'Are any locals are being used on this operation?' Peter pushed a cigar into his mouth.

'No, because everyone knows everyone else in Wales – apparently. No smoking,' Bill snapped.

'I won't light it. It's my dummy,' Peter answered laconically.

'Trevor Brown and Peter Ashton.' Dan pointed to Trevor and Peter before Peter's belligerence elicited a tirade from Bill. 'Bent coppers turned dealers after being kicked off the force. Representing a consortium of bent coppers trading in supplies of confiscated drugs. They're looking to contact local dealers with a view to expanding their merchandise to include the new drug. They're moving into a suite in a five-star hotel on the Bay. Be vigilant if you see them out and about. A slip up could cost them – and you.'

Andrew whistled. 'And what did you two do to deserve that berth?'

'Our time in hostels for the homeless when you were rolling little balls across greens,' Peter retorted.

'No previous knowledge!' Bill shouted.

'Sarah Bell and Chris Rivers, minor dealers and ex-cons, supplied by Brown and Ashton. They're moving on to the estate where the party was held that resulted in three dead and four hospitalised. Brown, Ashton, Bell and Rivers will be the only four in open and regular contact.'

'Good luck, you brave young things.' Peter winked at Chris and Sarah.

Dan ignored Peter but Bill glared at him.

'Michael Sullivan and Maria Sanchez,' Dan pointed to the two Americans. 'Columbians who want in on the new drug, looking to contact any South Americans operating on the Bay. Lee Chan, targeting the Triads, Tony Servini, the Italian Mafia. Tom Patel, hoping to infiltrate the Asians, Hassan Eidi, Somali, Ibrahaim Milgi, Kurd, Justin Lebov, Albanian, Veenay Singh, Indian, Alexander Markov, Russian.'

'How did we find out about this drug?' Peter asked.

'Good question.' Dan spoke even more slowly than usual. 'It first appeared about a year ago. The locals found a few pills on personal users. It was never traced back to a dealer, although the locals suspected a connection to the housing estate. They decided the quantities were too small to worry about. Then it surfaced at the party in the penthouse and on the estate. Since then large quantities have been touted in clubs on the Bay. "Samples" have been sent to the major dealers offering the formula and marketing rights.'

'That rumour or definite?' Trevor questioned.

'Definite, the locals intercepted the merchandise and half a dozen letters when they picked up an independent dealer on the Bay. He probably would have delivered them if he hadn't been high as a kite. The drugs were of a lower concentration than the one found in Jake Phillips's and Alec Hodges' bloodstream. We think there are two sorts out there, "safe", as much as any illegal substance can be, and a lethally high dose. So far there have been no more instances of any of the side-effects that Jake Phillips, Alec Hodges and the others are exhibiting.'

'Locals had a tip-off?' Trevor suggested.

'No,' Bill answered. 'He took a curve on the wrong side of the road and hit a mini-bus. But at least we now know what we're looking for. All he could talk about when he was arrested was his "Black Daffodils". Wanted to know if his pills were safe.'

Bill Mulcahy pointed to the two sets of Briggs and Riley suitcases and 'carry-ons' stacked in the corner of Trevor's office. 'Yours are red, Collins.'

'Ashton?' Peter corrected.

Bill clenched his teeth. 'We're in the bloody

'office …'

'Getting into character,' Peter interrupted.

'This is an undercover operation not a fucking school play …'

'Grey ones mine?' Trevor stated the obvious but he had watched Peter wind up their superior too many times to want to watch a repeat performance.

'Packed with designer clothes and shoes in your sizes. Top of the range – money – not taste. Toiletries, electric razors, personal papers, passports with immigration stamps going back five years. You're well travelled. USA, Caribbean, Africa, South America … watches.' Bill opened a box and handed each of them a gold Rolex.

Trevor turned his over. 'This real?'

'Asset confiscation from convicted dealers.'

'I'll wear mine with pride.' Peter exchanged his stainless steel waterproof watch for the Rolex. He held out his wrist. 'Not sure I like it.'

'It's not yours to like or dislike. It's police property,' Bill reminded him.

'It's Peter Ashton's and he likes it.' Trevor replaced his own watch.

'Ashton has no taste,' Peter complained.

Bill lifted a couple of wallets from the box. He opened one and checked the name on the credit card before handing it to Peter.

'Slightly worn but nice. Aspinal no less. Custom made or …'

'Asset confiscation.' Bill confirmed. 'There's a secret pocket we've stuffed with Sim cards in the bottom.' He pulled apart what looked like solid stitching to reveal a gap. 'You've two credit cards apiece plus two thousand pounds cash for incidental expenses. Pin numbers on all the cards are the same as the last four digits of your direct line telephone numbers here. Every penny spent on expenses to be accounted for. Any discrepancy will be taken from your salary.'

'We claim for all food, drink, accommodation and incidentals?' Peter checked.

'Go easy on the drink and incidentals,' Bill glowered.

'Ashton has expensive taste and not all of it is tacky. He enjoys fine malt and Havana cigars.'

'As does Collins,' Bill sniped.

'Just getting into ...'

'Character?' Bill narrowed his eyes. 'Say that once more and you'll be paying for your own drinks – and incidentals.' He reached into the box again and handed them leather cases. 'Sunglasses, value five hundred pounds a pair. Guns – Glocks, semi automatic. You are both up to date with weapons training?'

'I am,' Trevor assured him.

'Me too, Boss.' Peter examined the gun and ammunition. 'Confiscated?'

'No registration or history attached to either.' Bill pointed to two piles of clothes on the desk. 'Casual outfits, shoes and underwear. Change here before you drive to Wales. Go over your covers until you can recite them backwards. You're coppers turned bad, jumped up working class Flash Harrys. You only have one goal and God, money. You'll do anything to get it.'

'I never thought the day would come when I'd

44

see you in Versace and Hugo Boss, Peter.' Dan entered the office with a small, nervous looking man. 'Meet Ferdi.'

'Hello,' Trevor greeted him warily. Whatever else "Ferdi" was, he wasn't a fellow officer. 'I'm sorry about your nephew, Dan.'

'Thank you.' Dan abruptly changed the subject. 'Ferdi's been given top clearance.' Dan slowed his speech even more than usual. 'He's a hairdresser and make-up artist.'

Peter grinned. 'You want Trevor to shorten his hair, lose the moustache and pluck his eyebrows.'

'Over my dead body,' Trevor growled.

'Think back to your police college lectures on identity and recognition,' Dan lectured him. 'People remember facial hair before features.'

'It'll grow again.' Peter's words were sympathetic, the grin on his face anything but.

'You're both going to get haircuts. Very short haircuts,' Bill emphasised.

'Mine can't get any shorter?' Peter ran his hand over his thick, brown, close cropped hair.

'Shaved.' It was Bill's turn to smirk. 'You're tough guys. We need you looking the part. Easiest way to change someone's appearance, is shave their head and stick a pair of sunglasses on them. Eric Darrow might have a long memory and you'll be sniffing around his clubs. He also owns shares in the hotel you'll be staying in.'

'Lighten up, boys, or is it boyos. It'll grow again.' Dan's smile was as broad as Bill's.

'While Ferdi works on you, memorise your back stories. Ex-coppers, ex-military service, ex-husbands …'

'That's a lot of exes,' Peter commented.

'On the plus side, you have houses and yachts in Spain,' Dan handed them two more files.

Peter flicked through his. 'Do these properties exist?'

'They exist,' Dan confirmed. 'Ownership in the name of your cover.'

'Can I change Collins to Ashton by deed poll when this is finished?'

'You can stop buggering around and wasting time, Sergeant,' Bill ordered. 'Soon as you're changed and ready to go, in my office; the goods are packed.'

The 'goods' were four bags of cocaine and eight of marijuana.

'We've seized more Charlie and grass in the last six months than anything else,' Bill explained.

Trevor picked up one of the packs. Both cocaine and marijuana had been packed into plastic envelopes, each containing a gram.

Dan lifted two laptop cases on to Trevor's desk. 'These contain functioning laptops with all the standard programmes.' He unzipped the main section and showed them the latest in wafer-thin, lightweight notebooks. 'Leads, spare batteries, in these front pockets.' He unzipped the back section. 'Place to put the files with photographs of your yachts and Spanish property.'

'We like boasting?' Peter sat on the edge of the desk.

'You've met enough bloody dealers to know

how they behave.' Bill's temper was still simmering.

'They also have false compartments, Put files in the paper compartment and no one will notice this flap even when the case is open.' Dan tugged at a small tag that had been folded into the underside of the handle of one of the cases. He jerked it and, it opened. He divided the bags of drugs and packed half of them into the case.

'Very neat.' Trevor packed the remainder of the drugs into the second laptop case.

Peter frowned at Trevor. 'If I saw anyone who looked like him on my beat, I'd run him in on suspicion. Do the locals know about us?'

'They know uncover operatives are moving in. They don't know who they are, where they're from, or where they'll be. Should you get picked up, we'll ensure you get released. But only after a visit from your solicitor. His card is in your wallets along with other contacts you may find useful. We'll call a taxi to take you to the train station. Your car is parked there.' Bill pulled the keys from his pocket.

'Only one,' Peter complained.

'Treat it with kid gloves. It's worth seventy-eight grand plus.'

Peter's eyes lit up like a child who has seen the Christmas presents. 'Tell me?'

'Granturismo Maserati, we want it returned in the same state you receive it.'

'Oh boy – or should it be boyo. Come to Daddy,' Peter snatched the keys from Bill.

'Senior officer drives.' Trevor tried to grab them back.

'The senior officer sits in the back so he can be chauffeur-driven by his sergeant,' Peter contradicted him.

'You'll sit side by side. You two are partners in every sense of the word, except one,' Bill took a deep breath. 'I shouldn't have to warn you ...'

'You don't,' Trevor broke in. Now the preliminaries were over, he wanted to be on his way, so he could wrap up the case and get back to Lyn.

Peter responded to Bill's withering look. 'No more jokes.'

'It's bad enough you wind me up, *Ashton*,' Bill emphasised, 'without making the Inspector's life hell. Remember not only does he have a cooler head, he outranks you. You can get "into character" on the drive to the station. Good luck.'

Dan watched them pick up the laptop cases. 'I don't have to remind you ...'

'About hackers, bugs, listening devices? No, you don't,' Trevor broke in.

'Scramblers in your bag for the telephones. We don't know what we're up against or what resources they have, so only use them in an emergency when you can't access your mobiles. We've packed them together with the usual torches, CS gas canisters, cable ties and burglars' tool kits in the carry-ons. Sweeper.' Dan held one up. 'It picks up all the listening devices we know about but they get more sophisticated every day. These,' Dan handed each of them a mobile phone with built-in camera, 'are clean. Use the Sim cards in them for calls you don't mind the other side knowing about. Taxis, takeaways, dry-cleaners …'

'We know the drill, Dan.' Trevor slung the laptop case over his shoulder and picked up his suitcase and carry-on. He went to the door. 'If Lyn phones …'

'We'll put her through on that mobile and doctor the number to make it look as though she's calling from Spain. We'll also warn her people could be eavesdropping.' Dan glanced at Bill and stepped out into the corridor before lowering his voice. 'I slipped four dozen extra Sim cards in your case. Destroy each one after you've talked to her.'

'What about me and my lady love?' Peter asked.

'Talk nicely to Trevor and he might give you a few extra Sim cards.'

Bill joined them in the doorway. 'If you have the slightest suspicion your cover has blown, contact Andrew. We'll pull you out immediately. Day or night. The last thing this station and your wife needs is a dead hero.' Bill held out his hand. Trevor shook it.

'I'm expendable?' Peter mocked.

'Bolshie sergeants are two a penny.' A grim smile hovered at the corner of Bill's mouth. 'Let's hope you close down this supply chain before any other poor sod is killed or has his brain turned to soup.'

'As requested, interconnecting suites on the top floor, with balconies and sea views, Mr Brown, Mr Ashton.'

Peter gave the receptionist, a blonde with blue eyes and model figure, the benefit of his most practised smile along with a credit card. She swiped it, packaged a set of card keys in an envelope and handed it to Peter along with his card. 'The brown card key is for the room, the blue for the safe. You will need to programme your own code. The safe will only lock after the code has been entered.'

'Thank you.' Peter winked at her.

Trevor handed her his American Express card and she repeated the registration procedure.

'If we can do anything to make your stay with us more pleasant, Mr Brown, Mr Ashton, please ring down. The suites have twenty-four-hour room service.'

'That's good to know.' Peter followed Trevor and the bell boy into the lift. The bell-boy pressed the buttons and they rode in silence to the top floor.

The boy opened the adjoining doors to their suites, unlocked the communicating door and proceeded to give them the full conducted tour, walking ahead of them and opening doors as he went.

'Mini-bars in the bedrooms, full-sized bars in the lounges. En suite marble bathrooms with separate shower units. If you need more of our exclusive Italian toiletries, sirs, ring housekeeping.' He went to the control panel on the wall. 'Air-conditioning, interactive satellite television, your safe is hidden here and in the same place in the other bedroom. The telephones in the bedrooms have different numbers to the ones in your lounges. You will find them on your check-in cards. They all have voice mail facilities. Easy connect high-speed Internet in the lounge and both bedrooms. Hairdryer, trouser press …'

Bored, Peter walked out onto one of the balconies that opened from every room. Trevor cut the boy short, gave him a ten pound tip and saw him out. He went to the bar in one of the lounges, took two cold beers from the fridge, opened them and joined Peter.

'Nice view.' He handed Peter one of the bottles, then looked up at the ceiling and checked the walls for signs of cameras and bugging devices. He noticed Peter doing the same. It had been a while since either of them had worked undercover, but they knew the drill.

'Where do you want to go tonight?' Peter wiped the top of his bottle before drinking.

'Casino.'

'Time to unpack and make ourselves at home. Bags I the blue and cream suite, you can have the brown and beige.'

'They're identical.'

'To your eyes.'

They went inside. Trevor opened his laptop, shook out a few sample packs of cocaine and marijuana and stowed them in the inside pocket of his suit.

'Fill mine up too.' Peter handed him his jacket. 'In case we get separated.'

Trevor looked at him quizzically.

'You know me, always on the look-out for local talent.'

'What kind of talent?' Trevor asked suspiciously.

'The usual and unusual.' Peter glanced at his watch. 'Time for another beer and a couple of hours shut eye.'

'Shut-eye before or after a steak?' Trevor closed the laptop case.

'Before. Clubbing and gambling is best done on a full stomach. Wake me in two hours if I'm still asleep.' Peter kicked off his shoes and stretched out on the Emperor-sized bed in his chosen room.

Sarah stared out of the window as Chris drove them down the motorway and over the Severn Bridge. They sped past wooded hills, valleys and alongside the plush, new suburbs of Newport before heading south towards the sea.

Chris and Sarah had worked out of the same station for three years but he was used to seeing her in uniform or one of the sober trouser suits she wore in the office. Not figure-hugging jeans and a thin strapped top that left nothing to his imagination. Even her hair was different. She usually wore it in a neat French pleat, not hanging loose over her shoulders. The undercover boys had taken care of every detail: her make-up was thicker and brighter and her garish jewellery suited her cover. The large gold hooped earrings, bangles, chains and gem-studded watch were very different from her own discreet silver studs and watch.

His torn jeans and T-shirt sporting the logo of a whisky company wasn't the casual wear he would have chosen for himself, either. He wondered about the sports bags they'd been given. He'd stowed them into the back of the van along with the German shepherd dog they'd been given – after a crash course in dog handling. Neither of them had bothered to check what undercover had packed for their use. Possibly Sarah, like him, preferred not to think about her clothes until she had to.

'You ever live on a council estate?' he asked.

'No. You?'

'I policed one after I left college. I was warned that this one is rougher than most when I was given the Tasers and hand guns.'

'Let's hope we won't have to use them.'

'Worried?'

'Slightly.' She hoped he wouldn't realise she was lying. 'You?'

'Slightly,' he flicked the indicator on the five-year-old anonymous white van he was driving and pulled into the inside lane. 'Our new city.'

They drove past a neat development of red-brick homes after they turned off the motorway. 'It doesn't look too bad. How far out is the estate?'

'Two miles from the city centre.' Chris followed a slow-moving stream of traffic into a commercial street that had more charity shops and boarded premises than retail stores.

They entered a close-built network of Victorian terraces. After a mile, the terraces ended and an estate of 1960s pebble dashed houses began. A few sported curtains at the windows and neat gardens but, the deeper into the estate Chris drove, the more rubbish-strewn the streets and unkempt the houses became.

At the end of a wide thoroughfare, half a dozen tower blocks loomed out of a sea of burned out cars, broken prams, bicycles, rotting carpets and smashed furniture. Grimy toddlers and babies, most naked from the waist down, stared at them from doorsteps and pavements.

'What floor we on?' Chris asked Sarah as he looked for, and found, the name of their 'home' block.

'Third. Inspector Evans ...'

'Dan,' Chris said sharply. 'We might be alone in a clean van but, from this moment on, we have to remain in character at all times.'

'... Dan said the lift often doesn't work. There are empty ground-floor flats, but they've all been vandalised.'

'There's plenty of parking space.' Chris slowed the van at the entrance to a low-walled area marked with faded numbered parking bays. 'All carpeted with broken glass.'

'So we park on the street?' Sarah suggested.

'Little option.' He stopped the van, walked around to the back and let out the dog.

'Good boy, Tiger. We'll get you some water in a minute.' Sarah clipped on the lead. The dog sat patiently at her feet while Chris lifted out the sports bags.

'Let's see what the housing association has given us. It's supposed to be clean and furnished. And from now on ...'

'We talk for the audience.' Sarah led the way into the block. The hall and stairwell reeked of faeces and urine; the walls were smeared with graffiti – and worse. She hit the lift button. Nothing happened.

'I'd feel safer on the stairs than in a metal box,' Chris said. 'You have the keys?'

54

She took a key-ring from her denim bag.

'Three floors isn't so bad,' Chris commented unconvincingly as he trailed behind her with the bags. The dog bounded up but both of them were breathless when they reached the third floor. Sarah opened the door to the flat and they walked into a large, light living room.

There was a strong chemical smell, and Sarah rushed to open the windows, but she was prevented from opening them more than a couple of inches by safety locks. The dining table and chairs were cheap veneer, still wrapped in plastic sheeting, as was the beige vinyl three-piece suite. There was a television and a DVD player.

Chris dropped the cases onto the nylon carpet and they walked through to a tiny inner hall that had four doors. Two led to double bedrooms, identically furnished with new double beds, like the furniture in the living room, swathed in plastic. There were chests of drawers and built-in wardrobes. The bathroom walls were covered with six-inch white tiles. The basic three-piece suite still bore the brown paper strip that had been glued around the edges to protect it in transit. The tiny kitchen had two cupboards, a fridge, with small freezer compartment, bottom of the range cooker and microwave, all new. Sarah opened a cupboard that held three saucepans, a frying pan, and four-piece crockery and cutlery sets.

Chris opened the fridge. It yawned back at him, empty. 'I'm starving. Let's find a shop. The dog could do with a walk anyway.'

'We can introduce ourselves to our neighbours,'

Sarah returned to the living room.

Chris took a bowl from the cupboard and filled it with water. He put it on the floor. 'Here, Tiger, this will do until we can get the dog bowls out of the car.' The dog dived on the bowl and lapped up the water. Chris buried his fingers in his fur. Shouts and screams echoed down from the floors above them.

Sarah picked up the dog lead. 'I have a feeling we are going to be grateful for the presence of our four-legged friend while we're here.'

CHAPTER FOUR

Peter opened his eyes to see the sun sinking slowly into the sea and the bay bathed in a soft golden light. He left the bed and stood in front of the balcony doors for a moment admiring the view. After showering and making liberal use of the complimentary toiletries in his bathroom, he slung a towel around his waist and joined Trevor in his lounge.

Trevor hung up the telephone. 'I heard you moving. I've ordered steak, salad and potato salad twice.'

'I would have preferred chips.' Peter helped himself to a beer.

'Your waistline wouldn't. Salad is better for you.'

'So is porridge. We're not with our women now.'

Trevor allowed the complaint to pass.

'You're wearing a suit,' Peter commented after his third swig of beer.

'I even have a tie in my pocket.'

Peter finished his beer and tossed the can into the waste bin. He returned to his own quarters, dressed, slapped on a layer of cologne and returned to the lounge where Trevor was watching the news.

'When do you want to visit Chris and Sarah?' Peter asked.

'Tomorrow. We'll telephone to give them advance warning.'

Peter knew Chris and Sarah had been given supplies of cocaine and marijuana as befitting their covers of "small time" dealers. 'You think they'll need more stock?'

'If Chris is as good as he thinks he is.' Trevor rose at a knock on the door. He opened the door. The waiter wheeled in a table and set it up in front of the window.

'We'll serve ourselves.' Trevor handed the boy a ten pound note and ushered him out while he was still muttering 'thanks you's.

Peter pulled a chair up to the table and cut into his steak. 'I could get used to this.'

'I'll tell your lady love what you said.'

'If she was along, it would be just about perfect.'

Trevor thought of Lyn and their life together in their own house. 'For a short break, maybe.'

'You look like a chick flick ad,' Peter mocked. 'Your steak's getting cold and we have a hard night's gambling ahead of us.'

Trevor took the hint. But as he cut into his steak he thought of Jake Phillips and hoped it would be only money that he and Peter would be staking.

The shop was a culture shock to Sarah but Chris had seen others like it when he had pounded the beat. The windows were boarded with steel shutters. Only a steel door left slightly ajar, and a Lotto sign fixed high on the wall, outside the reach of all but the most determined vandal, indicated that it was open for business. Next to it was a sign, NO DOGS.

Chris studied the street. Apart from a gang of teenage boys who were kicking a ball around there wasn't anyone in sight.

'Stay with Tiger. What do we need?'

'Everything,' Sarah said.

Chris walked through the steel door. Fluorescent lights illuminated a central island of shelves loaded with confectionery and tinned and packet goods. The fresh food section behind them held four brown bananas and three wrinkled apples. The glassed-in meat counter held a single tiny lamb chop. There was no salad or vegetables.

Chris picked up a basket and threw in toilet rolls, soap, a box of the least sugary breakfast cereal on offer, two cartons of long life milk, a plastic-wrapped loaf of sliced bread, a jar of instant coffee, because there was no ground, and he couldn't remember seeing a cafetiere in the kitchen, a bag of sugar and half a dozen eggs. A chill cabinet yielded a slab of pale, plastic-wrapped cheddar, a tub of butter substitute, and a packet of bacon. He opened the freezer cabinet and found beef and chicken burgers and frozen chips. He carried his haul to the counter. Two Asians stood behind it. They eyed him suspiciously. He returned their stare before recalling his shaved head and the coffin-shaped earring and facial studs Ferdi had given him 'to blend in'.

He lifted the basket on to the high level of the counter and one of the Asians started scanning the contents. Chris glanced around the shop again before asking, 'Do you have beer?'

'Cabinet behind me, sir.'

It was only then Chris noticed the shelves protected by a wire grill that sported a large padlock. He recalled seeing Sarah drink vodka and Coke at a retirement celebration. 'Two six packs of lager and a bottle of vodka.' He almost added

59

'please' before remembering he was a hardened ex-con. 'And a large bottle of Diet Coke.'

The man nodded. 'Sixty-eight pounds and seventy-four pence.'

Chris almost complained before deciding that anyone brave enough to operate a business on the estate was entitled to charge a premium to cover the cost of security, loss through theft and wear and tear on nerves.

He opened his wallet and handed over seventy pounds. The man took it, counted out his change and finally opened the alcohol cabinet. He and his colleague bagged Chris's purchases, added a large bottle of Coca-Cola and handed them over.

Chris blinked as he walked outside. The sunshine was blinding after the interior of the shop.

Sarah was crouching next to the dog, petting it while she talked to a painfully thin, nervous, pockmarked young man. Chris stepped back but remained within earshot.

The boy held up a spliff. 'This is my last.'

'I'm not buying, I'm selling,' Sarah whispered. 'Grass and Charlie. Best quality and price for miles.'

'How much is the grass?'

'A gram?'

'An ounce.' The boy began to shake and Sarah guessed that he either was, or aspired to be, a small time dealer. 'I got money.'

'How much?' Sarah asked.

He pulled two crumpled notes from his back pocket and looked at them. '£30.'

'If we let an ounce go for less than £43 our

wholesaler will string us up.'

The boy's face crumpled. 'That's all I got until my next giro.'

'We can do a swap,' Sarah rose to her feet. 'Got any black daffodil?'

Trevor and Peter walked into the casino at eleven o'clock. They lingered at the entrance for a moment to gauge the atmosphere.

'I just *love* neo-Nazi Classicism.' Peter pitched his voice loud enough to carry to the bouncers.

Over the years Trevor had learned to ignore fifty percent of Peter's observations. But when it came to the décor, he had to agree. The initial impression was temple created by Las Vegas-based interior designer, with overlays of Hollywood, ancient Rome, Egypt and China. It had certainly been executed with no eye to economy or taste.

Massive gilded figures of naked women held up a vast, domed navy blue ceiling studded with blinking star lights. Ornate gilded pavilions, hung with sheer crimson curtains housed the gaming tables. An indoor 'terrace' bordered with silk greenery and 'sculpted' resin nymph ornamented water features, was lined with gaming machines. A bar ran the length of the football pitch sized room, opening at each end into triangular stages around which nubile young dancers in G-strings pole danced.

Peter scanned the tables. 'I'm for Blackjack.'

'You feeling lucky or fancy your chances with the blonde?' Trevor had already spotted two potential 'sleight of hand' deals going down between bouncers and punters. Ten years ago he'd suspected, but never been able to prove, that Darrow had actively encouraged his employees to 'make a little on the side' so when the police moved in, as they frequently did, Darrow could throw up his hands in despair, and say, 'I had absolutely no idea. It's so difficult to find honest staff these days.'

It was a plausible way of taking the heat from his own operations, as well as extending his market. He and Peter had also suspected Darrow of supplying his workers through a third party, but the man who'd promised to deliver evidence of Darrow's involvement, had simply disappeared. As so many of Eric Darrow's 'business' acquaintances had done before – and, according to police reports – since.

'My hand is itching,' Peter scratched it. 'Here's to my first hundred grand.'

'I'll help you make it.' A dark-haired girl sidled up to Peter.

'No thanks, love, I'm allergic to girls with moustaches. But, if I win, I'll give you enough to buy a lady shave.'

The girl brought her hand back and slapped Peter soundly across the face. Bouncers moved in but Peter laughed as the girl sauntered off. 'You win some, you lose some. She doesn't like my style of courting.'

Trevor wished that, just for once, Peter had settled for a low profile. But he wasn't surprised by Peter's behaviour. Low profile had never been Peter's style, and big-time drug dealers needed to attract attention from the right – or depending on how you looked at the situation – wrong – kind of people.

Peter walked to a blackjack table. He opted for the game whenever they went undercover in a casino. If the game was straight and the decks weren't marked, it had the best odds. And Peter was a good player. He didn't declare his winnings because he played with his own money. He said it was enough of a bonus to get paid while he was at the card table.

Trevor joined the crowd at the roulette table. He recognised a few faces. Alfred … Harding. He forced himself to think of him by his cover; he was stacking half a dozen fifty-pound chips on red. Next to him were two sharply dressed West Indians. Alfred hadn't lost any time in making contact. But infiltrating the supply chain wasn't difficult when you could offer cheap merchandise. He didn't doubt Bill and Dan had supplied all the operatives as liberally as they had him and Peter.

Lee Chan walked through with a group of Chinese who disappeared through a door at the back of the room. Trevor guessed they were on their way to a private poker game. He had never known a race enjoy gambling as much as the Chinese. It wasn't so much a pastime as a way of life.

The two Americans, Maria and Michael, were playing the slots and exchanging banter with a group of swarthy, well-dressed men and women. Trevor walked past them on his way to the bar and picked up their transatlantic accents. The only other operatives he saw were the Albanian, Justin Lebov and the Russian, Alexander Markov, who were rolling dice.

'How can I help you, sir?' A girl who looked as though she'd raided her big sister's wardrobe and make-up box accosted him. The voice was deep, the accent Eastern European.

'Isn't that the other way around? You want a drink?'

'I thought I'd die of thirst before you asked,' she answered shamelessly. She turned to the barman. 'Champagne cocktail, large, please.'

'And for you, sir?' the Polish barman smiled at Trevor.

'Vodka, straight on the rocks.' Trevor wondered if every restaurant, bar and casino in Britain would close if the Eastern Europeans left the country overnight. He took his credit card from his wallet and handed it to the barman. 'Start a tab and have a drink yourself and make it a double.'

'Thank you very much, sir.'

Trevor wasn't being altruistic. He had picked up more useful information from waiters, barman and bouncers over the years than from police narks. He perched on a stool next to the girl.

She touched her glass to his. 'I toast your winning streak.'

'Thank you … ?'

'Masha.'

'A real live Russian?'

'A real live Bulgarian.'

'How long have you been working here?'

'In this casino, six weeks. In the UK a year.'

'You like it here?'

'I love it,' she gushed. 'After a month I was able to send enough money home to my mother to buy a washing machine and a television. Another two years and I'll have enough to buy a dress shop.'

'Which game do you recommend?'

'Roulette.'

Trevor knew she'd been primed by management. Roulette had the worst odds in favour of the gambler and the best for the house. 'Try again.'

'Dice. I always bring people luck at dice when I stand beside them.'

Trevor noticed an enormous bouncer cross the room. He looked him in the eye when he approached. 'Evening.'

'Evening, sir.' The bouncer shouted to gain the barman's attention. He took the bottle of mineral water the boy handed him.

'Not allowed to drink on duty?' Trevor knew no bouncer was allowed to consume alcohol on the job, but it was as good an opening gambit as any.

'Only the hostesses are, sir.' The man winked at Masha. 'So, how do you like our little Bulgarian, sir?'

Trevor glanced across the room. He couldn't see any sign of Eric Darrow but what he could see were CCTV cameras covering every inch of the room. Had he and Peter been rumbled? Or was Darrow cautious with all newcomers?

Trevor decided to play friendly. If the bouncer was looking for information he should be satisfied with their cover story. If he was looking for something more, he and Peter had strapped the Glocks to their shins.

'Your Masha is pretty and obliging,' Trevor complimented. Masha beamed.

The man leaned with his back against the counter so he could continue watching the room. 'New in town?'

'Why you asking?' Trevor hardened his voice.

'Your mate has won two and a half grand in the last twenty minutes.'

'Lucky streak,' Trevor said. 'He'll lose it again before the night is out. He always does. He never knows when to call it a day.'

As if to confirm his words, a collective sigh rippled through the crowd of onlookers gathered around Peter's table.

'Told you,' Trevor sipped his drink.

'Boss warned us to be on the lookout for scammers.'

'Sorry, we can't oblige. Your boss will be richer when we leave. Your job is safe.'

'And there's me thinking your mate had a sure-fire system.' The bouncer shifted his bulk on to a stool but his attention remained riveted on the room.

'If he had, we could give up work for play.'

'What line you in?'

'I need another cocktail.' Jealous of the attention Trevor was showing the bouncer, Masha wrapped her hands around Trevor's arm.

'I'll buy you one later. Where are the toilets?' Trevor asked the bouncer.

'I need a slash myself, I'll show you.'

It was only when the bouncer moved that Trevor realised just how large he was. Shaved head, thick neck, he could even see his oversized muscles banding his arms and thighs through his evening suit.

Trevor didn't answer the bouncer's question until they were washing their hands in the deserted toilets, which, from the utilitarian décor, Trevor guessed were staff. 'I buy and sell merchandise.'

'I guessed.' The bouncer dried his hands on a paper towel and offered it to Trevor. 'Jude.'

'Just Jude?' Trevor shook it.

'Williams. I work here three, sometimes four, nights a week. It pays the rent and covers my extras at the gym.'

'And your steroids.' Trevor didn't voice the thought.

'What you selling?'

Trevor lowered his voice. 'Grass, Charlie, good quality.'

'Price?'

'Quantity?'

'I'll take five grams of Charlie – if the price is right.'

Trevor knew the street value of good quality cocaine was based on a profit margin of 95%. He reduced it to 80%, but warned Jude, 'that's an introductory, rock bottom deal.'

'I'll take it.'

From the speed of Jude's take-up Trevor realised he'd pitched too low. 'My partner and I represent a consortium ...'

'I only take what I can shift in the gym. If you've steroids ...'

'We haven't. But we're looking to buy as well as sell. We've a ...' Trevor deliberately hesitated, '... a captive market. And from what we've heard Black Daffodil could be right for it.'

'Every bugger in town is after that at the moment. You don't want to go meddling with that stuff.'

'Why not?'

'Friend of mine got hold of some. Her wholesaler said it came from a good source. The Tafia …'

'Tafia?' Trevor interrupted.

'Welsh mafia,' the bouncer explained irritably. 'The Black Daffodil wasn't a regular line and there wasn't a lot of it. But my friend can always find punters willing to experiment if the price is low enough. She bought some and sold it on to the bottom end of the market in good faith. But there was something wrong with the batch. Her customers got a trip of a lifetime. For some it was their last.'

'So Black Daffodil is tainted?'

'That's the only bad lot I've heard about. But there's only one way to test merchandise and I'm not volunteering.'

'We were hoping that Black Daffodil would be the answer to our prayers.'

'That depends on what you prayed for,' the bouncer grinned.

'Profitable goods for a large and ready market.'

'I've heard there's Black Daffodil samples on offer. They won't be plentiful. Word is the manufacturer's looking to sell the rights, not just the merchandise.'

'How much?'

'B D pills wholesale at £2 a pop.'

'Retail?'

'I've heard of punters paying £5.'

'A single pill?' Trevor was sceptical.

'When they can get them.'

Trevor recalled Bill telling him 48 could be produced for a pound. No wonder every major dealer was after it. 'I'll exchange the Charlie for a sample. If I like what I get, there'll be more orders. A lot more,' Trevor promised.

'That's no good to me unless I'm already doing business with whoever buys the rights. You setting up a stall round here?' Jude asked suspiciously.

'Not in competition with the locals,' Trevor reassured him. 'When I said a captive market, I meant it.'

Jude looked bemused for a moment before his thin-lipped mouth curved into a smile. 'The slammer! I done pokey. Dog handlers and wardens are swine.'

'If Black Daffodil is all it's cracked up to be, easily transportable and undetectable to sniffer dogs, we're very interested. But can you get it?' Trevor pressed.

'Like I said, I can ask around. When do you want it?'

'Tomorrow?'

'You interested in the rights?'

'Possibly,' Trevor hedged.

'You'll have the Charlie tomorrow?'

'I will.'

A barman walked in, nodded to Jude, walked into a cubicle and shut the door.

Jude motioned his head towards the door. 'If I can't get what you want, I'll have the cash.'

The last thing Trevor wanted to do was play

straight dealer. 'You'll try?'

'My gym's in the city centre.' Jude fished a card out of his shirt pocket and handed it to Trevor, who pushed it into his wallet. 'I'll be there tomorrow from four till six.'

Trevor returned his wallet to his pocket.

Jude smiled as they headed back to the bar. 'Masha's waiting for you.'

'It's a good time to check on my friend's losing streak.'

'You don't gamble?' Jude asked.

'Only on dead certs.'

'After two years here I don't even put the odd tenner on a gee gee any more.' Jude turned to the main door.

Trevor's phone vibrated in the pocket of his jacket. He moved to the edge of the crowd around the blackjack table and discreetly checked the messages. There was only one from Chris.

HIT GOLD

Trevor smiled. There was nothing he or Peter could do before morning, but it was good to know that they didn't have to rely on Jude to come up with the goods. He fingered the keys and sent a return message.

C U SOON

Peter pulled off his tie as they walked into his suite. 'At one stage I was five grand up.' He shrugged off his suit jacket and tossed it beside his tie on to the bed.

'A wise gambler told me the only number that matters is the one you are up at the end of a session.' Trevor handed Peter a malt whisky, sat in a chair and lifted his feet on to Peter's bed.

'I said that?'

'You did.' Trevor lifted his glass. 'Here's to a speedy wrap.'

'And the fall of bloody wise arses.'

'How much you down?'

'What makes you think I'm down?' Peter demanded.

'How much?' Trevor repeated.

'Two hundred.'

'Given that you played for four hours you could say that was cheap entertainment. And the dealer was pretty.'

'Very.' Peter smiled.

'Drink up, we have places to go and people to see tomorrow.'

'Our gofers?'

'Sent a message. They hit gold.'

Peter whistled. 'Well done, gofers. I'm amazed.'

'Only because you don't want to believe anyone is as good as you when it comes to marketing.'

'I give credit when it's due.'

'I also want to call in the estate agent's.'

'You want to move to *Wales*?'

Given the theatrical emphasis Peter had put on the last word, Trevor thought it would be disappointing if their role-playing didn't have an audience. 'This city is booming. The right property here would be a gilt-edged investment. A penthouse with rental prospects appeals. It's a sin to leave hard-earned money lying idle.'

Peter opened the balcony doors and stepped

outside. Trevor joined him. The sky was navy blue, punctuated by golden lights on the ground and silver stars above.

'If the gods smile on us, we might also personally pick up the first batch of our preferred merchandise tomorrow.'

Peter faced him. 'You …'

'Made contact and put in an order for a sample.'

'Major player?'

'Minor but …'

'He has connections,' Peter finished for him.

'He confirmed that the merchandise rights are up for sale.' Trevor finished his drink. 'I'm for bed.' He left Peter's bedroom.

'First one up rings down for breakfast. Fried bread, black pudding – the works,' Peter shouted after him.

'I heard you. Muesli, skimmed milk, porridge, fruit juice …'

'There's only so much winding up a man can stand.' Peter returned to his bedroom and reached for the bottle of whisky Trevor had left next to his bed.

'He who dishes it out must also learn to take it,' Trevor called back.

'Always have to have the last bloody word, don't you.' Peter poured himself a generous measure of malt.

CHAPTER FIVE

The offices of Jones, Jones and Watkins were on the second floor of a mezzanine walkway, sandwiched between a Thai restaurant and an exclusive dress shop. Trevor knew it was exclusive because there were no prices on the garments in the windows and Lyn had taught him the meaning of the word 'exclusive' in relation to women's fashion.

He glanced at the properties on offer in the estate agent's window. Apart from two commercial units, both small and on the Bay, they were all apartments ranging in price from studios at a hundred and eighty thousand to penthouse duplexes for millions.

Peter pushed open the door. Trevor followed. A smartly dressed young girl left her desk and greeted them.

'How can I help you, sirs?'

Peter smiled at her. 'In many ways, darling. Would you like me to list them?'

The girl blushed and Trevor pushed Peter aside. The girl had used the standard – 'there's no get out, you have to answer me one way or another' – opening Masha had used; a transatlantic greeting that had found its way into every supermarket and fast-food outlet in the UK. Trevor hated it but it didn't warrant Peter's quip.

'We're interested in the new tower block penthouse development.'

'That is a very popular development, sir. Our Mr Horton is dealing with it. He is with another client at the moment. Have you registered your interest?'

73

'That's why we're here,' Trevor informed her.

'Could I have your names please?' She poised a pen over a notepad.

'Brown and Ashton.'

She made a note and gave them another empty smile. 'If you'll excuse me, I'll see how long Mr Horton is likely to be.' She disappeared into a back office and emerged a few seconds later.

'He will only be another ten minutes. In the meantime, perhaps you'd care to look at our brochure.' She pointed to a seating area at the back of the open-plan office and offered each of them a leaflet. 'Can I get you coffee? Or would you prefer tea?'

'Coffee, strong, black, four sugars.' Peter took the brochure from her.

'And you, sir?' She turned to Trevor.

'Black coffee, no sugar, thank you.' Trevor sat beside Peter.

Peter opened the brochure. 'Something strike you about the room dimensions on the cheapest option?'

Trevor checked them. 'Not particularly.'

'They're half the size of the rooms in the council flat I grew up in with my Mum and six brothers in Birmingham.'

Peter had never lived anywhere near Birmingham and only had one brother. But when Trevor checked the sizes against the photographs of the rooms, he realised the mock ups had either been taken with a very clever camera or furnished with child scale fittings.

'Mr Brown, Mr Ashton, so sorry to keep you

waiting.' Andrew emerged from the office. The front door opened and Trevor caught a glimpse of Alfred Harding leaving.

'Your secretary kept us amused.' Peter held up the brochure.

'I have detailed plans and models in my office. Hold all calls, Judy.'

'Yes, Mr Horton.'

Andrew shut his office door as soon as Trevor and Peter were inside. He held up a gadget and switched it on. 'No bugs, no eavesdropping devices. This building is squeaky clean.'

'I saw Alfred leaving. Did he pick up anything last night?' Trevor asked.

'Rumours that the club is being used to launder money.'

'Knowing Darrow, I believe them.' Peter finished his coffee.

'Belief doesn't constitute evidence,' Andrew retorted.

Peter gave a cold smile. 'Well done. I didn't know you could bite back, T-off.'

Because his office was the opposite end of their home station to Peter's, Trevor rarely saw Andrew and Peter together. He had forgotten about the ongoing feud between them. A feud that was so old he couldn't remember the origins of it – if he had ever known them. 'Did Alfred say anything else?' Trevor knew there was no point in asking Peter to cool it.

'The Darrows are running massage parlours and brothels through dummy companies.'

'That is old news,' Trevor sat back in his chair.

'His staff aren't old. According to what Alfred was told by one of the hostesses in the casino last night, in Darrow's down-market parlours, locals have been replaced by girls trafficked by gang masters. The hostess, who goes by the name of Alice, picked up Alfred and asked him to help her. Gave him the usual sob story, she's Jamaican, and was conned into coming to this country to take a nanny's job. When she reached Heathrow she was sold to the highest bidder, gang-raped and ended up in one of the downmarket brothels. It took her six months to graduate to the casino. She told Alfred she's watched all the time. She also said she's paid in drugs not cash. Most of the girls are users but she insisted she was clean and sold her 'cut' to one of the bouncers for cash.'

'Did Alfred get the name of the bouncer?' Peter dumped his empty cup on Andrew's desk.

'Fred, he's Asian. This Alice lives above a massage parlour. She works there by day and the casino by night. She told Alfred that she owes the gangmaster who brought her in five grand in expenses, which is why she works twenty hours a day and more.'

'Alfred believed her?' Trevor checked.

Andrew shrugged. 'It's an old story but believable. Lee was here at nine. On his way home after an all night session. Upstairs must have given him good references. He tapped into a private poker game. Said all the players could talk about was laying their hands on the merchandising rights to Black Daffodil. Officers using dogs busted two of the Triad shipments last month. Half a ton of heroin packed into Chinese knick knacks being shipped in from Taiwan and Hong Kong.' Andrew pushed his chair back from his desk and lifted his feet on to the corner. 'Servini and Patel called in briefly. They both said the same thing. The Mafia and Asians know about Black Daffodil but haven't a clue who's making it, haven't bought samples and aren't interested in the auction.'

'Obviously not in the running to widen their business interests. Markov and Lebov call in after their success at the tables last night?' Peter took his cigar box out of his pocket.

'So you weren't just playing blackjack,' Trevor observed.

'Buggers won two grand playing craps. Used their own money too so they don't have to hand it over,' Andrew said enviously.

'They called in?' Peter repeated.

'Ostensibly to register interest and report that they got wind of an auction. The manufacturer of Black Daffodil is offering the formula to the highest bidder. The Albanians have come in at twenty million. The Russians, fifty.'

'When's the deadline?' Peter questioned.

'They're trying to find out. You two got anything?'

Trevor glanced at his watch. 'Chris struck lucky and picked up merchandise. We're on our way there now.'

'I knew that boy was ambitious the first time I laid eyes on him.'

'I'm surprised you recognise ambition, given that you're lacking in that quality yourself, T-off,' Peter baited him.

Andrew bit back. 'One day I'll punch you on the nose.'

'Promises, promises,' Peter mocked.

'Hopefully, at four o'clock this afternoon, we'll pick up our own sample of 90 Black Daffodils, wholesaling at £2 a piece,' Trevor steered the conversation back on course.

'Big dealer?' Andrew looked interested.

'Small cog. But there's always the hope he'll lead us to someone bigger. Now we know there's an auction, I'll ask him to put in a bid for us.'

'With monopoly money?' Peter jeered. 'Whoever's behind this will want to see gilt-edged securities.'

'Andrew, get back to Dan and the super, and see if they can doctor something up that will bear scrutiny by the seller.'

'Will do,' Andrew nodded to Trevor. 'And, if your man leads you higher up the chain …'

'It won't be the top,' Trevor broke in. 'Whoever's manufacturing and marketing this stuff has the sense to lie low and let minions do his dirty work.' He left his chair and walked to the window. He peered through the blinds and looked down on their car parked in the street below. 'If Black Daffodil is being manufactured on that council estate, Chris or Sarah might have heard about the factory.'

'Let's hope they have. Then we can wrap this case and get back to real life. This is my first taste of undercover work,' Andrew divulged, 'and I'm glad it will be my last.'

'Serious police work too rough for you?' Once Peter started needling his colleagues he never knew when to stop.

'I'm here, aren't I?' Andrew snapped.

'A present if reluctant hero,' Peter agreed. 'I thought it would take a crowbar to prise you away from the golf club. Don't tell me you had a sudden attack of conscience and volunteered for this job.' Peter left his chair.

'It's no secret that Dan promised me a pension upgrade if I stayed on to see this case through.'

'Ah, money,' Peter nodded.

'Unlike you, working solely for the love of the job?'

'The perks,' Peter smiled. 'All expenses paid in a five-star hotel is just about bearable.'

'I thought the chance to live in a luxury flat on the Bay, a short drive from an exceptionally good golf course, was too good to miss. But that was before I discovered that I don't have any free time to drive to the course, let alone play on it.'

'Free time is something we've all kissed goodbye for a while.' Peter went to the door. 'I've a funny feeling about this one. Usually we face a stone wall at the beginning of an operation. There's too much information flying around.'

'Given the number of operators upstairs has put out there, I'd be more worried if the information wasn't coming in.' Andrew stacked their cups.

'That's all you know, "Mr first time undercover". Take it from a superior who knows. There are way too many leads.'

'The trouble with you is you like the difficult

life,' Andrew mimicked Peter's taunting tone.

'That's exactly what I'm saying, T-off. I don't like the difficult life, but undercover operatives have no choice but to live it. And it's the kind of life you know nothing about. Experience has taught me – and Trevor – that fortune doesn't smile on the likes of us unless she's lulling us into a false sense of security before splatting us like flies.'

'Breakfast, or rather brunch, is ready.' Chris forked the oven chips and chicken burgers he'd cooked in the frying pan onto plates. Kept awake half the night by their noisy quarrelsome neighbours playing their televisions at full blast, he and Sarah had fallen into a deep sleep as dawn broke. As a result they'd overslept.

Sarah walked into the kitchen from the living room where she had been watching TV. She stared in dismay at the plate Chris handed her. 'Do you call that breakfast? I don't even call it food.'

'There was nothing resembling food in that shop. I'd like to see what you would have come up with if you'd gone in.'

'I guarantee I would have found something better than this and the beefburger sandwiches we had yesterday.' She took the plate he handed her. 'One week of your idea of a diet and I'll put on a stone. Where's the salt and vinegar?'

'There isn't any.'

'No salt and vinegar?' she echoed in disbelief.

'Forgot, sorry,' Chris apologised.

'After our bosses call, I do the shopping.'

'Only with an escort.'

'Why? Sneezy wasn't so bad and no one else would talk to us.'

Chris dumped the frying pan in the sink. 'Is that the name of the boy who sold you those four Black Daffodils?'

'The only one he would give me.'

'I can't wait to see Doc, Happy, Dopey ...'

'You've been spending way too much time with Peter.' She held up her plate. 'Want to watch the news? It might make us forget we're eating cardboard.'

'By immersing ourselves in the troubles in the Middle East and gang warfare in London?'

'I found an old film on one of the channels. It's a weepie.'

'News will do. I'll be with you as soon as I've fed the dog.' Chris tipped a generous helping of the dry dog food into the stainless steel bowl he'd brought up from the car. He refilled the water bowl but he didn't have to call the German shepherd. Tiger recognised the sound and smell of his food being poured. He ran in and stood patiently, tail wagging, waiting for Chris to set the bowls on the floor.

'You know that dog food doesn't look half bad,' Sarah watched Tiger wolf it down.

'Would you like it with skimmed or semi skimmed milk?' Chris followed Sarah into the living room, sat on the sofa and balanced his plate on his lap.

'How about freshly squeezed orange juice?'

'They didn't have oranges. And stop complaining.'

'Soon as we've eaten, I'll take another walk to that shop. I won't be gone long and you never know. They might have had a delivery from a greengrocer.'

'Or we could wait for our visitors and leave after they've gone. The dog could do with a walk and we could drive back via Asda,' he suggested.

'That would be cheating.'

'No one said anything to me about where we should buy our groceries.' He pulled a black bit from an oven chip before forking it into his mouth.

'These aren't wonderful at the best of times, but they are better cooked in the oven than a frying pan. As the manufacturer advises,' Sarah criticised.

They stopped eating at a timid knock at the door of the flat.

Chris turned down the TV. 'Sneezy?'

'He said he'd stop by if he tracked down more Black Daffodil.'

'He might have been here sooner if someone hadn't been soft enough to give him half a gram of cocaine for four pills. Unlike us, he probably had a great evening.'

A disembodied voice wafted through the keyhole. 'Dog girl. I got what you want. Let me in. Quick!'

'Dog girl?' Chris left the sofa. 'As opposed to cat woman. Who am I, Batman or the Joker?'

'A Peter clone,' she retorted irritably. 'Go easy on Sneezy. I feel sorry for him.'

Although Chris wouldn't have admitted it to Sarah, he pitied the junkie, and probably for sounder reasons. During his stint patrolling a council estate he had seen first-hand the effects of the despair long-term unemployment caused and the moral bankruptcy and crime it led to. Along with his colleagues he'd faced daily battles with an army of social rejects who'd taken the easy route out of society that pills, alcohol, bongs or syringes offered. 'Family' was too strong a word to describe some of the groups drawn together by accidents of birth and the need to remain together so they could receive maximum state benefits.

Blighted before they even began their schooling, kids turned to crime almost as soon as they could walk and talk, because, contrary to government thinking, in his opinion no amount of sympathetic teaching or well-meant 'schemes' could compensate for the absence of a home life. But sympathy didn't stop him from reaching into the oversized pocket of his cargo pants and wrapping his hands around the Taser he'd been issued, or checking that the handgun Dan had slipped him was still in his back pocket.

He looked through the spy hole and saw the skeletal boy hopping from one foot to another. Was Sneezy desperate for a fix? Or was his uneasiness down to something more sinister?

Chris pulled back the three deadbolts but left the safety chain on. He wondered if the Housing Association fitted high security locks on all their high-rise property, or just the ones they rented out to the police. The links on the chain were sound, the door and frame were steel-reinforced. Not burglar proof. He had seen similar ones sliced open by acetylene cutters. But it was solid enough to deter the casual thief. He opened the door a few inches.

The door thudded back as far as the chain would allow. Metal cutters sliced through the links and the door crashed against the wall. A fist flew over Sneezy's shoulder. Chris ducked. Not quickly enough. The blow connected with his cheek bone instead of his jaw and sent him reeling across the room.

Sarah jumped up. Her plate, burgers and chips crashed to the floor. She turned and saw four men burst in. Sneezy stood, gnawing his knuckles, behind them. He caught sight of her staring and ran.

Alerted by the commotion, Tiger charged in from the kitchen. The man who'd thumped Chris, pulled a knife and waved it in front of Chris's eyes. Tiger flew across the room, sank his teeth into the man's hand and forced him to drop the weapon. Chris saw one of the men pointing a pistol at the dog. He pulled out his gun and fired. He knew, even as he squeezed the trigger, that the angle was wrong. The bullet ricocheted off the steel door and hit the man's shoulder. The thug yelped and dropped his pistol. The third man slammed Chris into the wall.

Tiger pinned the man who'd pulled the knife to the floor. His companion tried to drag the dog away, but Tiger sank his teeth further into the man's hand. Blood spurted, spraying the walls.

Sarah reached down the side of the sofa in search of the Taser she'd hidden there. Her fingers closed around it as the fourth and largest man grabbed her by the neck and dragged her backwards. There was no time to fire. She lifted it and, with all the strength she could muster, hit him on the side of his head.

'I likes girls who fight back.' He grabbed the Taser, wrenched it from her and pointed it at the dog.

Sarah screamed. 'Tiger!' too late.

He fired.

Tiger yelped and rolled, lifeless, on his side.

The man tightened his grip on Sarah and yelled at his companions. 'Get that bloody dog out.'

The thug who'd dropped the knife dragged Tiger's body outside, slammed the door and turned on Chris who was slumped, barely conscious, in the corner, legs stretched out in front of him, back to the wall, pointing his gun at the men.

One of them picked up the pistol. Chris fired. His bullet hit his target's thigh. The second man flung himself on Chris and grabbed the gun. It fired twice in quick succession. Chunks of plaster flew down from the ceiling. He grabbed Chris's head and slammed it against the wall. The lout who'd taken out the dog kicked Chris in the chest. Dazed, nauseous, Chris was too far gone to fight.

Sarah's assailant locked his fingers into her hair and dragged her backwards into the inner hall. She screamed and lashed out furiously to no effect before instinctively resorting to the moves she'd been taught in self-defence sessions. She flung herself forward, caught the man off balance, planted one foot on the floor and kicked back at his shins with the other, before swivelling round and grabbing his genitals.

He screamed but knotted his fingers even more tightly into her hair before slapping her soundly across the head with his free hand. He threw her into one of the bedrooms, stepped after her and locked his arm around her throat. She could hear Tiger scratching and whimpering outside the door and fought all the harder.

'You want it rough?' Her attacker lifted her head to his. His teeth were black and broken. She reeled as a wave of stinking beer breath wafted over her. Determined he wouldn't get the better of her, she brought back her elbow and thrust it into his solar plexus. The breath hissed from between his lips but his grip remained firm.

He thrust Sarah on the bed, jumped on top of her and pressed the full weight of his arm across her neck, cutting off her air supply. She reached up and dug her fingernails into his eyes and cheeks, scraping and tearing at his skin. He relaxed his hold for an instant. Utilising every ounce of strength she possessed, she propped herself up. He brought back his hand and punched her across the head. Ringing filled her ears. Darkness crept inwards from the corners of the room when he punched her again – and again – and again –

The last thing she heard was shouts from the living room and Tiger scratching at the door in the outer hall. Random thoughts sparked through her mind.

'Please don't let them hurt the dog or Chris. Please don't let them hurt the dog or Chris … Please …' She plunged downwards into a swirling mist.

Peter drew up outside the tower block, glanced at the rubbish strewn parking area and remained on the road.

'This is it?' Trevor leaned forward and looked upwards.

'The address we were given.' Peter removed the ignition keys.

'You see what I see?'

Peter glanced through the window. 'Parked pizza delivery van?'

'Pizza delivery painted on the side but no telephone number or logo. Not keen to advertise and not very bright. Take a look at the driver watching the door of the tower block.'

'Could be he's waiting for someone to deliver a pizza.'

'At midday around here?' Trevor said sarcastically.

'You're right; Giro bunnies don't leave their bed until sundown.'

'Could be Chris and Sarah's deals have annoyed the local supplier and that's his driver. Is there another entrance to the block?' Trevor asked.

'It's worth taking a look.' Peter started the car and drove around until they faced the back of the building.

'No door.'

'Boarded up windows on the ground floor.'

'Bring the torch,' Trevor ordered.

Five minutes later Peter had located a loose board and they were inside an abandoned ground floor flat. It was pitch black and the electricity had been cut off. The fetid air stank and the floor was littered with syringes and other debris they were reluctant to examine.

'Third floor,' Trevor checked after recalling the

briefing notes he'd memorised.

'Third floor,' Peter confirmed. 'You know what I hate most about these bloody places. The stench. Stick this in Westminster and it would be advertised as a spacious luxury block with panoramic views from the top floors. Why do some people live like bloody pigs?'

'Don't insult pigs.'

'I keep forgetting you grew up on a farm. At least pigs don't inject themselves with bloody crap.' Peter kicked half a dozen syringes aside, shone the torch on the floor and picked his way towards the door.

CHAPTER SIX

Chris was soaked in blood and hurting but he sensed very little of the blood was his. He pushed thoughts of Aids from his mind. That was something to consider later – if he survived.

The man he'd shot in the shoulder was kicking him, the one he'd wounded in the thigh was lying across him and the third was punching his head. But he was too concerned for Sarah to consider his own predicament. She had stopped screaming. The silence emanating from the bedroom was worse than her cries. Ominous and foreboding.

For all the talk of and insistence on equality in the force, he felt he should have protected her. Instead, he was helpless, cornered by three thugs. While ... what? His partner was being raped ...

'Don't fuck with us. This is our turf. No bastard is going to move in and undercut us.'

Chris groaned when the steel toe-capped boot connected with his ribcage.

'Give us your gear and we might let you crawl away.' The man palmed a knife that dropped down from his sleeve.

Chris gritted his teeth and braced himself for more pain.

The man rose slowly into the air. He hovered there, his feet dangling six inches off the ground as his two companions rolled away. Chris stared, mesmerized as the two wounded men struggled to rise.

Tiger bounded up to him, licked his face, turned,

bared his teeth and snarled at the two men who'd backed against the wall. Chris watched his assailant continue to sway, apparently unsupported for what seemed like minutes although it could only have been seconds before he crumpled to the floor.

'Ups a daisy, sunshine.' Peter leaned over Chris and offered him a hand. Chris allowed Peter to heave him upright. He perched, breathless and light headed on the windowsill. Tiger was lying at Trevor's feet. Dog and man were glaring at the two men against the wall. It was only then Chris saw the gun in Trevor's hand. Tiger continued growling, anticipating an order to attack. The men watched the dog – in between eyeing Trevor's gun.

Chris's head cleared. 'Sarah …' He staggered upright. 'The bedroom …' he lurched towards the inner door.

Peter kicked the man he'd hauled off Chris towards the other two before charging after Chris into the inner hall.

Sarah was lying on the bed. A man was leaning over her, pulling down her jeans. Peter pushed Chris aside, slipped his hand into his pocket, brought it out and slammed the back of his fist against the man's head. The would-be rapist grunted and rolled off the bed onto the floor.

Chris saw the dull glint of brass. 'Knuckleduster?'

'When you play with the big boys you need their toys. See to Sarah.' Sarah was a good-looking girl and despite the often hard-edged banter he'd exchanged with her, Peter admired her. He wanted to kill the man who'd almost succeeded in violating her. If he and Trevor had stopped on the way for fish and chips as he'd wanted to, they would have been too late …

Chris folded the duvet over Sarah. 'I'll give you a hand with him.' He pointed to the man on the floor.

'I'll put the rubbish out. You check Sarah, wash the blood off yourself and change your clothes.' Peter locked his fingers into the back of the man's collar, dragged him through the door and closed it behind him. He hauled the man into the living room and dropped him in front of the two who were upright and the one who was lying in front of them.

Trevor eyed the four men. The one Peter had brought in was unconscious and had the beginnings of a bruise spreading out from behind his ear. The thug Peter had lifted off Chris was balanced precariously on his left leg, his right trouser leg soaked in his own blood. Of the two he had cornered, one had blood running down his arm; the other was nursing a bloodied hand.

Trevor couldn't risk blowing his and Peter's cover. Neither could he allow the thugs to run wild or attack Chris and Sarah again.

'We need to get them downstairs,' he said to Peter.

Peter had worked so closely with Trevor over the years he knew exactly what he was thinking. 'I'll bring in their driver.'

He returned five minutes later with a stocky man who was sweating from more than his excess weight.

Trevor waved his gun. The man lined up

alongside his companions.

'Empty your pockets on the floor. All of you. And his.' Trevor nudged the man who was still unconscious with the toe of his shoe. He hadn't looked at the dog, but Tiger lunged forward. The men moved. Wallets, keys, cigarettes, condoms and packets of drugs piled up at their feet. Peter picked up the drugs, opened the packs and sniffed them.

'Crystal meth, Pot, E's, Charlie, GHB …'.Peter opened one packet wet his finger dipped it into the white powder and tasted it. 'Smack.'

Trevor motioned with his gun. 'Stuff everything back into your pockets. Then downstairs.'

The man with a bullet in his thigh whined. 'He's out of it. I can't walk …'

'Then we'll drop the pair of you over the banister. Unless you prefer to slide down on your arses.' Peter pushed him off balance. The man soon dragged himself away.

Twenty minutes later, stomachs heaving at the latrine stench, Peter and Trevor watched the driver and battered and wounded men haul their comatose friend into the downstairs flat.

Trevor cleared an area with his foot for the dog and ordered Tiger to stay. Leaving the door open enough to allow in a sliver of light, he motioned Peter aside.

'My carry-on is in the boot.'

'Cable ties and a gas canister?' Peter asked.

'Give our tame copper a ring. He'll be interested in this little lot and what they're carrying.' Trevor didn't bother to lower his voice.

Peter left.

Trevor stepped back into the flat. 'We know who you are, and where your families live.' Trevor had no doubt that the local force could supply details if he needed them. 'Tangle with us, or our friends again and you'll take a short walk off a steep cliff. One word from you about what's happened here and we'll get to you inside, because that's where you're going. Don't even think about calling in favours to even the score. Try, and there'll be a bloodbath. In your houses, not ours.' He paused. 'Understood?'

The men's eyes shone in the subdued light of the torch.

'This is now our estate. If as much as one hair on either of our operatives' heads is touched, you and your families won't live to see another sunset.'

'Bastard ...'

'He's got a death wish. Can I kill him?' Peter had returned. The man fell gibbering to the floor, when Peter pulled out his gun.

Peter handed Trevor half the ties. 'I asked the tame one for five minutes grace.'

They set to work fastening the men's ankles together and their wrists securely behind their backs. They went to the door and waited. Peter activated and threw in the C S gas canister when they heard the first siren.

'Remember, this is our estate.' Trevor closed the door on the sound of coughing. He raced back up the stairs behind Tiger and Peter.

Trevor and Peter sat on the chairs of the three piece suite, leaving the sofa for Chris and Sarah. Someone – Trevor guessed Chris – had righted the furniture and tried to wipe the blood from the walls. Smears remained.

Chris saw him looking at them. 'I only had soap and water. I need to go to the shop to buy a few things.'

Trevor took a sweeper identical to the one Andrew had used in the estate agent's office from his pocket. He switched it on and walked around the flat, checking every room. 'I think the place is clean.'

'Forget the shop; we need to get the two of you out of here.' Peter made a face as he drank the instant coffee Chris had made.

'Why?' Sarah asked. 'Those men are in custody – they'll stay there – won't they?'

'I phoned Andrew. He contacted the locals for us. Even if those thugs have someone on the inside of the local force prepared to lose relevant paperwork, I know Bill. He'll make sure they are remanded in custody. The drugs and weapons they were carrying, even without the charges of intimidation and assault, are enough to keep them inside until they go to trial. Hopefully we'll have this operation wrapped by then.' Trevor set his cup on the coffee table.

'You need an Aids test,' Peter warned Chris.

'I'll see about it.'

'Phone Bill on one of your disposable Sim cards,' Trevor ordered. 'He'll arrange it and check ups for both of you after the beatings you took. Ask him to run health checks on the men to see if any of them are positive.'

'I'll do that.' Chris knew what the odds were of a

drug user having Aids and he didn't doubt that the men were users.

'This afternoon,' Trevor ordered.

'We will. But if the men have been locked up there's no reason why we can't stay on here,' Sarah pleaded.

'After what you've just gone through?' Trevor knelt before Sarah and lifted her chin gently to expose the bruise that had spread across her neck.

'That party was held on this estate. Sneezy found us four Black Daffodils within an hour, so we know it's available ...'

'There could be two kinds.' Trevor told them what Jude had said about suspect pills being the cause of the deaths of the people on the estate. He looked at Sarah's face, taut and ashen and Chris's cuts and bruises. 'Peter's right, we have to get you out.'

'A couple more days might make all the difference,' Chris added his plea to Sarah's. 'With those men inside there's a vacancy for a dealer around here.'

'Let some other bugger take the risk,' Peter left the chair and went to the window.

'We're already here. There's no sense in bringing in new agents who will need time to get as far as we have.'

'Sarah has a point,' Chris said firmly.

'You two don't know when to give up, do you?' Trevor wasn't sure whether he should praise or argue with them.

'See it from our point of view, sir ...'

'Trevor,' Trevor corrected Sarah.

'Trevor,' Sarah continued. 'You've been in this job for ever …'

'Thank you very much for making me feel like Methuselah,' Peter said.

'I didn't mean it that way,' Sarah said hastily. 'Plain clothes is a step up for us.'

They stiffened at a knock at the door. Chris dragged himself off the sofa and went to the spy hole. Trevor and Peter pulled out their guns and moved stealthily behind him.

'Who is it?' Chris shouted.

'Moselle. Sneezy said he's sorry for what happened. They followed him. He didn't see them until it was too late. He needs stuff real bad. There's no one else he can go to round here now.'

Trevor nodded to Chris and stepped behind the door. Peter moved the other side and stood flat against the wall.

Chris pulled the bolts back. A girl held out a bundle of grubby notes. 'Sneezy feels bad about Jon's boys.'

'I don't buy your "they followed him" story.' Chris made no attempt to take the money.

'I told Sneezy you wouldn't. They paid him a visit because he was late picking up his stuff. They beat this address out of him. But we heard the coppers have them.'

'That was quick,' Chris growled.

'We saw them being dragged into the police van. And, like I said, there isn't anyone else dealing except you around here now. Please, you have to help us. We need Charlie … we're desperate … I wouldn't be here if we weren't.'

Peter pocketed his gun and moved into view. The girl looked about twelve. Skinny as most addicts were, with sores around her nose and mouth – a legacy of glue sniffing before she moved on to the hard stuff? Her eyes were enormous, too large for her white, pinched face, her pupils dilated.

Chris took the notes she offered. He counted them out as though he had all the time in the world, watching her grow more and more agitated with every passing second. Eventually he pulled a gram bag of cocaine from his back pocket and handed it to her. 'Tell Sneezy there's another like this for free when he brings me more Black Daffodil. In person.'

'You just want to find a bigger dealer than Sneezy,' she challenged.

'That's right.' Chris didn't attempt to lie.

She walked away then turned back at the top of the stairs. 'Want me to put the word out that this is a new shop?'

'Yes.' Chris tried another tack. 'Can you arrange a meet with the supplier of Black Daffodil?'

She shook her head. 'Only Sneezy knows who that is.'

'Then tell Sneezy we need to see him – urgently.'

'Sneezy's afraid to come here after what he did to you.' She eyed Peter warily.

'Remind him I'm offering free goods. That gram won't last for ever.'

'I'll tell him but I can't make him come here.' She hesitated. 'You're crazy, you are. Black Daffodil killed my friends. Stick to weed and Charlie. You know where you are with them.'

Chris and Peter watched her run down the stairs.

Peter drove out of the estate and took a turn that led away from the city.

'Why the scenic route?' Trevor asked when they left the estates behind them and drove past trees, fields bordered by hedgerows, grey stone walls and the occasional farmhouse.

'Because I saw you looking at your watch.' Peter swerved into a parking area screened by birch. Although there were no people in sight he parked the car as far from the picnic benches as possible. 'After that estate a ploughed field looks remarkably clean.' He took a pack of cigars from his pocket.

'Bill won't appreciate a bill from the rental company to remove the smell of tobacco from the upholstery.' Trevor took his mobile phone from his pocket, opened the back, removed the Sim card and stowed it in the glove compartment. He extracted one of the disposable Sim cards from his wallet, placed it in his phone, closed the back and stepped outside. The air was fresh, fragrant, and cool after the suffocating heat of the concrete-walled estate. He switched on the phone and waited for it to pick up the signal before dialling Lyn's mobile. She answered on the third ring.

'Hello … is anyone there?'

'It's me.' His voice sounded unnaturally deep and husky. 'How are you? Both of you?'

'Burgeoning, blooming,' the tone of her voice changed and he visualised her moving into determinedly cheerful mode for his benefit. 'Bending your credit card as I promised we would.'

'Bend it all you like. Whatever you're buying, get the best. You both deserve it.'

'You have no idea how expensive the best is.' He detected a slight catch in her voice.

'You have the emergency number safe?'

'Yes.'

'You've given it to your mother?'

'Stop worrying. I'm fine. I saw your other half's other half last night. We went out for a meal.'

'Is she OK?'

'Missing her paramour almost as much as we're missing you. Tell him she said it was good to eat in a healthy place for a change.'

'I'll pass on the message. Take care of yourselves. Long to see you.'

'And me you, although it's only been a day and a half. Remember, we both love and need you very much.'

'Love you back.' Trevor ended the call, took out the Sim card and cracked it between his fingers. There was a McDonald's on the way back to the city. Peter would want to drop in there. He'd never known a man so addicted to fast food. And a bin in a public toilet was a good place to dump incriminating evidence.

He returned to the car. Peter was still in the driving seat, listening to the news on the radio. He'd opened all the windows and was thoughtfully holding his cigar outside the car. He looked quizzically at Trevor.

'She's fine, they both are.' Trevor sat beside him. 'She and Daisy went out for a meal.' Trevor opened the glove compartment, retrieved the Sim card he had put in there and returned it to his phone. 'Daisy commented that it was nice to eat healthily for once.'

'Irritating woman lives on carrots, spinach and lettuce leaves.'

'She looks fantastic on it.' Trevor closed the back of his cell phone and glanced at his watch. 'It's only two o'clock. We don't have to be in the city until four. Why don't you call her?'

'In my own good time.'

'It wouldn't kill you to admit you're besotted.'

'I feel guilty as hell leaving those two babies in that council flat.' Peter turned the key in the ignition.

'They're experienced officers and I should have known better than to bring up a personal subject with you.'

'Those jokers might not be the only the dealers operating on the estate looking to get at Chris and Sarah for having their nose pushed out of joint.'

'The front door on the flat is solid. They're armed,' Trevor reminded him. 'Provided they don't make the mistake of opening it to the wrong people again, they'll be fine until morning. We can look in on them again then. Did Andrew say anything about telling the locals they're undercover when you passed on the location of the thugs?'

'He said that the locals have been alerted that Chris is an-ex con. They've been warned to leave him and his girlfriend alone unless the situation is life-threatening because serious crimes is hoping Chris can lead them to a major dealer.'

'So the locals won't interfere?'

'Not unless bullets fly or Andrew calls them again. He said the police patrols on the estate were told not to show a higher than normal profile before or after Chris and Sarah moved in, for fear of frightening off the big man.'

'How did Andrew intend to explain away our call about the thugs we left in the ground floor flat?'

'By telling them the tip-off came from one of the big man's henchmen who'd been ordered to clear the decks of local operators so Chris and Sarah could begin trading.' Peter took a tin from the side pocket in the car door.

'I suppose a big man in the background would make any other dealers' pet thugs wary of tackling Chris and Sarah.'

'With luck, after our success in taking those scumbags out of circulation, the opposition will have one of us down as the big man.' Peter squashed his cigar in the tin.

'Will the local force buy the story?'

'Bent or straight, I see no reason why they shouldn't.' Peter closed the tin and returned it to the side pocket.

'Smoking is a filthy habit,' Trevor said.

'So Daisy keeps telling me.' Peter put the car into gear and reversed.

'Do it around my offspring and I'll throttle you.'

'I don't doubt you will. Back to the city?'

'Via Macdonald's.'

'You hate burgers.'

'Their coffee's good and I want to get rid of the Sim card.'

'I'd forgotten how careful you have to be about

every nit-picking, microscopic thing; and how it plays on your nerves.'

'Even all expenses paid in a five-star hotel?'

'Especially in a five-star hotel, all-expenses-paid,' Peter answered. 'Can you think of a less likely place you and I could afford to move into semi-permanently?'

'The taste of luxury has spoiled you for everyday life?'

'Knowing the only people who can afford the kind of luxury we're living in are the bad guys.'

'Everyday life has compensations five-star hotels don't,' Trevor smiled.

Peter saw the smile. 'Only for those who believe life is fair and crime doesn't pay.'

CHAPTER SEVEN

Peter and Trevor found Jude Williams working with weights in the main area of the gym. He saw them and made a show of lifting the bar high above his head before dropping it on the stand.

'What do you think?' He climbed off the bench and waved his arm expansively.

'About what?' Trevor was mystified by the question.

'Is this the sort of place you'd like to take out full membership?'

Trevor saw people watching them and realised Jude was providing an explanation for his and Peter's presence. He hadn't considered that Jude might be a member of staff but it made sense for a minor dealer to hold down two part-time jobs. It would double his customer base. And selling gym membership and conducting tours of the facilities would give Jude a convenient cover to set up meetings with suppliers and customers.

Trevor nodded. 'From what I've seen. I might consider joining if I leave the hotel.'

'I'd say the standard of this gym is on a par with that of a five-star hotel.' Jude picked up a towel and slung it around his neck.

'How do you know where we're staying?' Trevor asked suspiciously. There was only one five-star hotel on the bay.

'I asked around.'

Peter gave up waiting for Trevor to introduce him and offered Jude his hand. 'Peter Ashton.'

'Jude was worried about you last night. He thought you'd invented a system to beat the blackjack dealer. I told him you average an annual five grand loss.'

'Last year it was nearer ten.' Peter winced as Jude closed his fingers around his. 'Some grip you have there.'

'Sorry, used to guys who work out.'

'Not wimps like me.' Peter parried his hard look.

'Join and I'll come up with a tailor made exercise and diet plan that will turn you into ...'

'An even more handsome Adonis?' Peter interrupted.

Jude backed down. 'Want the full tour?'

'Why not?' Trevor gazed at the treadmills, exercise bikes, elliptical trainers and stepping and rowing machines. He saw Peter looking at them and wondered if the same thought was going through his mind. The hollow tubing of an average exercise machine could be used to conceal a sizeable shipment of drugs. Perhaps he'd been on the job too long. Not so much meeting trouble halfway, but seeing it when it wasn't there.

'This place is well-equipped and, as it's pretty close to office closing time, it doesn't seem to be over-used,' Trevor remarked.

'Come back at six. We operate a booking system on some of the machines.'

'What else you got here?' Peter asked.

'Hot tubs, sauna, swimming pool, massage – straight massage,' Jude added in response to Peter's leer. They left the workout area and walked down a corridor lined with curtained cubicles. Most of the curtains were open and half a dozen men were conducting a conversation about football while being oiled and pummelled by a team of male and female masseurs. Jude hadn't lied about the 'straight massage'. Judging by their looks, the masseurs had been chosen solely for their skill.

'Cold pool,' Jude opened a door and showed them a deserted white tiled room with a pool in the centre.

'More like a bloody fridge pool.' Peter retreated from the blast of freezing air.

'Hot tub.' Jude opened another door. Steam wafted out to meet them from an empty, bubbling tub. 'We have twelve rooms like this, each hot tub can seat six, but we have a corporate one that caters for twelve, fifteen if you're prepared to get cosy.'

'Convivial as long as none of your colleagues have any nasty skin diseases,' Peter observed.

'We have to enter the pool area through the changing rooms.' Jude took them down another corridor and pushed a door marked MALE CHANGING ROOM.

It was deserted. Jude turned a corner, pulled a bunch of keys from his pocket and unlocked a second door. 'Staff quarters.' He opened a locker and lifted out a brochure. 'Here you are, Mr Brown. All the details of the club are in there, including individual and corporate membership fees.'

Trevor flicked through the pages. The last one was thicker than the others. When he examined it he saw two had been stuck together. He peeled back the corner of the topmost one and saw rows of pills encased in cellophane. He realised why Black

Daffodil had acquired its name. They were shaped like daffodil trumpets.

'Ninety,' Jude whispered. 'I may not be able to get more before the rights are sold. It's rumoured the deadline on the auction of the formula is close.'

'The Havana cigars I promised you.' Trevor took a wooden cigar box from his pocket and handed it to Jude.

Jude flipped the lid. 'Good to do business with you, Mr Brown.' He stowed the box in his locker, turned the key and led the way back, stopping to lock the door to the staff quarters.

'Will we see you in the casino tonight?' Trevor asked.

'My night off. I'll be there tomorrow.' He raised his voice. 'The pool is through here. You'll have to stay behind the footbath.'

'Excuse me.' A plump, short, balding man, with a towel tied around his waist, pushed past as they entered the shower area, only to back off when Peter glared. 'Sorry, Jude. Didn't realise you were showing people round.'

'Prospective members,' Jude explained.

Trevor held up the brochure. 'Impressive facilities.'

'Best in the city,' the man looked at Trevor and Peter for a moment. 'Excuse me.' He disappeared into the changing room.

Peter looked pointedly at his watch. 'We have another meeting.'

Trevor led the way back to the changing room. 'If you walk us out Jude, we can discuss that corporate membership.'

'As I said, Mr Brown, I'm not sure we can cater for the numbers you are looking to place.'

'We have a very large customer base, very large,' Trevor emphasised. 'We're hoping to supply all of them with regular sessions.'

'I will be in a position to give you a better idea tomorrow.'

'We'll discuss exact numbers then. But, as my colleague has pointed out, we're late for a meeting. I've learned not to keep estate agents waiting.'

'You buying property here?' Jude fished.

'Looking at a penthouse on the bay.' Trevor headed towards the main door of the building.

Peter pulled out his phone and opened it. 'Vibrate.' He explained when Jude looked at him. 'Text just arrived.' He hit a few buttons and held the phone high to get a better view of the screen. 'Do you have a bar or restaurant here?'

Trevor checked the time. It was almost five and they needed to get the pills to Andrew ASAP so he could ferry them to the lab.

'Juice and salad bar in the basement,' Jude answered.

'No alcohol – no fast food?' Peter continued to fiddle with his phone.

'You can't get faster food than salad. You only have to wash it in mineral water. And alcohol wouldn't be healthy in a gym.'

'No point in getting fit if you can't abuse your body afterwards.' Peter closed his phone and returned it to his pocket.

'I have a client coming in at five. See you again, gentlemen.' Jude left them at the door.

'What was the text about?' Trevor asked when they were outside.

'Later.' Peter unlocked their car.

'As we're going to arrive after closing, thanks to you, I'll phone the agents.' Trevor speed-dialled the number.

'Jones Jones and Watkins how may I help you?'

Trevor recognised the voice of the girl they had met that morning.

'Trevor Brown. I need to clarify a few points with Mr Horton.'

'We're about to close, Mr Brown. If you'd like to ring back in the morning …'

'This won't take a moment. It could make the difference between closing a deal and looking elsewhere.'

'I'll put you through, Mr Brown.'

'Andy Horton.'

Trevor climbed into the car alongside Peter. 'I have to see you right away, Mr Horton. Could we call round in the next ten minutes?'

'As long as it is ten minutes, Mr Brown.' Trevor knew Andrew was talking for the benefit of the staff when he added, 'the rest of the staff are about to leave for the day. Knock on the door when you arrive.'

'I appreciate your time, Mr Horton.'

'So what was all that discussion about a bar?' Trevor asked Peter as they left the centre of the city and headed for the bay.

'You didn't see him?'

'See who?' Trevor asked irritably.

'Could be something, might be nothing. Tell you

later.'

'There are times when I wish someone other than me would work with you.'

Peter grinned at him. 'Admit it, you love me really.'

Andrew opened the door when he saw Trevor and Peter step on the mezzanine. He ushered them straight into his inner office. To Trevor's surprise Alfred and Dan were there.

'Alfred will be leaving in ten minutes in case anyone's watching, which will have given him exactly fifteen minutes here.' Dan informed them.

'Apparently I've put down a deposit on a flat. A studio resale on the second floor of a five-year-old block,' Alfred folded a sheaf of papers and pushed them into the inside pocket of his suit jacket. 'No five-star accommodation for poor me.'

Dan came straight to the point. 'Andrew said you might have Black Daffodils.'

Trevor looked quizzically at Peter.

'I mentioned Chris and Sarah struck lucky and we were going mining for more,' Peter perched on the edge of Andrew's desk. It was gloomy in the office. The blinds were closed and Andrew hadn't switched on the lights.

Trevor handed Dan the brochure and the screwed up corner of newspaper that contained the four pills Chris had acquired from Sneezy. 'We bought the brochure from our seller. The odd ones came from the housing estate. Our seller might not be able to get more. It's rumoured the auction of the formula is about to close. Chris and Sarah are advertising a cocaine for Black Daffodil deal that might bring in more, and hopefully a line to contacts higher up the chain.'

'We've heard about the auction closing from other sources.' Dan peeled open the back pages.

Peter looked at the pills. 'Pretty.'

'Very,' Dan agreed. 'I'll get these to the lab. Alfred?'

'The people I've met are looking for the inventor, manufacturer and developer ... '

'Aren't we all,' Peter broke in.

'Not to waste them. A conference was held this morning. My people know they can't outbid the Russians so they're out to kill Black Daffodil before it hits the streets. They realise that something this cheap could wipe out their trade.'

'It doesn't take a genius to predict that it will do that,' Trevor agreed.

'They've arranged a meet with the seller in the club tonight so they can make him a fake offer in the hope of getting to the manufacturer so they can put a price on his head. As for the meet – other than "one hour after midnight" I've no idea what time, at what table, or even if it's in the main area,' Alfred concluded.

'Stick to your new mates like glue,' Dan ordered. 'I've called all the operatives and asked them to be in the casino at eleven.'

'Have you alerted the locals?' Trevor asked.

'No. One informant could blow this case and your covers. Alfred's friends aren't the only ones who are thinking waste.' Dan hunched forward on his chair. He looked like a giant sitting on kindergarten furniture. 'Lee called in at midday. The Chinese are also out to kill the Russian deal before it's made. Their trade is worth millions and they're not about to give it up.'

'They going to make a fake offer too?' Peter tapped a cigar from his box.

'Lee's trying to find out more. We gave him good credentials, but he's the new boy from Hong Kong.'

'Albanians still in?' Trevor asked.

'Upped their offer to fifty-five million this afternoon according to Justin. They're planning to talk to the vendors in Darrow's club tonight but he doesn't know their identity. Markov heard that the Russians are prepared to go as high as sixty million, but he suspects that's big talk to put off the rival bidders. Maria and Michael have been invited to dinner by the Columbians tonight.'

Peter whistled. 'Lucky them, I love tortillas and enchiladas washed down with tequila.'

'Michael offered to part bankroll the purchase of the formula in exchange for a share of the profits. He and Maria think the Columbians are about to make a bid.'

'So, the Russians and Albanians want to buy. The Columbians possibly and the Chinese and Jamaicans are out to kill whoever's making the stuff. And someone in the local Tafia passed on tainted pills.' Trevor summarised the information Jude had given him about the tainted pills that had killed three addicts on the estate.

'The Italians?' Peter looked to Dan.

'Tony has seen evidence of a trade in

111

amphetamines, nothing else. The Dons are predicting all out war over Black Daffodil and they want to keep their operatives out of it.'

'Wise people,' Alfred left his chair.

'You have the disk?' Dan asked.

Alfred patted his pocket.

'Get back to Andrew the minute you have an ID on the manufacturer or vendor …'

'I'll fix a meeting,' Alfred assured him.

'Even if it's four in the morning,' Dan cautioned.

'No respect for my beauty sleep,' Andrew grumbled.

'How can you respect anyone who dreams about little balls rolling across greens when there are so many erotic things to fantasise about,' Peter chipped in.

Dan moved to the chair behind the desk when Andrew showed Alfred out.

'What about the Asians?' Trevor asked.

'Tom has come across evidence of people-trafficking for the sweat shop and take-away trade and tax fraud. Nothing that links them to Black Daffodil. On the face of it, they're not interested. We're preparing to second him to the trafficking team.'

'The Somalis?' Peter recalled all the options that had been covered at the briefing.

'Too concerned with importing khat and growing hash to concern themselves with anything else. The small-time criminal fraternity on the Bay – mixed ethnicity not solely Somali or much of any one race – is a closed community. Milgi and Eidi haven't come up with anything either. All the indications point to Black Daffodil being a home-grown Welsh product.'

'Not least the name,' Trevor mused.

'Upstairs asked the locals to step up their efforts to track down everyone who was at that party in the penthouse who might have seen the assault on Jake. Or Jake and Alec spending time with any particular group of people. From the statements they've taken so far, you'd think it was a church youth club get-together. Given the number of witnesses who saw and heard that party from the street and the number of guests questioned, it beggars belief that they can't find a soul prepared to tell us what went on there.'

Andrew returned, saw Dan sitting behind his desk and took the chair next to Trevor.

'No more crazies or deaths?' Peter queried, before remembering Jake was Dan's nephew.

'No.' Dan's reply was curt. 'But we can't be sure whether a batch went sour or someone tried to copy it and got it wrong, or whether it was a deliberate attempt to damage Jake, Alec and the junkies.'

'If Jake had been rumbled, the others could be a blind,' Trevor said thoughtfully.

'I've been through Jake Phillips's reports with a toothcomb,' Dan countered. 'There's nothing in them that suggests anyone suspected him to be anything other than a film student.'

'Does anyone else think that the Darrows are behind Black Daffodil?' Peter selected a cigar from his box and removed the cellophane wrapper.

'We have no evidence.' Dan pushed a DVD across the desk towards Trevor. 'Ignore the label. It's not a DVD of the property you've expressed an interest in. The locals interviewed Jake and Alec's flatmates, Damian Darrow and Lloyd Jones, about the party. These are edited highlights. Don't expect too much. They both deny knowledge of any drug taking and assault. Don't leave the disk lying around your hotel room where it can be played by a maid. After you've watched it – somewhere quiet – return it to me. Darrow and Jones are being called in again tomorrow with their solicitor so the locals can go through their statements again.'

'Pity about the solicitor. Bring back the good old days when we could torture the truth out of scum.'

'And when was that?' Dan raised his eyebrows at Peter.

'Before my time, guv.'

Dan pursed his mouth in irritation. 'Alec Hodges has been interviewed again. Not that he's coherent. I listened to the recording.' Dan opened his notebook and quoted, '"… I wanted to screw Kelly but Jake got her … Damian gave me Ally … he had Cynara … Lloyd got Lucy … Ally was all right but I wanted Kelly …" there's more of the same.'

'Damian?' Trevor repeated.

'Alec didn't mention a surname. Although he lives with Damian Darrow, and the Darrows are under investigation for people trafficking and money laundering we can't be certain whether the Damian he was referring to is Darrow, or not.'

'It's bloody obvious.'

'Bloody obvious isn't evidence, Peter.' Dan was uncharacteristically curt. 'All the witnesses saw girls at that party who have since been identified as working girls. But we have no proof they were

Darrow's working girls.'

'Proof … proof …' Peter said. 'As fast as we look for hard evidence, the Darrows hide it along with the millions they kive from ignorant punters stupid enough to hand over their hard-earned cash.'

'It's possible that whoever's behind Black Daffodil paid the working girls to pull in punters? It wouldn't be the first time dealers have used girls to market their goods.' Trevor pocketed the DVD.

'The locals have checked out all the Kellys, Allys and Lucys in the city's parlours.' Dan took a slip of paper from his notebook. 'There are three girls of those names working in one on the bay. It's the address at the top of the list. Call in there, and try to see the girls. They may open up to you in your undercover guise. Last time the locals raided a parlour they suspected the Darrows of owning, none of the girls would talk, even when they were threatened with prosecution, gaol and publicity.'

'You think they'll talk to a punter?' Trevor asked.

'Before the police – yes. It's a long shot but worth pursuing, given how little information we have about what went on at that party,' Dan answered. 'One of them might have seen Jake or Alec or something significant.'

'And they won't be in the least suspicious if we drop Jake and Alec's names casually into conversation?' Peter suggested caustically.

'Not if the person who's doing the dropping is sympathetic,' Dan replied.

'We'll be risking our cover.'

'You're dealers after relaxation. Where better to

find it than a massage parlour? And while you're there, take a good look at the other girls. The locals suspect some are underage. They're kids, they're terrified of the law and they're even more terrified of whoever's pimping them. There are more addresses, if Kelly, Lucy and Ally aren't in the first place. The girls are frequently moved from one parlour to another.'

'Hence the ads in the personal columns "All New Girls",' Peter replied. 'It conjures images of skips out back crammed with girls in stockings and basques, lying back with their legs over the side while they swig vodka straight from the bottle.'

'Only to you.' Trevor scanned the list Dan had given him. 'Impressive portfolio. They all Darrow's?'

'Not that we can prove. Legal department's been working on the tangle of registered companies for months.'

'Lucrative sideline to any business when you consider the turnover of just one of those places.' Trevor folded the list into his wallet.

'Call into the first parlour tonight, either on your way back to the hotel or before you go to the casino,' Dan ordered.

'Mid-morning is quieter,' Trevor returned his wallet to his pocket.

Dan glanced at his watch. 'Seven is a good time. After the office-closing rush hour and before the evening gets going. And, as you well know, time is the one thing we are short of.'

Peter made a face.

'It wouldn't be the first time you've visited a

brothel,' Dan reminded.

'The last time I went I wasn't courting.'

Trevor burst out laughing.

'What's so funny?' Peter demanded.

'The idea of you "courting".'

'Glad you find the situation amusing.' Peter pulled out his cigars.

'No smoking in these offices,' Andrew warned.

Peter held up his cigar. 'Dummy.'

'Wind-up artist.'

'That's me.'

Trevor left his chair. 'Come on, we have a brothel and a casino to visit.'

'After a five-star steak, chips and brandy in our private dining room. And I might, just might, make the brandy a double,' Peter gave Dan a defiant look. 'You'll be at the casino tonight?'

'No, but Andrew will. Bill and I will be listening in.'

'You've bugged the place,' Trevor guessed.

'There were problems with the power supply. They were rectified earlier today.' Dan opened the door for them.

'Tonight is going to be interesting.' Peter pulled out his lighter.

'Remember the law,' Dan warned. 'Light that outside, Peter, there's a good boy.'

CHAPTER EIGHT

Trevor and Peter returned to their hotel, showered and ate steak with chips, at Peter's insistence, before locking themselves in the bathroom in Trevor's suite. Trevor set his laptop on the toilet seat and they sat on the floor, backs to the door, to watch the DVD. Peter had brought in four bottles of beer, he opened two and handed Trevor one.

Damian Darrow appeared on screen. Dressed in a heavy knit cream silk shirt and faded jeans, sporting a gold linked bracelet, gold Rolex and sovereign rings, he looked affluent and unconcerned. Or in Peter's terms, 'bloody smug and arrogant'. He was sitting in a chair that had been bolted to the floor of a standard interview room but if he was intimidated by his surroundings, or the two officers who faced him with their backs to the camera, he showed no sign of it. A table stood between him and the officers. On it was a solitary cup and saucer. Damian's solicitor, a middle-aged woman, sat next to Damian, notepad and pen in hand.

'Baby Darrow knows where the camera is and he's playing full-on to the gallery.' Peter wiped the top of his beer bottle and drank.

Damian began to speak in mid-conversation and Trevor recalled Dan mentioning 'edited highlights'.

'I work hard and play hard and the party was both. I'm launching a new band. They're ...'

The interviewer interrupted. *'You invited Jake Phillips and Alec Hodges to this party?'*

'I'm a close friend of Jake and Alec, as well as their landlord.'

'Were they both in your flat when the party started?'

'I don't know. I don't clock them in or out of my penthouse.' He emphasised the last word.

'Likes to show off, like Daddy.' Peter sipped his beer.

'You didn't spend the day with Jake or Alec?'

'I spent the day with my band, advising them on technique and performance. Jake and Alec are adults, they have keys. Where they go and what they do is entirely their own business.'

'Jake Phillips is in a coma, Mr Darrow. The doctors don't expect him to recover.'

'You can't blame me for what happened to Jake. I wasn't there.'

'Where is "there", Mr Darrow?'

Damian gave a theatrical sigh and spoke to the officers as though they were two-year-olds. '"There" is Jake's bedroom. And if you want my opinion, I think Jake fell off his balcony when he was drunk.'

'You saw Jake Phillips drink alcohol?'

'Of course I saw Jake drink bloody alcohol. It was a party. I don't know what kind of parties you go to but ...'

The interviewer cut in sharply again. 'What time did you last see Jake at your party?'

'I don't know. I wasn't watching the clock.'

'Who was he with when you last saw him?'

'A crowd of people.'

'Men? Women?'

'Both.'

'Do you remember anyone in particular?'

'I invited over a hundred people to that party ...'

'You have a list of guests?'

'A list of music professionals and people who own clubs. I was looking for bookings for the band.'

'So the only people present were music professionals?' The interviewer's voice remained bland and professional. If he was sceptical, there was no trace of it.

'Everyone in film school knows they're welcome when I throw a party. It's open house.'

'So film school students were present as well as professionals from the music and entertainment industry.'

'And casual friends, acquaintances and neighbours. It's easier to invite them than deal with complaints about the noise.'

'Girls?'

'Obviously girls. They make up around fifty percent of the population.'

'Including prostitutes?'

Damian sighed theatrically. 'I booked and paid for strippers.'

'How many strippers?'

'Eight.'

'That must have been expensive.'

'Expense isn't a consideration when I entertain friends or host a business event.'

'You booked the girls just to strip?'

'I wouldn't have stopped them from indulging in

extra-mural activities, if they'd wanted to.'
  'You knew they were prostitutes?'
  'I knew they were strippers.'

'Cool bugger.' Peter drank from the bottle.
  'Too cool,' Trevor observed.

'Do you or any of your flat-mates have girlfriends?'
  'Dozens.'
  'Jake and Alec?'
  'We're not gay if that's what you're suggesting.'

For the first time Trevor detected a note of
exasperation in Damian's voice.

'Do Jake and Alec have any particular girlfriends?'
  'Not that I've noticed.'
  'Prostitutes?'
  *'We're studying at film school. Actresses and
drama students queue at our door in the hope we'll
use them in our projects. We don't need to use or
pay prostitutes.'*

'Answer's too detailed. Baby Darrow's getting
irritable.' Peter finished one bottle and reached for
another.
  'Sound interviewer,' Trevor remarked. 'Calm
and collected. Not the sort to lose it.'
  'If that's a snipe …'
  'It's a nothing. Listen.' Trevor flicked back the
disk to the point where Peter had begun talking.

'Were there any drug dealers at the party?'

'None I invited.'

'You know drug dealers?' The interviewer's voice remained even.

'Not personally. I've seen them around. It's difficult not to. I don't go looking for them. That's a police job, not that you seem to be doing it.'

'Do you use drugs?'

'Never.' There was no unusual emphasis in Damian's reply.

'Did Jake or Alec use drugs?'

'Not to my knowledge.'

'Did you call the emergency services?'

'No.'

'Did anyone call them from your flat?'

'You logged the calls. You'd know the answer to that better than me.'

'Although Alec Hodges was ill and Jake had been thrown from the window you didn't call the emergency services?'

'I didn't know Jake had gone out of the window, and the last time I saw Alec at the party he just seemed a bit hyper.'

'What do you mean by hyper, Mr Darrow?'

'Antsy, jumpy, like he'd had too much excitement or alcohol – which he probably had.'

'Or taken drugs?'

'If he had, I didn't see him doing it. And, as I keep telling you, I don't police my friends.'

'Even if it involves using illegal substances in your home.' The interviewer paused before continuing. 'Someone did call the police.'

'Obviously, as they walked in uninvited.' Damian leaned as far back in his chair from the interviewer as space would allow.

'Did you see either Jake Phillips or Alec Hodges take a girl into their bedrooms?'

'No.'

'A witness stated that he saw Alec Hodges enter his bedroom, with ...' There was a rustle of paper as the officer conducting the interview consulted his notes. 'A prostitute known as Ally.'

'The only Ally I know and hired for the evening is a stripper.'

'You didn't see her with Alec?'

'No'. Damian yawned.

'Did you see Jake go into his bedroom with a girl called Kelly?'

'No.'

'Did you know that Alec Hodges had taken drugs?'

'We're not back to that are we? I told you I don't know anything about illegal substances.'

'Did you hear noises coming from any of the bedrooms?'

'Not that I recall.'

'Some of your guests reported that they heard the sound of moaning and screaming coming from that area of your flat.'

'It was a party. There was a lot of noise in my penthouse – music, laughter; if I heard a scream I would have assumed it was one of delight.'

The interviewer wasn't to be so easily fobbed off. 'Did you, or did you not hear a scream, Mr Darrow?'

'I repeat, not that I can recall.'

'When did you realise that something had

happened to Jake Phillips and Alec Hodges?'

'When the police told me Jake was lying on an awning on one of the balconies below mine.'

'Then what happened?'

'Your boys and girls were there so why fucking ask me these useless fucking ...'

The solicitor whispered something to Damian.

'No! I want to get this over and done with so I can get out of here.'

'Not one word of sympathy or regret for Jake who's lying in a coma, or Alec Hodges who's in a secure psychiatric ward.' Trevor stretched his legs and carried on watching.

'You read the report, who did call the police?' Peter asked.

Trevor pressed pause. 'A passer-by who saw Jake being dropped out of that window.'

'He's positive about the dropping?'

'He said he saw two pairs of hands lift Jake over the balcony.'

'You think whoever it was would have checked for an awning if they wanted to do away with him. Could it have been down to drunken antics?'

'Drunken antics on the eleventh floor?' Trevor pressed play again.

'What did you do when the police told you that Jake Phillips had been thrown from one of the balconies of your penthouse, Mr Darrow?'

'They asked to see his room. I showed them the corridor outside the bedrooms. We found Alec Hodges lying on the floor and the police called the

124

paramedics. But you know all this ...'

'He's losing it again,' Peter remarked.

'No one thought to call the paramedics before for Alec?'

'Anyone who saw him would have assumed he was drunk.'

'So he often got drunk. Is that what you're saying?'

Damian's temper rose to the surface again. *'Don't put bloody words into my mouth. Alec got drunk now and again but no more than the rest of us. We're students ...'*

'We were talking about what happened after the police arrived.'

'They rounded us up, bagged our hands, drove us down here and treated us like common criminals. Strip searched us. And didn't your officers just enjoy humiliating us? They took our fingerprints, photographs, DNA samples, and you didn't find anything on me ...'

'May I remind you, Mr Darrow, that one of your flat-mates, Jake Phillips, is in a coma, and another in a psychiatric ward?'

'And instead of being allowed to visit them I've been dragged down here ...'

The interviewer proved relentless.

'Are you aware that some of your friends and acquaintances are drug users?'

'You can't go to film school without picking up the odd conversation about this or that person smoking a joint, or sniffing a line of Charlie.'

125

'You know the street names for drugs?'

'Given the amount of coverage the media gives drug abuse, you'd have to be fucking blind and deaf not to know.'

'Have you ever personally bought or sold drugs?

'How many times do I have to tell you I don't take, buy, or sell banned substances of any description?'

'Have you ever seen Alec Hodges take a banned substance?'

'No.'

'He's lying.' Peter set his half-full beer bottle on the floor beside him.

'You have lived with Alec Hodges for nearly two years?'

'Somewhere around that.'

'And you never saw him take any banned substance?'

'No.'

'How can you be sure?'

'Because all I've ever seen Alec do is drink. We're students. Do you know what that means? We work. We spend all our time writing, directing and producing films. We study techniques and, after a hard day at the college or working on our individual projects, about all we're up for is a couple of beers.' Damian turned to his solicitor. 'How long do I have to sit here and put up with this shit?'

The solicitor didn't answer but the officer interviewing Damian did.

'Until you have answered all our questions, Mr

Peter held up his empty bottle. 'Another beer?' he asked Trevor.

'Just one. We have to have our wits about us tonight.' Trevor pressed pause on the remote control.

'After what we've eaten, two beers aren't going to tip us over the limit.' Peter opened the other two bottles he'd brought in. Trevor pressed 'play' on the remote. Damian faded. A few seconds later the camera zoomed in on Lloyd Jones who was sitting in the chair Damian Darrow had occupied, in the same interview room.

He was a very different character to his friend and landlord. Damian Darrow was blond, suntanned, good-looking and knew it. Lloyd was the male equivalent of female mousy. He could have played the dream Hollywood hero's ugly 'best friend'. And that was just his looks. Obviously nervous and uneasy, cringing, obsequious, he reminded Trevor of a beaten dog, anxious to please even though its spirit was broken.

Peter looked up at the screen. 'Ah-hah.'

Irritated, Trevor paused the disk – again. 'What?'

'Remember the gym. When I was asking your bouncer friend Jude about a bar or restaurant on the premises.'

'When you were asking him inane questions when I wanted to get to the estate agent's – yes.'

'You didn't notice?'

'I'm not in the mood for guessing games.'

'You didn't take a good look at the guy who

stared at us when he tried to push past by the swimming pool?'

Trevor thought for a moment. 'He was overweight ...'

'Not so overweight that he didn't galvanise himself and dress in record time so he could follow us to the door and watch us climb into our car.' Peter slipped his hand into the pocket of his bathrobe and brought out his mobile phone. He flicked it to camera, then photographs, called one up and showed it to Trevor. 'Lloyd Jones.'

'You recognised him?'

'How could I? I'd never seen him before the club and now this recording. But he was watching us and he looked shifty ...'

'Shifty isn't evidence,' Trevor reminded him. 'That gym isn't far from the penthouse. Perhaps it's the best around.'

'Could be all he wants to do is build muscle and tone up,' Peter agreed. 'Living with a boy with the looks of Damian Darrow wouldn't be easy for the likes of Lloyd Jones when it comes to reeling in girls. But for all that there's something about him that's ringing my alarm bells.'

'We haven't much time before we're due at the casino. Do you want to watch the interview?' Trevor didn't wait for Peter to reply. He pressed play.

'Did you see either Jake Phillips or Alec Hodges take any illegal substances at the party, Mr Jones?'

'No.' Lloyd's hands shook as he answered.

'Did you see Alec Hodges lying on the floor of

the corridor?'

'Yes'

'Did you check him?'

'I saw that he was breathing. I thought he was drunk.'

'You've seen Alec Hodges drunk before?'

'Sometimes.'

'Often?'

'No more often than the rest of us.'

'Where were you when Jake Phillips was thrown from that window?'

'I don't know.'

'You can't recall?'

'I don't know when he went out of the window.'

'He's been coached,' Peter commented.

'Who told you what had happened to Jake?'

'I don't know.'

'You don't know every much do you, Mr Jones?'

'It was a party. I was busy.'

'Doing what?'

'I was with a girl.'

'Her name?'

'She didn't tell me.'

'You didn't ask?'

'No.'

'How long were you with her?'

'An hour or so.'

And you didn't ask her name?'

'It was a party.'

'Who invited her?'

'She was one of Damian's girls ... friends.'

129

'"Damian's girls".' Peter repeated. 'It's easy to see who's top dog in that penthouse.'

'All four living in Damian Darrow's penthouse were heavily subsidised by Damian.' Trevor sipped his beer.

'Lloyd Jones seems more nervous than the interview warrants.'

'He could be the nervous type.'

'More likely simply lying.' Peter took the remote from Trevor and pressed play.

The solicitor – the same woman who had sat with Damian briefly conferred with Lloyd before shaking her head.

'Supplied by the Darrows?' Peter asked Trevor.

'I'll check with Dan.'

'Were you aware that some people were taking banned substances at the party?'

'I saw people taking pills and smoking spliffs on the balcony. But they were all doing it out of Damian's sight ...'

'I do *so* love a good fairytale, 'Peter mocked.

'I didn't take any and I didn't force anything on anybody. I've given a blood and urine test ... I didn't want any of this to happen.. Not to Jake and not to Alec ... I hate drugs ... so did Jake ... we warned Alec but he always wanted to experiment. Said it broadened the mind and Jake and I were

small-minded petty jumped-up working-class arseholes…' Lloyd's shoulders began to shake. His sagging, bulbous, nondescript features crumpled and he sobbed uncontrollably.

'End of interview with Mr Lloyd Jones. We are awaiting the results of blood and urine tests for drugs and alcohol …'

'"I didn't take any and I didn't force anything on anybody?" Strange choice of words when you consider what happened.' Peter dumped his empty beer bottles in the bin next to the sink.

Trevor ejected the disk. 'That gives us something to think about.'

'Want me to lock this in my safe?' Peter returned the disk to the box as Trevor closed down the machine.

'We'll post it through the estate agent's letter box on the way to the parlour.' Trevor turned as the door handle moved. Quicker than Peter, he unlocked the door and opened it. A startled maid looked from him to Peter, and turned crimson.

'I brought clean towels, Mr Brown.' She thrust them at him and ran.

Peter burst out laughing. 'Look at us.'

They were both wearing hotel bathrobes.

Peter draped his arm around Trevor's shoulders. 'Well, sweetheart. I guess word will get out. Not only are we a couple of tough drug dealers, but gay tough drug dealers. I like it. It gives me an excuse to sit back and do nothing when we visit the parlour.'

'Gays don't visit parlours.' Trevor shrugged off Peter's hand.

'Latent gays do. This adds a whole new dimension to my character.'

Trevor narrowed his eyes in exasperation. 'Make believe, Peter. Make believe.'

CHAPTER NINE

Trevor slipped his card key in the top pocket of his suit and checked the name of the parlour Dan had given him before folding the paper and pushing it into the hidden space in his wallet. He opened the safe, took out seven hundred pounds and the American Express credit card before punching in the code he'd chosen – Lyn's birthday – and locking it.

Peter walked through the door that connected the two suites, dressed in a dark green casual suit.

'What **are** you wearing?' Trevor asked.

Peter looked down. 'I'm not sure about the colour either. The shirt's nice though, linen …'

Trevor sniffed. 'I'm talking cologne, not clothes.'

'I don't know what it's called. The bottle was in my suitcase.'

'Stick to the complimentary stuff in your bathroom,' Trevor advised. 'You smell like a Turkish brothel.'

'And what would you know about a Turkish brothel?'

'Not much,' Trevor admitted.

'Ever been to Turkey?'

'Istanbul, twice.'

'Ah-hah! Caught you out.'

'Ah-hah nothing.' Trevor was irritated by the knowing grin on Peter's face. 'I went there years ago with Mags.' Trevor fell silent. It had been years ago. And he couldn't recall the last time he had thought of, or spoken about, his previous and only live-in girlfriend before Lyn.

'Mags – there's a blast from the past.'

'A cool one. You know something,' Trevor was genuinely surprised. 'I can't remember what she looked like.'

'Since the divorce I've managed to blot out every memory I had of my wife, which is just as well. There weren't any pleasant ones – not after we married. Do you want to take the car or a taxi?'

Trevor hesitated and replayed the conversation they'd just exchanged in his mind. It had been personal. They had to be more careful. Had either of them said anything Trevor Brown or Peter Ashton wouldn't? They were both supposed to be divorced so Peter's reference to his ex-wife was fine. Mags? There were Turkish stamps in Brown's passport and Brown could have had a dozen girls in his past called Mags …

'We'll walk. I've checked the street map. It's not far.' He looked Peter in the eye and Peter gave a slight nod to show he understood. Believing themselves safe in the bathroom they had let their guard down when they'd been watching the DVD – and afterwards – had the maid been listening at the door?

She'd tried the door handle, which had alerted them. That suggested she hadn't been. But probability wasn't good enough undercover. They had to be more careful. An instant, that's all it took to lose a cover – a case – and in an extreme cases a life.

'The girls who come highly recommended are Kelly, Lucy, Ally and Cynara. I've been told on good authority they cater for our tastes.'

'Cynara? Dowson's poem Cynara?'

'She's a redhead.' Trevor crossed to the bar and checked there was beer in the fridge for later. 'You read poetry now?'

'You're not the only man in the world who possesses a poetry book. Good name for a working girl, Cynara. Says it in one. "For I have loved thee Cynara in my fashion". You playing tonight?'

'Roulette,' Trevor said decisively.

'The mug's game.'

'Only for losers. I feel Lady Luck blowing my way.'

'Bet you a grand, my winnings will be up on yours this time next week whatever game you opt for,' Peter dared recklessly.

'We start even.'

'I'm not carrying my loss forward?'

'I was hoping.'

'No chance. Bet on or off.'

Trevor held out his hand. 'On.'

Peter shook Trevor's hand. 'Now I have to think of something I can do with that grand to rub your nose in it.'

The massage parlour Dan had ordered them to visit was, like Eric Darrow's casino, sumptuous, up-market and had the stamp of the same Hollywood-inspired interior designer. Whichever dummy company was ostensibly running it, Darrow's influence was evident. Thick cream carpets, antique green and gold washed walls, reception area furnished with French Empire desk and cream leather armchairs, soft piped music and erotic, artist-signed prints on the walls.

A middle-aged woman, dressed in a business suit, was sitting behind the desk filing her nails when Trevor and Peter walked in. She set the file aside and gave them a professional smile.

'Good evening, sirs. And how may I help you?'

Trevor gritted his teeth. That phrase again! 'A friend recommended this as a good place to relax.'

'A friend, sir?' Her smile hardened.

'A Mr Smith?'

The woman's smile broadened. 'We offer discretion above all else.' She handed each of them a cream leather folder. Our catalogues, photographs of our masseurs, and price lists. We accept all major credit cards.' She showed them into a small ante-room, furnished in the same style as the reception area. 'Can I get you something to drink? Tea? Coffee? Wine?'

'We're fine, thank you,' Trevor sat down.

She closed the door. They flicked through the lists of girls.

Peter hit a photograph with his forefinger. 'I'll take Kelly for a massage.'

Trevor nodded. From her photograph Kelly looked young and vulnerable. Despite his hard-boiled exterior, Peter had a track record of extracting information from the bullied, put-upon waifs and strays that formed an inevitable part of the criminal fraternity. 'I'll go for Lucy.'

'More your type,' Peter teased. 'Older, harder, brassier … more silicone …'

Trevor picked up the phone. 'Two straight

massages, Lucy and Kelly.'

'Straight massages, sir?' she repeated in surprise. 'Lucy is a very talented girl who usually works out of our executive suites. And Kelly has regulars who like her number three. I recommend her …'

Trevor glanced down the menu. 'We really do want number ones, just a massage,' he reiterated.

'Number ones it is, sir.' The tone suggested their custom wasn't worth bothering with.

Deciding they may need more time to talk to the girls Trevor added, 'It's possible we may change our minds. In which case we'll make a financial adjustment.'

'A straight massage will be seventy pounds each for thirty minutes. You may leave your credit cards at the desk and pick them up when you have finished.'

'It says fifty.'

'There is a minimum charge of seventy pounds at peak times, irrespective of menu. The girls will be topless.'

'And, if we don't want them topless?' Trevor didn't know why he was arguing. It wasn't as though it was his money that he and Peter were spending. A streak of prudery born out of his close, loving relationship with Lyn?

'The girls can leave their tops on, if you prefer, but there'll be no reduction.'

Trevor hung up. He and Peter left the ante-room, went into reception and handed over their credit cards. Trevor opened his wallet, pulled out a twenty pound note and gave it to the receptionist. She looked at it quizzically.

'Your tip.'

'Thank you, sir.' If she found the gratuity strange after Trevor's argument over the fee she didn't comment. She handed each of them thick, lavender-scented bath sheets. 'I'll show you to your rooms. The girls will be with you in a few minutes.'

Trevor removed his suit and shirt and wrapped the towel around his waist, over his boxer shorts. If he could be certain that Lucy wouldn't be using oil, he would have left his trousers on. He stretched his muscles. His shoulders were tense, but he doubted Lucy was a trained masseur.

'Hi, I'm Lucy. I hope you like having fun.' Lucy, who was as well-endowed as her photograph suggested, joined him. She was wearing a pink G string, a smile and nothing else. Trevor noticed that she was as muscle-bound as a body-builder.

He sat on the couch which was twice as wide as a standard masseur's. 'Shoulder massage.'

'Why don't we go into one of the executive suites,' she cooed. 'They cost a little more but they have hot tubs. We'll be more comfortable there. And, there's one special suite that caters for ...' she licked her lips, '... interesting tastes.'

'I want a shoulder massage and I have an appointment in half an hour.'

'Can't you phone them and delay it.'

'There's a twenty in it, if you stop the hard sell,' he interrupted.

She pouted. 'It's your choice – and loss.' Her tone changed and lost its warmth. 'Lie face down and I'll loosen you up. Coconut or olive?'

He looked at her over his shoulder.

'Oil.'

'Coconut. There is a shower in there?' He eyed the inner door.

'Of course. And for an extra tenner on the tip you're going to give me, I'll scrub your back. And for an extra twenty I'll …'

Peter stripped to his shorts, covered himself with the towel and was sitting on the couch when Kelly came in wearing a thong. She was so thin below her pert, silicone-enhanced breasts he could count every rib.

He'd been prepared for someone young, but not a child who should have been in school. He looked into her eyes but her pupils weren't dilated. He couldn't see any obvious signs of needle marks on her arms or track lines on her back. Had she managed to stay off mainlining? So far?

'We have an executive suite with a hot tub …'

'Spare me the sales pitch, love. I really do just want a massage.'

'We get paid …'

'I know how you get paid.' He pulled his wallet out from under him, and peeled off five twenty pound notes. 'Your tip.'

'For a massage?' Her eyes rounded.

'A friend mentioned your name.'

She was instantly wary. 'Who?'

'Like me, he's a friend of Jake Phillips.'

'Jake …' She backed towards the door, dispelling any notion he'd had that Dan had sent them on a wild goose chase.

'The door's closed. No one is listening,' he said,

more in an attempt to find out if anyone was, than to reassure her. He didn't doubt that the girls would know if the rooms were bugged. 'I'd like to know what happened to Jake last Saturday night. You were there. Weren't you?'

Kelly turned her back on him and headed for the door. For an instant he thought she was going to run. Instead, she sank down on the floor, buried her face in her hands, and burst into tears.

'Why you asking about the party last Saturday night? You weren't there, were you?' Lucy squinted suspiciously at Trevor.

'I heard about it.'

'Given the TV and newspaper coverage, you'd have to be blind and deaf or an idiot not to know about it.'

'Must have been some party. Did you enjoy it?'

'I'm a working girl. It was work.'

'I know Alec and Jake …'

'I don't.' Her retort was too quick.

'But you *were* at the party?'

'So were a lot of others.'

You're a working girl who gets around.'

She eyed him cautiously. 'You a copper?'

He turned the question back on her. 'Do I look like a copper?'

'Can't tell these days.'

'I'm self-employed.'

'If you say so. You paid for a massage. That's what you're going to get. Talk is extra.' She dribbled oil on to his back and began pounding. As he'd suspected, she didn't have a clue about massage. He felt as though he was in a steam press.

Trevor tried another tack. 'I asked about the party because it seemed like a good marketing idea.'

'You in marketing?'

'No. But I'm thinking of moving to the Bay.'

'And setting up a parlour?'

'Not my line of work, but it pays to entertain prospective clients.' Trevor winced as she knuckled his back.

'What business you in?'

'Now who's asking the questions?'

'Business people on the Bay like to help each other out.'

'You own this parlour?'

She snorted. 'I wish.'

'Does the owner organise parties for clients?'

'This is a strictly on the premises parlour. And we don't do house calls either.' She moved from one side of the couch to the other, and pulled a curtain across to screen it from the rest of the cubicle.

Trevor had time to catch a glimpse of a small indent in the ceiling and he guessed there were hidden cameras the girls knew about and could block out. He suspected there were others they weren't aware of. One of the biggest sources of amateur porn films was brothels.

'I've finished your back. Want me to do your front? We don't have to tell anyone. That tip you said you'll give me …'

'No, do my back again.'

'You will give me twenty?'

Trevor reached for the wallet he'd tucked into

the towel.

Lucy lifted her hands to her hair. A business card floated down and landed on his wallet. The name Lucy was printed above a mobile number. He looked quizzically at her. She lifted a finger to her lips. He slipped the card into his wallet.

'Here,' he took a twenty-pound note from his wallet, but held on to it. 'I'll make it forty if you'll tell me, where I can get some of these Black Daffodils everyone is talking about?'

Her voice hardened. 'What makes you think I know anything about Black Daffodil?'

'Bright girl like you, working here on the Bay. You see things. Know people. Who do I see?'

She snatched the note. 'I haven't the faintest idea what you're talking about.'

Instinct told him she knew something. But she clearly wasn't prepared to talk. Was it because she was implicated in the assault on Jake? Had someone threatened her? Or bought her silence?

She didn't seem the type that would frighten easily. He looked pointedly at his watch. 'Ten minutes I have to be off and I'll need five of those for a shower.'

'Come on love,' Peter coaxed Kelly. 'Crying isn't going to help Jake or you.'

Kelly swallowed her tears and wiped her nose in her hand. Peter handed her the towel, reached for his clothes and began to dress.

'You've been so nice. I have to ...'

'You don't have to do anything, love,' Peter pulled on his trousers and zipped them up, before buttoning his shirt. 'Sit down.' He lifted her up on to the couch. She was so light and fragile he was afraid of crushing her.

'No one was ever nice to me before except Jake. He was lovely, a really kind man and … and … he's …'

'If Jake was as kind as you say he was, he wouldn't want you to carry on like this.' Peter slipped his arm around Kelly's shoulders and hugged her.

'Jake and me grew up on the same estate. He was a lot older than me. He was my sister's friend not mine. They were the same age, but he never used to tease me or hurt me like the other boys. His mam was nice too. She used to give me and my sisters biscuits and cakes whenever we went round there.'

'Well, there you are then, more than one person has been nice to you. Jake and his mam.' He smiled at her and she smiled back at him through her tears.

'I'd get a right telling off if management knew how I was carrying on. We're supposed to smile and pretend to be happy all the time. Even when we can't stand the client … especially when we can't stand the client.'

'That can't be easy,' he commiserated with her.

'It isn't. Some of them expect you to do horrible things.' She shuddered.

'Why you here, love?' Peter asked.

'What do you mean?' She retreated towards the wall.

'There's no way you're sixteen.'

Her voice grew shrill in alarm. 'I am too.'

'You're young, you're pretty. You're not a user.

But if you stay here you soon will be.'

'I need the money.'

'There are other jobs.'

'None that pay the money this one does. I have … a friend who needs stuff.'

'Stuff?' he repeated.

She turned aside.

'Charlie?' he ventured.

She nodded. 'It's expensive. She promised to try and get off it but it's hard. She's cut down …' her eyes widened in panic. 'You're not a cop are you? If you are I'm supposed to press the panic button.'

Peter slipped his hand into his pocket of his suit and pulled out two packets. 'I wouldn't be giving you these if I was a copper?'

She took them from him and stared at them in wonder. 'There has to be a couple of grams there.'

'There are.'

'I haven't enough money to pay for them.'

'I don't want any.'

'Then what do you want?' she demanded suspiciously.

'This is no life for a pretty young girl, Kelly …'

'You one of them religious nuts?' She shrank even further away from him.

He burst out laughing. 'I've been called many things but no one's accused me of being a religious nut before.'

'Because if you expect me to pray with you …'

'I'm not a religious nut. I don't want you to pray with me, I just want to talk to you about Jake and what happened to him in the party.'

There was a sharp rap on the door. Kelly jumped.

'Who is it?'

'One of your regulars is here, Kelly,' the receptionist spoke through the door. 'He wants to see you right away.'

'I paid for a massage,' Peter snapped back.

'I'll send one of the other girls in, sir.'

'I don't want one of the other girls.'

Kelly looked at him before opening the door. 'Sorry.'

It was only when he turned around that Peter realised she'd taken the drugs he'd given her.

Peter left the massage parlour, crossed the road and looked around for Trevor. He saw him leaning on the railings that fenced off the sea, staring at the last faint glimmer of light on the horizon that separated sky from water. There was no one else within a hundred yards. Even in pensive mood, with his shaved head and grim expression, Trevor appeared intimidating.

Peter joined him. 'So, how was it for you?'

'The rooms are bugged.'

'So I discovered. I got Kelly to admit she knew Jake; was at that party and was financing someone with a coke habit, but she was hauled out. I hope they don't do anything more to her than they already have. I'll contact Andrew. It's time the locals raided the place.'

Trevor glanced over his shoulder. Peter noticed.

'We're being ridiculous with all this checking and double-checking. If anyone *is* watching us, it's because we look shifty on the basis of our haircuts alone.'

'Did you get anything out of Kelly?'

'As I said, my session was cut short. The receptionist said one of Kelly's regulars had come in. She charged out like a rocket after pocketing the present I'd given her.'

'Drugs?'

'And cash.'

'You think she was ordered out because she was talking to you?'

'Yes. She was ordered out mid-flow.'

'A working girl as young as Kelly would have any number of regulars.'

'Suppose for argument's sake that Damian Darrow is behind the manufacturing of Black Daffodil.'

'I don't buy that,' Trevor dismissed.

'Because he hasn't the nonce?'

'Because he has all the money he could spend in one lifetime. And, he can get more any time by touching up Daddy who is making too much out of his semi-legit businesses to get mixed up in something like Black Daffodil.'

'Even for the millions the Russians are offering?' Peter lifted his eyebrows.

Trevor thought for a moment. 'I take your point. Eric Darrow is a greedy bastard.'

Peter looked up and down the street. 'I want to get in touch with Andrew and arrange protection for Kelly but I can't phone here.'

'The hotel is ten minutes away. One of our bathrooms is as good a place as any,'

They retraced their steps along the front with its mix of neon-lit restaurant facades, and luxury flats.

By tacit agreement they crossed the road and walked on the quiet side.

'When you say protection, you going to ask Dan to assign Kelly a babysitter?' Trevor quickened his step to keep up with Peter.

'I'd like the locals to take her into protective custody. I don't want her to end up like Jake – or worse. And if the locals are right and the Darrows do own that parlour and, punish her for saying too much – not that it was useful – there's no saying what they'll do to her. After seeing that interview I suspect young Darrow can be every bit as vicious as his old man.'

'The locals will need a reason. They can't just go into that parlour and whisk her out.'

'She's under-age.'

'She told you?'

'No, but I know a kid when I see one.'

'She could be using a friend or relative's identity.'

'She could. But if the locals need another excuse they could pick her up as a material witness to Jake's attempted murder.'

'Only if she admits to seeing something at that party,' Trevor warned.

'Did Lucy tell you she was there?'

'Yes. But like Damian and Lloyd, she was too busy to see what was going on.'

Ten minutes later after a hurried call to Andrew, Peter took a disposable Sim card from his phone and crushed it between his fingers. He wrapped it in a tissue, pushed it into his pocket and made a note to dump it in the first public bin they walked past. He unlocked the bathroom door and walked through the bedroom into the lounge. Trevor was watching TV.

'I see you're watching the usual news on a loop crap.'

Trevor didn't turn away from the screen. 'Sorted?'

'Yes.'

'Then it's the casino. Get your wallet ready.'

'It's jumping up and down in my pocket at the thought of getting fatter.' Peter picked up his card key. 'Let's go.'

CHAPTER TEN

The casino was busier than it had been the night before. Peter made a beeline for the same blackjack table he had patronised the previous evening. Trevor went to the roulette table and watched the state of play. He ordered a double vodka on the rocks from one of the waitresses and shook off the hostesses who tried to pick him up.

Alfred was standing opposite him on the other side of the table. He was with half a dozen of his 'new friends' all tall, black and handsome in well-cut suits and silk shirts. Trevor found it strange that dedicated teachers, nurses, and other essential workers could never aspire to dress or live as well as criminals who flouted the law.

Trevor watched Alfred place ten one-hundred-pound chips on red. He lost, shrugged in keeping with his undercover character and took another thousand pounds from the stack in front of him.

A group of expressionless Chinese entered the casino and walked to the back of the room just as they had done the night before, Lee among them. They disappeared through the same door. Trevor looked for but saw no sign of Maria Sanchez or Michael Sullivan, then recalled Dan telling him that they were having dinner with the Columbians.

He watched the roulette wheel for twenty minutes before using his American Express card to buy a thousand pounds worth of chips. He returned to the table and placed fifty pounds on red. It wasn't a bet that required much attention.

One of Alfred's companions whispered in Alfred's ear. A few minutes later they left the table and walked through the door that led to the private rooms and toilets. Peter was sitting at the blackjack table apparently engrossed in his game but Trevor noticed he had also clocked Alfred's disappearance. Unlike the previous evening, the Russian, Alexander Markov and the Albanian, Justin Lebov, were with different groups, both were playing dice. He checked his watch. Eleven forty-five. An hour and a quarter to go before the 1 a.m. deadline for the Yardies to make their offer on Black Daffodil. The ball landed on red. He scooped up his winning chips. Time to make another bet.

Lee picked up the cards he had been dealt and fanned out his hand cautiously so no one could see what he was holding. He played with the chips on the piles in front of him. He took six and pushed them forward.

A cord lassoed around his neck.

He choked when it tightened. His head jerked and slammed into the high back of the chair behind him.

'Mr Policeman?' Hostile eyes glared upside down into his. 'Your body has Chinese blood. But your loyalties are not with your race.'

Lee would have protested if he'd been able to make a sound.

'Perhaps you had a forefather whose soul wasn't tainted. They would have told you about the old country. The old ways. What warriors do to traitors? Which part of your body can you do without, traitor policeman?'

Lee's eyes widened in panic. He could barely breathe. Speech was impossible. His neck burned. His wind pipe was being severed.

'Blink when I mention which part of your body you can dispense with. Your right arm?'

Lee fought to keep his eyes open, unblinking.

'Your right leg?'

Lee focused on a spot on the ceiling. He concentrated with all his might. His eyes were dry, burning but he dare not close his eyelids.

'Your left leg?'

The pain in his neck and eyes was excruciating – intensifying.

'Your head?'

The suggestion provoked subdued laughter. Lee tried to raise his hands to loosen the rope around his neck. He couldn't move them. They had been looped together behind the chair and it hadn't even registered.

'The left arm? That is all that remains. The instrument if you please.'

A machete flashed before Lee's eyes. Air hissed past his left ear. He glimpsed a black tarpaulin being thrown on to the carpet. Tape was plastered across his mouth sealing his lips. More was wound around his chest pinning him to the back of the chair. His legs were fastened at the ankles. His chair rocked precariously and landed on its side. Pins and needles shot through his hands as the bonds were cut on his wrists.

The men around the table moved in on him. One held his legs in an iron grip. The noose around his neck cut through his skin into his flesh. He felt droplets of blood crawl down towards his collar. His right arm was pinned to the floor. His left extended over the tarpaulin. A rope was passed around his bicep and tightened. A short stick was placed beneath the rope and turned, twisting and tightening the tourniquet. The pain was excruciating, overriding even the pain in his neck.

The room faded to grey. The machete caught the light as it sliced downwards, a dart of shimmering silver in the gloom. His severed arm lay on the tarpaulin; pumping out blood. His first thought was the pain wasn't as great as he had feared.

The last thing he saw was the clean-cut, bloodied amputation above his elbow.

Trevor was three hundred pounds down, when he spotted Andrew playing the fruit machines. He watched him surreptitiously for a while, saw him hit a jackpot, pile his winnings into a cup, and allow himself to be picked up by one of the hostesses.

Trevor didn't know if it was his imagination or if tension was building in the room. The atmosphere seemed to have changed, sharpened, heightening his senses. He moved on from betting black or red to betting on numbers and to his surprise began to win modest amounts more often than he lost. But his attention remained focused on what was happening around him, rather than the outcome of the spinning of the roulette wheel.

'So where's the deal going down?' Alfred looked around the deserted gents.

The man Alfred knew as 'Bozo' pulled a couple of short, plastic straws and a packet from his pocket. He walked past the sinks to the marble work surface in front of the mirrors at the end of the run. Leaning against the wall, he took a flat metal card case from his inside jacket pocket and opened it out. There were no cards, only a glossy metal surface. He shook the powder on to it. Using a credit card, he cut the powder into two lines. He handed Alfred one of the straws.

'I'm OK.' Alfred held up his hands.

'No one turns down a free one when we offer it, man. Hurry up. Someone could come in.'

Given that two of their companions were standing in front of the door, blocking it, Alfred felt it unlikely they'd be disturbed, but he took the straw, turned his back to Bozo and held the straw over the line. A sudden and excruciating pain in his kidneys caught him off balance. He clamped his hands on the worktop but it was too little, too late. By the time he hit the floor all sense of feeling and being had left his body.

When Alfred's four companions returned without him, Trevor was worried, but he had a hundred and fifty pounds worth of chips riding on the wheel. He couldn't have given a toss what happened to it, but he knew the people around him would find it odd if he walked away before the wheel stopped spinning. The last thing he could afford to do was jeopardise his and Peter's cover.

The wheel had never spun so long. Even when it slowed, the ball bounced from one slot to another.

Trevor managed a deprecating smile when it became clear he had lost. He pocketed his remaining chips, except for one twenty-pound chip which he handed to the girl manning the wheel and two ten-pound chips which he gave to the girls who'd been shovelling the losing chips into black bags.

Pockets bulging, he walked quickly – but not too quickly, to the back of the room. He opened the door that led to the corridor that housed the private rooms and toilets and went into the Gents. Blinding white-tiled floors, wall and worktops gleamed vacantly back at him. The air smelled of antiseptic and the pine-scented hand-wash in the porcelain dispensers. A single dripping tap echoed 'pings' that shattered the silence. There were no other sounds. The piped music and buzz of conversation in the casino had been closed out, two doors and several feet away.

He looked along the line of cubicles. All the doors were open except for the one at the far end. He approached it cautiously, and knocked. When no one replied, he pushed it. It held firm, locked on the inside.

'Is anyone there?' His voice resounded hollowly, alongside the drip of the tap.

He went into the adjoining cubicle, locked the door, climbed on to the toilet seat and looked over the top of the partition. Alfred was slumped on the lid of the closed toilet seat. His suit jacket lay on the floor at his feet. The right sleeve of his shirt was rolled up. A rubber tube had been tightened around his upper arm and a hypodermic syringe stuck in the crook of his elbow. His head was tilted back; his dark brown eyes open, staring, devoid of the warmth that had animated them in life. Cold, dead they gazed blindly into Trevor's.

Trevor leaned back and almost lost his balance. He clutched the top of the wall to steady himself. Alfred was a good man, a sound copper, a reliable colleague. He had met Alfred's wife and three children – two boys and a girl. Seen what a devoted husband and father he was. And now – now – in the space of a less than half an hour Alfred had been transformed from living, loving, happy family man and dedicated police officer to corpse.

Trevor climbed down off the pan, sat on it and sank his head in his hands. He retreated into the persona of cool, emotionless, trained officer. He had seen Alfred leave the floor of the casino with four men and those same four men return without him half an hour later. He had no doubt that they had murdered Alfred. The one thing he could be one hundred percent certain of was that Alfred was no drug addict.

The question he had to ask was: had Alfred slipped up and inadvertently blown his cover, a mistake that any one of them working on this operation was capable of. Or had someone discovered Alfred was an undercover police officer and shopped him to the gang he'd infiltrated? If it was the latter, they could all be in danger? Lee, Maria, Michael, Justin, Alexander – Peter – him.

Nauseous, he rose to his feet. The place was still empty but for how long? How many people had seen him leave the casino? He hadn't been invited to join a private game so there was only one place he could be.

He left the cubicle and looked for CCTV cameras. There was one set over the door. The lens was trained on the washbasins and wouldn't cover the area in front of the cubicles. He should have checked for CCTV before he entered the cubicle, climbed up and looked over the dividing wall. Between that omission and the conversation he'd had with Peter, he was making too many slip-ups for a married man about to become a father.

He conjured images of Alfred's wife and children and considered how the news of Alfred's death would affect them as a family and individuals. How it would blight Alfred's children's lives. Would Lyn ever …

He pushed the unbearable idea from his mind before it formed.

He walked to the sink, ran a basin of cold water, plunged his hands into it and splashed his face. Two questions dominated his thinking and he couldn't provide an answer to either. Had Alfred slipped up? Or was there a leak?

He relegated both to the 'be thought of later' compartment. He had a more immediate and pressing problem.

The door opened and two men swaggered in. They went to the urinals. He switched off the tap and left, walking straight back to the casino.

He had to alert Andrew without putting either his own or Peter's cover at risk.

Peter was still playing blackjack, apparently engrossed in the game, although he was looking around the room at intervals as he had done all evening. Andrew was at the bar chatting to the hostess who was wearing a transparent silk dress. She was sipping a champagne cocktail – the preferred 'in-house' hostess drink.

There was no sign of Lebov, or what was more disturbing, his friends. Markov was playing dice. Trevor went to the bar, ordered a drink and smiled at Andrew. 'Mr Horton, what a surprise.'

'Mr Brown, I don't talk business outside the office,' Andrew shook the hand Trevor offered him.

'Neither do I, Mr Horton. Just sampling some of the entertainment on offer in the Bay.'

The girl who was with Andrew coughed loudly.

Trevor apologised. 'Where are my manners? Would you and the lady like a drink?'

'Mine's a champagne cocktail.' The blonde sidled up to him. Andrew had obviously been trying to give her the brush-off.

'Malt whisky, straight.' Andrew eyed Trevor warily.

Trevor turned to the barman. 'Malt whisky, champagne cocktail and vodka on the rocks. Any vodka as long as it's Russian and have one yourself.' Trevor handed over his American Express card.

'Let me help you with those, Mr Brown.' Andrew took the champagne cocktail as the barman swiped Trevor's card.

'I heard a good joke today,' Trevor lowered his voice, 'but it's not fit for the lady's ears.' He leaned close to Andrew and whispered. 'Alfred's dead. His body is in the Gents.'

Andrew went white and Trevor slapped his back.

'Isn't that hilarious?'

'Yes … yes,' Andrew stammered, 'poor taste, Mr Brown, but hilarious. If you'll excuse me, I've forgotten to tell my area manager I will be out of the office tomorrow morning. Dental appointment. I'd better phone him right now before I forget again.'

'There's nothing worse than suffering with your teeth,' Trevor sympathised. 'Excuse me,' he beamed at the girl who was already halfway down her cocktail. 'Lady Luck is calling.' He rattled the chips in his pocket and returned to the roulette table.

Trevor had placed his bet, red nine, and the croupier had spun the wheel when two uniformed police officers entered the casino. One was speaking into a mobile phone. They drew aside the bouncers manning the entrance. After a few minutes the bouncers closed the doors and stood with their backs to them, facing the room.

Trevor watched the floor manager run towards the police officers. It was too early for Andrew to have called anyone. He glanced over to the door leading to the toilets and saw Andrew, mobile in hand, looking as mystified as he was.

There was a banging on the door. One of the officers spoke to the bouncers who were manning it. They opened the door and a dozen uniformed officers filed into the casino. The music stopped, a lift door opened and a man stepped out. He marched up to the most senior officer present, a superintendent. He didn't speak particularly loudly but a hush had fallen over the room and his voice carried over to the roulette table.

'Good evening, Superintendent Williams.'

'Good evening, Mr Darrow.'

'Do you mind telling me what is going on?' Eric Darrow had phrased the question politely, but his manner of asking was anything but.

Trevor had seen many 'super' criminals in his time, but none quite like Eric Darrow. Yet his physical presence wasn't impressive. Five feet eight inches, he might have once been as blond, slim and athletic as his son. If the stories he liked to tell about his past glories as an international rugby player had any truth in them, he may have been even fitter. But now, in his early fifties, his body had run to fat and he was at least two stone heavier than when Trevor had last seen him. The final vestiges of colour had left his thinning, silver grey hair. His eyes were as blue and as bright as Trevor recalled. They were also as vicious.

Trevor saw nothing to alter the impression he had formed the first time he had met the man. Eric Darrow was the same slimy bastard he remembered from ten years back, when Darrow had evaded every single question he and Peter had asked, never giving a straight answer to any one of them, while repeating his threat to sue them, the force, and use his connections to 'have their jobs'.

Darrow's eyes flicked over the room. Trevor knew he'd changed even more than Darrow, since they had last met but that didn't stop a sick feeling rising from the pit of his stomach.

What if Darrow recognised him – or Peter? Then he realised. He was a professional police officer yet Darrow had the power to intimidate him.

What chance did the Kelly's of this world have if

even he, with the full backing of the police force, couldn't stand up to and confront the man?

Darrow posed in front of the lift that opened on the walkway that ringed the room. He looked down on the customers and police officers who were standing on the floor of the casino, three feet below him. He was obviously trying to emphasise his status as owner of the casino and also give the impression that it was he, not the police, who were in control of the situation. He barked an order. A few moments later a bouncer ran up to him and handed him a radio microphone. Darrow switched it on and addressed the room as if he were a politician at a rally.

'Ladies and gentlemen, no one regrets this interruption to your evening's entertainment more than me. The police have informed me that a human body part has been discovered in the car park outside the casino. They refuse to tell me anything more – or what part of the human body the part is.' He paused. If he had expected laughter he was disappointed.

'The officers insist on taking the names and addresses of everyone here. I realise this is an infringement of your civil liberties, but the police have the power to detain potential witnesses to what may – or may not –' he laid heavy emphasis on the last three words, 'turn out to be a criminal offence.'

A hubbub broke out.

'The police have also insisted that we suspend all gaming.' Eric Darrow held up his hand as people began to shout questions. 'I doubt they have the authority to do so, but to save any unpleasantness I have agreed. I have instructed my staff to give everyone a voucher on leaving the club, which will entitle you to ten pounds worth of free chips the next time you visit.'

The police officers began to divide the people into groups,

Alexander Markov, Peter and Trevor were moved into one group of twelve men. Justin Lebov and Andrew into another. Rookie constables moved along the groups with notepads and paper, taking down names and addresses. Most customers tossed business cards at the officers but the police had been well briefed. They took no card at face value and demanded corroboration from a second document.

Trevor studied the line and saw that it was going to be a slow process. He watched Peter push a cigar in his mouth only to receive the customary, 'No smoking,' reprimand from a bouncer.

Before Peter could give his 'this is just my dummy' reply, an officer came running from the back corridor and Trevor knew that neither he nor Peter would see their beds before dawn.

CHAPTER ELEVEN

Hours later, after everyone in the casino had been 'processed', a short journey in the back of a police van, and two and a half hours spent in a waiting room with 'other potential witnesses', Trevor, Peter and Alexander were escorted out of the ante-room and away from the half a dozen self-proclaimed 'hard cases' who 'had previous form'. It took another ten minutes of 'shuffling' before they ended up in the same room as Dan and Andrew. Dan closed the door. A few seconds later Bill appeared, grim-faced and exhausted. He pulled a chair out from under the table and sat down.

'What the hell's going on …' Peter began.

Bill silenced him with a curt, 'Alfred's dead.'

'I found his body.' Trevor was relieved that he could finally tell Peter and Alexander.

'I phoned Dan as soon as Trevor passed on the news.' Andrew's face was ashen, drained of colour.

Trevor wondered if it was down to the strain they were under or the fluorescent lighting.

Dan picked up the thread. 'The locals moved in and took control of the casino before I had time to call them.'

'What body part was found?' Alexander asked.

'Lee's arm.' Bill leaned his elbows on the table.

'It's a Triad torture,' Dan explained. 'If they think someone has betrayed them, they kidnap them and ask which part of their body they can do without. They remove whichever leg or arm the victim decides on, wait a week or two for the wound to heal, then return and ask them which other part they can do without. Sometimes the victims are kept alive for months before being killed or starved to death. They usually start with the left arm. That's what we found.'

'Has it been identified as Lee's?' Peter didn't want to believe it.

'It has his ring on the index finger and the Rolex we issued strapped to the wrist. There was blood in the back room the Chinese had hired. Not much, but enough to cross match. We're waiting on results. But don't get your hopes up. It's Lee's all right. Locals think they put down plastic sheeting when they severed his arm. We've had wind of it happening to Triad members before – but not anywhere as public as a casino.'

'Lee could still be alive?' Andrew asked earnestly.

'As Dan said, it's almost certain he is.' Bill covered his eyes as if the light was too strong – it wasn't. 'Locals have everyone they can spare out looking for him. But we're dealing with the Chinese. They could have hidden him in any one of a thousand places around the Bay and, that's without starting on the yachts. Eighteen have sailed out in the last two hours. He could be on his way to France, Ireland or the Med.'

'What happened to Alfred?' Peter asked.

Trevor related in a few words how he found him.

'We won't have the PM results until tomorrow. As Trevor said, there was a needle in his arm. But from the angle there is no way that he injected himself. There was also a swelling on the crown of

163

his head and bruising on his back, so he was assaulted before he died. If he was lucky, he didn't know what was happening to him.' Bill tensed the muscles in his jaw. 'And that's not all.'

'What can be bloody worse than this …' Peter began.

'Maria Sanchez and Michael Sullivan were found floating in a stolen tender on the bay ten minutes ago. Both had been shot in the head.'

Andrew swayed and gripped the back of his chair. 'There's no mistake …'

'Not a chance,' Bill muttered.

Trevor stared down at the floor.

Peter bit the cigar in his mouth in half. He spat the threads of tobacco that clung to his lips into a tissue. 'There's a leak inside the force.'

'It looks that way,' Bill concurred.

'What about the others? Are they still out there?' Trevor asked.

'We've pulled in everyone who wasn't at the casino tonight. Tony, Tom, Veenay and Hassan are in safe houses.'

'You're watching them?' Peter asked.

'Every operative on this case was thoroughly screened,' Dan insisted. 'I staked my life – and yours – on your collective integrity.'

'Justin?' Alexander looked at Bill.

'Justin is with the rest of the Albanians, in a cell. One of them was carrying half a pound of heroin.'

'Typical,' Alexander said, 'no finesse or style.'

'Solicitor's getting him out now,' Bill said. 'There are a couple more things. We checked everyone's families. Lee's wife is missing.

According to a neighbour she left the house in her car around midnight. The neighbour was still up; Lee's wife's saw her light, knocked on the door, gave her a key and asked the neighbour if she would feed their cat. She explained that she'd had a call from a hospital to say Lee had been in an accident and she didn't know when she'd be back. Her car was found abandoned at the local hospital, a twenty-minute drive from her house.'

'There was no sign of her?' Peter said.

'As *yet*,' Bill emphasised.

'What about our families?' Trevor asked urgently.

'All fine, all being watched,' Dan reassured him. 'But Kelly has disappeared from the massage parlour.'

'Was she reported missing?' Peter clenched his fists.

'No. After you called Andrew, we sent in two men. They visited an hour apart. Both asked for her. Both were told that she wasn't working because she was ill.'

'She was fine when I was with her,' Peter said fiercely.

'Upstairs are pulling in every undercover officer and closing down this operation with immediate effect.'

'Isn't that rather drastic?' Alexander asked.

'Not when you consider what happened to Alfred and Lee,' Bill answered.

'They were both murdered by the gangs they infiltrated,' Peter murmured more to himself than anyone else.

'Thank you for stating the obvious, Sergeant,' Bill snapped. 'That's why we're holding the men who accompanied Alfred to the Gents. Locals have taken the tape from the CCTV in the bathroom, hopefully before it could be tampered with. We're waiting on forensic tests. We're not expecting fingerprints but we might strike lucky with DNA.'

Trevor said, 'Lee is in the hands of the Triads and they have to be behind the abduction of his wife. Alfred was killed by the Yardies. Maria and Michael were almost certainly shot by the Columbians, all of which means that whoever's behind the sale of Black Daffodil has tipped off the gangs. The undercover operatives were targets – not of whoever is marketing the formula of Black Daffodil – that person or persons is far too clever to point the finger at themselves – but the people they penetrated. And everyone else who has made contact with a gang will remain a target until we unmask the leak and show the gangs how they have been used.'

'If they're prepared to be shown.' Bill looked doubtful.

'No one will cease being a target because "upstairs" has chosen to shut this operation down,' Peter stated. 'The Russians know Alexander. The Albanians know Justin. And, as they're sitting here and not lying in the mortuary like Alfred, Michael and Maria, or locked up somewhere and being tortured like Lee, that means either their contacts are slower off the mark, or the gangs haven't been informed that they're undercover cops yet.'

'We need to find out who is behind this leak,'

Trevor looked to Bill.

'How?' Bill asked.

'Leave Peter and me out there for another twenty four hours,' Trevor suggested. 'But bring in Alexander and Justin. They're working with gangs that aren't going to shy away from murder. Peter and I have been working with minor dealers. We haven't reached the big boys but our faces are known. Every local dealer on the Bay – big and small – must have been alerted to our quest for Black Daffodil by now. We'll start by calling on Chris and Sarah ...'

'They are all right?' Peter checked.

'They were both fine when I came in here. I risked telephoning them. I warned them to keep their doors and windows locked. I also took the precaution of ordering an out-of-town team to move into an empty flat on their floor.' Bill turned to Peter. 'What do you think of Trevor's idea?'

Peter glanced from Trevor to Bill and finally to Dan. 'Trevor's right. We've played the part of lone operators moving into existing territory. We're no threat to anyone other than the small-time dealers who supplied us with Black Daffodil. And, if there is a local police informer, the chances are he's passed on information about us and Chris and Sarah working for a Mr Big.'

'Whoever passed on information about Alfred, Lee, Michael and Maria wasn't local,' Dan warned. 'He or she had gold star information on our operation.'

'There could be two informers,' Peter explained with unusual patience – for him. 'One who leaked

167

information about this operation, and possibly another who has access to information about police operations on the council estate. You must have been concerned about that scenario. If you hadn't, you wouldn't have imposed an information blackout on the local force about Chris and Sarah.'

Dan nodded cautiously, 'Agreed.'

'It can't hurt Trevor or me if the smaller dealers assume we're are part of a bigger operation, especially if they believe we have serious muscle behind us. The other informant we're looking for has to be someone in on this operation. But who is he – or she – going to pass on information about Trevor or me to? The small fry won't dare tackle us after that last show in the tower block. And, as we haven't approached any of the big dealers or gangs, they have nothing on us that they could see as a threat.'

'Peter has a point.' Dan said to Bill.

'There's one person they haven't thought of,' Bill observed, 'and that's whoever's behind Black Daffodil. Because he is set to make millions from a deal with the Russians – provided we don't interfere.'

'But if we flush out whoever it is, we will close the case,' Trevor said optimistically.

'At considerable risk to yourselves. Do you two really want to go back out there?' Bill asked.

Peter left his chair. 'Think about it, Bill, what have we got to lose? Only our lives and you told me mine was expendable.'

'Yours,' Bill replied, with a ghost of a smile, 'not Trevor's.'

'Call a taxi to take us back to the hotel,' Trevor suggested. 'We'll drive up to the estate tomorrow and talk to Chris and Sarah. If they haven't tracked down the main supplier of Black Daffodil on that estate you can pull them out.'

'And then?' Dan asked.

'Peter and I keep asking questions and see what we come up with until tomorrow evening when we'll think again.'

'Ask questions? Who are you going to ask?' Bill demanded.

'Eric Darrow for one. It's his city. Even if he isn't mixed up in Black Daffodil I bet he knows who is.' Peter went to the door.

'Sergeant …'

'I know. Go easy. Don't I always?' Peter gave his superiors a broad, artificial smile.

'No you don't.'

'Twenty four hours isn't long. We'll do what we can.'

'I'll keep him in check.' Trevor joined Peter. 'Send for that car. I'm sleeping on my feet.'

Peter lay on the emperor-sized bed in his suite. He was bone weary, physically and mentally but couldn't stop tossing and turning. He stared up at the ceiling, grey, shrouded in shadows, then looked at the illuminated clock built into the headboard. The hands pointed to four thirty. He turned over his pillow, hit it several times, moved his head to what he hoped would be a cooler, more comfortable spot and closed his eyes, only for his mind to be drawn into a kaleidoscope of images.

Chris being beaten to a pulp by the thugs who had broken into the flat – Kelly huddled on the floor, head in hands as she sobbed her heart out for Jake Phillips because he was one of the few people who had 'been kind to her' – Alfred laughing as he walked to the door at the back of the casino, sharing a joke with men who were about to murder him. Maria and Michael playing the gaming machines in the casino, engrossed in conversation with their new Hispanic friends, never dreaming that less than twenty-four hours later they would cease to exist – Lee, serious and studious, walking towards the private room surrounded by Chinese gamblers.

Peter opened his eyes and looked at the clock again. Four thirty-five. Only five minutes since he had last checked the time. He pictured Daisy, her eyes flashing in anger in the restaurant when he was being his usual thick-skinned, pig-headed self because he didn't know how to tell her he loved her. Would she be getting a call from some low-life, as Lee's wife had, telling her that he was hurt and in hospital and needed her …

He moved his pillow again. The room was hot – airless. He couldn't breathe but he never could in air conditioned rooms. He left the bed, pressed the electric button that opened the balcony doors and stepped outside.

He had told Dan about Daisy – even going as far as putting her down as his next of kin, an honour that had been Trevor's until now. But whereas Trevor had asked Dan if Lyn was safe, he hadn't dared ask about Daisy because Andrew and Bill would scoff at the notion of him – the ultimate hard-headed cynical copper, having a girlfriend he actually cared for. Had Dan ordered a guard on Daisy? Was she in danger?

The false dawn that precedes the real one tinged the eastern horizon, painting the chill dark sea with even icier fingers. What was it about the sea that sent the price of property on the coast soaring out of the reach of most mortals? The eternal shifting movement of the waves? The white crests that foamed and dissipated only to reform in eternal motion? The plaintive cry of the gulls? The astringent smell of salt-laden air? He should know better than to ask. Philosophy wasn't good for someone in his line of work at any time, but was particularly unnerving in the early hours.

Police officers should be doers not thinkers. Thinkers had a habit of working situations out for themselves which led to disobeying orders – and pissing off superiors.

He left the balcony door open and returned to the bedroom. Picking up his cell phone he reached for his wallet, took out a disposable Sim card and removed the original. After inserting the new card he went into the bathroom, locked the door, turned on the shower and dialled Daisy's number.

Daisy heard the telephone and cursed. She fumbled blindly for the phone and it crashed to the floor. Why did people have to fall sick in the middle of the night and make her drop the phone and, what was even worse, open her eyes to find it.

Then she remembered. She wasn't on call. Hadn't been for years. She was working in reconstructive and plastic surgery. Plastic surgeons were never on call. They could schedule their consultations and surgery operations during civilised hours.

'Daisy Sherringham. This had better be good.'

'No names. It's me.'

'She squinted at the clock. 'Peter? Are you all right …'

'No names,' he repeated, 'I'm fine. I wanted to make sure you were.'

'I was. Do you know what time it is?'

'A quarter to five. I couldn't sleep.'

'I could. It was wonderful. Why did you wake me?'

'To ask you if you are all right.'

'I *was* fine.'

'Sorry I bothered you. Go back to sleep.'

'Don't you dare hang up now you've woken me,' she snapped irritably. 'Did you really telephone just to ask how I was?'

'I was worried about you.'

'What's going on?' She sat up in bed.

'Nothing.'

'Funny nothing. A squad came round tonight. They asked if anyone had telephoned me about you. When I said no, they asked if I'd seen any strangers hanging around my place or at work. I pointed out that there are always strangers hanging around my workplace.'

'You can't talk like this on the phone. I explained what it would be like …'

'I'm sorry my brain hasn't woken up and neither has the rest of me.'

'Were you asked to go somewhere?'

'Yes.'

'Somewhere safe?'

'So they said.'

'Then why are you still at this number and talking to me now?'

'I can't disrupt my entire life for you.'

'No one's asking you to.'

'Yes, you are. I'm your girlfriend, not your doormat. I have my job, you have yours. Besides, they told me they would be keeping a discreet eye on me, whatever that means. Is it something to do with the case you are working on?'

'Enough, if anyone's listening in they'll hit bonanza. There's another reason why I phoned you.'

'What?'

'I love you.'

It was just as well Daisy was in bed. She would have fallen over if she hadn't been. She couldn't believe what she was hearing. 'Do you mind repeating that? The line has gone peculiar.'

'I love you. Will you marry me?'

Trevor woke at five after less than an hour's sleep. He lay still, tensing his muscles and listening hard. Something had woken him. He wasn't sure what. Taking his gun, he left the bed and padded on bare feet into the lounge. He could hear a voice. Radio? Television? He checked both. Neither was switched on. He went to the door that separated his suite from Peter's. A light shone beneath it. He stood back and opened it before tentatively entering Peter's lounge. A table lamp was burning. There was a line of light beneath the bedroom door. He crossed the room, opened the door, stood back and glanced inside.

The room was cool. The balcony doors open, the blinds clacking in the slight breeze. He knocked the bathroom door. The voice fell silent.

Peter called out. 'Who is it?'

'The bloody bogeyman, who would sleep if he didn't hear voices in the middle of the night. You OK?'

'Never better.'

'I wish I could say the same.' Trevor sank down on Peter's bed. He leaned back on the pillow and closed his eyes … .

It could have been a few seconds, minutes or hours later when Peter shook him awake. Startled, he opened his eyes. 'Sorry,' he mumbled. 'I fell asleep.'

'On my bed.'

'Who the hell were you phoning at this hour?' Trevor watched Peter remove the Sim card from his cell phone.

'My lady love. I wanted to make sure she was all right.'

'I bet she thanked you for waking her in the middle of the night,' Trevor said sourly.

'As a matter of fact she did.' Peter poured himself a glass of water. He lifted the glass to Trevor. 'Want some?'

'Now I'm awake, yes.'

'No please or thank you,' Peter held it back. 'Tut tut. What example is that going to set the coming generation?'

'Hand it over.' Trevor took the glass of water

and sipped it. 'The best thing about living in a five-star hotel is there are always plenty of cold drinks on tap and I don't mean alcohol.'

'There would be in your house if somebody remembered to fill the fridge. I want you to be the first to know. I'm a reformed man.'

'That is too much to believe, even at this time in the morning.'

'I just asked her.'

'Asked who what?'

'My love to marry me.'

'You what?'

Peter stared at the water Trevor had tipped over his duvet. 'Now look what you've bloody well done.'

'It's not that wet,' Trevor remonstrated.

'Yes it is.'

'If you fold it over you can sleep in the other half of the bed.' Trevor rearranged the bedclothes.

Peter went to the door. 'I'll sleep in your bed thank you very much. You can have the wet one.'

Trevor lay on the dry bit. 'I'm too tired to move anyway. What prompted you to ask her now?'

'Until tonight I thought I had all the time in the world.'

'None of us have.' Trevor closed his eyes and thought about Lyn and the baby she was carrying. Their baby – his baby – she had been so determined she didn't want to know the sex but he half hoped – half wished it was a girl.

A beautiful grey-eyed, dark-haired girl exactly like her mother. And, given what had happened to Alfred and Lee, he hoped he'd live to see her.

CHAPTER TWELVE

Trevor was locked deep in sleep. He was dreaming that he was on a train that was going fast – and faster. He was being rocked from side to side. At first the movement was gentle then it became more and more violent. He tried to look out of the window, but all he could see was a blur of colours. Someone was calling his name ...

'Trevor ... .Trevor ...'

It changed sharply, in tone and urgency. 'Wake up you lazy sod.'

Trevor jerked bolt upright. He opened his eyes and stared blankly at Peter, his mind still lost in the nightmare world of a speeding, crashing train.

'Upstairs phoned your mobile. They couldn't get you because you were in my bed and bedroom and I was in yours. You have to be on the helipad on the roof in ten minutes.'

'What?'

'You thick or what?' Lack of sleep had made Peter more irritable than usual.

Trevor repeated, 'The helipad ...'

'Someone wants you to be somewhere urgently.'

'Fucking hell ...'

'They said there was nothing for you to worry about. Everything is going to plan and perfectly normal.' Peter was tired of having to speak without mentioning names. 'I suggest you shower, shave and dress.'

'No time.' Trevor threw back the bedclothes.

'There's time. It will take less than a minute to

get up on the roof. And you will be appreciated more by those who love you if you are clean and smell nice. Move it, out of my bed, so I can leave a note for housekeeping to change the sheets.'

Five minutes later, dressed, still damp from the shower, Trevor patted himself down. Wallets … keys … nothing he had on him, not even his clothes were his. Everything in the suite was Trevor Brown's. And for the next few hours Trevor Brown wouldn't exist. He could forget about his alter ego.

'Trevor?'

'I'm there.' Trevor headed for the door and saw Peter grab his suit jacket. 'What do you think you're doing?'

'There's no point in me staying without you. You're not brilliant, but you're all I have to cover my back. Rather than hang around here, I thought I'd go with you.'

'There's nothing you can do …'

'Except provide the glue you need to keep yourself together. Come on, you don't want to keep the helicopter waiting. It's rented by the hour.'

Trevor saw Dan standing on the fringe of the helipad on the roof of the hospital before they landed.

'Lyn?' Trevor demanded as he jumped down from the helicopter.

'She's fine. I spoke to the ward sister five minutes ago. She said the birth was imminent but she's been saying that for the last half hour. Second floor, ward seven,' Dan shouted after Trevor as he ran towards the lifts.

'Expectant fathers, eh?' Peter offered Dan a cigar.

'I'll talk to you when it's time for you to hold your wife's hand. Speaking of which, Daisy's here.'

'She would be. She works here.'

'You called her in the early hours.'

'How do you …' Peter looked at Dan. 'I might have bloody known. You packed listening devices and transmitters into our phones.'

'She must love you to let you call her at that hour.'

'She does actually. And if you were listening in, you'd know she agreed to marry me.' Peter still couldn't believe it. In spite of the murders, something wonderful had happened. And was going to carry on happening. He would be spending the rest of his life with the woman he loved.

He glanced at Dan. Exhaustion was etched into every line on his face. 'Have you slept since last night?'

'No. I had a couple of things to do.'

Peter could guess what the couple of things were. Dan would have taken it upon himself to see Alfred's family and tell them personally that he had been killed. He doubted that Michael or Maria had relatives in the UK but there were still telephone calls to make – to family and colleagues. And Lee?

'Any more news about Lee or his wife?' Peter asked.

'The arm has been confirmed as Lee's. But we knew that. The locals are searching for him but so far they've found no trace of him or his wife.'

'Kelly?' Peter asked.

'Nothing. She could have gone to ground. Chris and Sarah are fine.'

'You're not pulling them out?' Peter asked. 'I know we were going to do it this afternoon but, we're here …'

'They're waiting for a consignment of Black Daffodil.'

'Are you crazy?'

'They're being closely monitored.'

'Like Alfred, Michael, Maria and Lee, were being monitored?'

'We have first-class surveillance watching Chris, Sarah, the block and everything around them. If an ice cream van as much as stops in the street outside, we'll have it covered.'

'With a ground to air missile?' Peter suggested caustically.

'When you and Trevor have finished here you can go back and help them to close up shop.'

'And the leak?'

'Security are going through everyone's backgrounds again.'

'It has to be someone inside, Dan,' Peter said soberly.

'Stop reminding me.' The lift opened and Dan stepped inside. 'Let's find out if we're uncles.'

Daisy caught hold of Lyn's hand. 'Breathe.'

'I don't want to,' Lyn snapped. 'Trevor promised he'd be here. You said he knew I'd gone into labour …'

'They promised they'd tell him,' Daisy reassured

her.

'Bloody police! Bloody! Bloody! Police …' Lyn grimaced when another pain took hold.

Daisy winced as Lyn's grip on her hand tightened. 'Time for gas and air.'

'I'm going to hang on until Trevor arrives.'

'Of course, you are, darling.'

'And stop using that bloody voice on me.'

'What voice?' Daisy had trouble concealing her amusement. She had never heard Lyn swear as much as she had done since her labour pains had started.

'That bloody "I'm the doctor and I know best" voice. I'm a nurse, remember!'

'I remember. You sure you don't want me to call your mother?'

'I'm sure.'

'She's going to be furious that she missed this.'

'My parents have been looking forward to my cousin's wedding for months so they could catch up on the family gossip … argh! … that was a bad one.'

'And you really don't know whether it's a boy or girl?' Daisy asked in an attempt to distract Lyn. She knew full well that Lyn and Trevor had refused to ask the sex of their child but she wanted Lyn to think of something besides her ridiculous obsession to delay the birth until Trevor arrived.

'No, I don't know. But I bet it's a boy,' Lyn gasped.

'What makes you so certain?'

'A girl would never be this much trouble.'

The midwife bustled into the room. 'I'll just take

180

a look at you, Mrs Joseph …'

'I am NOT going to deliver this baby until my husband gets here,' Lyn insisted. 'And there's no point in you two rolling your eyes at one another. I am NOT …'

'You want the poor man to see what he's put you through.' The midwife checked the monitors.

'Exactly,' Lyn agreed through gritted teeth.

'I'm afraid your husband is going to be introduced to baby after baby's arrival.'

'You can't go in there without a cap and gown. Sir … sir …'

Trevor burst into the room, an auxiliary hard on his heels holding a cap, gown and mask. 'Hello, darling. Sorry I'm late.' He bent over Lyn and kissed her.

'What the hell have they done to you?'

Trevor touched his hairless lip and bald head. 'I'd forgotten about that.' He put on the gown and mask the auxiliary thrust at him.

'You look weird,' Lyn clenched her fists against the pain.

'Hello, Trevor. You do look odd.' Daisy greeted him.

'This is nothing.' He took hold of Lyn's hand. 'You wait until you see Peter. And congratulations.' He looked down at Lyn. 'Did Daisy tell you that Peter asked her to marry him and she said yes?'

Lyn turned to Daisy. 'No, she didn't.'

'He caught me when I was half asleep. I'm debating whether to change my mind. But that decision is for the future. Today you're having a baby and that's enough excitement.'

Another pain gripped Lyn. Daisy handed Trevor the iced sponge she'd been using to cool Lyn's forehead.

'You bastard!' Lyn picked up a pillow and hit Trevor with it. 'You said you would be here in good time for the birth.'

'You didn't tell me that you were going to be five weeks early.' He looked at the midwife. 'That doesn't mean there's going be a problem, does it?'

'Baby's heartbeat is strong, and Mum is doing fine. It's possible Mum was confused about her dates.'

'Don't talk to me as if I am an idiot or not here,' Lyn said crossly. 'I'm a nurse, I know dates …'

'Calm down, darling,' Trevor smoothed Lyn's damp hair away from her forehead. 'This isn't any good for the baby or you.'

'Is Peter outside?' Daisy asked.

'Yes.' Trevor answered Daisy. But he couldn't stop looking at Lyn.

'You don't have to go because Trevor's arrived, Daisy,' Lyn protested.

'Yes, I do. This is something the two of you should do together without an audience. Besides, I've my own man to see.'

'Daisy,' Lyn called after her as she went to the door.

Daisy turned back.

'Thank you.'

'My pleasure. And despite seeing all you've gone through in the last couple of hours and listening to all the cursing and swearing. I can't wait until it's my turn to do exactly what you're doing now.' She blew Lyn a kiss.

Daisy found Peter and Dan in the waiting room, drinking coffee.

Peter smiled at her.

'Trevor said that you might look as odd as him but you look even more thuggish.' She sat opposite him and Dan. 'You are Peter Collins, aren't you?'

'Very funny.' He ran his hand over his shaved head. 'Lice can be a problem where we're working.'

'It's not just the hair – or lack of it. It's the clothes.'

Peter fingered the lapel on his suit jacket. 'Real designer wear. No fakes.'

'Not to mention the Rolex. You look like a couple of …'

'Charming, eligible guys?' Peter finished for her. 'I was just telling Dan I'm about to make an honest woman of you.'

'After seeing you, I've changed my mind.'

'How are things going in there?' Dan inclined his head towards the maternity ward.

'They should be fine now. Lyn has been driving the midwives to distraction. She insisted she wanted to hang on until Trevor arrived. To our amazement, she succeeded.'

'This is the hospital you work in, isn't it Daisy?' Dan asked.

'Yes.'

'Is there somewhere private we can talk?'

'My office. I'll tell the ward sister to ring us there as soon as Lyn has given birth.' Daisy disappeared for a few moments before returning and leading them to the lift. They went up to the fifth floor and she walked along a deserted corridor, stopping outside a door she laid her thumb over the door panel.

'High security,' Dan commented when the door opened.

'Among other things I'm working on a confidential research project,' she explained. 'There are files on developmental procedures in here that some companies would pay a small fortune for. Especially some of the more unscrupulous American companies that specialise in cosmetic surgery. But enough of what I do, please come in and sit down.'

Two walls of Daisy's office were covered in bookcases. There was a desk and chair and four chairs set around a coffee table in the corner for conferences. Dan pulled a gadget out of his pocket switched it on and held it up.

'If you're checking to see if my office is bugged, Inspector, I assure you it isn't. The hospital sweeps these corridors regularly.' Daisy sat behind her desk.

'It's Dan, not Inspector.'

'Something's wrong, isn't it?' Daisy looked from Dan to Peter.

'The job's not going particularly well,' Peter admitted.

Dan coughed. 'Some of our undercover operatives' covers have been blown.'

'Yours and Trevor's?' Daisy adjusted the blinds to allow more light into the room.

'We don't think so,' Peter reassured her.

'Has anyone been hurt?'

'Yes,' Dan answered, because he sensed that Peter wouldn't.

'Anyone killed?' Daisy questioned.

When neither Dan nor Peter answered her question, Daisy clamped her hand over her mouth. 'Dear God.'

'Three operatives were murdered last night. One is missing, so is his wife, and that is why we are talking to you,' Dan explained. 'As soon as Lyn has given birth we'll put a guard on her and get you both out of here to a place of safety where you can be looked after.'

'Like where?'

'What does it matter where?' Peter asked.

'We'll try to make a pleasant place, but, wherever it is, it will be somewhere where you can be watched twenty-four seven,' Dan explained.

'Oh no you don't.' Daisy folded her arms across her chest. 'The last thing I need, are police officers following me around.'

'Daisy …' Peter didn't get any further.

'You can take Lyn and the baby wherever you like. And, I am in full agreement, they should be in a place of safety where they can live free from worry and Lyn can concentrate on bonding with her child. But I have a full-time job and I'm going to do it.'

'Look here, Daisy …'

'Look here, Peter,' she mimicked his voice perfectly. 'I'm your girlfriend, not your doormat. I have my job, you have yours.'

'But …'

'But nothing,' Daisy interrupted. 'There is no way that *I* am going to allow any mess that *you* have got yourself into ...'

'Mess?'

'Yes, mess,' she repeated, 'to interfere with my life or my work commitments. My patients rely on me to care for them, consult with them and when necessary carry out surgical procedures to better their quality of life.'

'Dan, tell her what we're up against,' Peter pleaded.

'I don't do domestics between people who have just got engaged.' Dan headed for the door.

'Oh no you don't. I need you to help me convince Daisy that she's in danger.' Peter tried to block Dan's path.

'I've told her what I think.' Dan frowned at Peter. 'Move, will you. Or do I have to remind you that I'm twice your size.'

'Order her to see sense,' Peter demanded.

'I can give you orders because I am your superior. But I can't order Daisy to do anything.'

'Not even when the order can save her life?' Peter challenged.

'Aren't you being a little melodramatic, Peter?' Daisy gave him a condescending smile.

'No, I am not. Three people are dead. One of my colleagues has disappeared. His wife received a telephone call telling her that he had been injured, and asking her to visit him in the hospital. She left their house and hasn't been seen since ...'

'Precisely, his wife. Think about it, Peter. I am not your wife ...'

'Yet.'

'Carry on like this and I won't be.' She watched Dan sneak out of the door behind Peter. 'No one knows about us. All we've had is a couple of dates …'

Dan closed the door behind him, stood in the corridor and listened to the argument raging behind him. It looked like Peter Collins, had met his match in temper − obstinacy − dedication to the job and a few other qualities it was difficult to put a name to.

'No! No! No! You might be a police officer but that does not affect me and I am not going to change my professional life to accommodate the vagaries of your chosen career.' Daisy left her chair, turned her back on Peter and walked to the window.

'Don't you understand what Dan and I are trying to tell you? Lee has disappeared and so has his wife …'

'I understand you. But for the tenth time. I am not your wife and from the way you are behaving right now I never will be.'

'Are you saying that my profession isn't important?'

'Are you saying mine isn't?' She turned the question back on him.

They glared at one another for a moment. Daisy saw Peter's mouth twitch. She started to laugh.

Peter dropped down into one of the chairs. 'This is bloody ridiculous.'

'That's the first sensible thing you've said in the last half hour.' She sat on his lap and kissed his lips.

'Truce.'

He kissed her back. 'On one condition.'

'What?' she asked warily.

'You tell me what kind of an engagement ring you'd like.'

It's a boy. He's all in one piece and has everything he should.' The midwife checked the baby's airways were clear which, given the noise he was making, seemed obvious to Trevor, cut the cord and wrapped the baby in a sheet before giving him to Trevor.

Lyn struggled to sit up. 'Let me see him.'

'He's perfect.' Trevor handed him over to Lyn. He crouched at the side of the bed, and gazed at both of them. He felt overwhelmed, yet happier than he'd ever been; as if someone had just shown him the meaning of life.

'He's beautiful.' Lyn pushed he little finger gently into the palm of the baby's hand.

'I need to clean him – and you – up, Mrs Joseph,' the midwife pushed a chair towards Trevor. 'But I suppose I can give Dad a few minutes grace.'

Lyn couldn't tear her gaze away from the baby. She lifted him in her arms and leaned back on the pillows. 'He is so – so – alive,' she murmured, watching in awe as he waved his tiny fingers and arms. The baby squinted, opening his eyes a fraction.

The midwife saw what she was looking at. 'His eyes will be blue for a while.'

'They're dark and they'll turn brown like his father's,' Lyn smiled down at the baby. 'Won't they darling?' She dropped a kiss on the baby's head.

'I'll be back in a few minutes, and, when I return, you,' the midwife pointed at Trevor, 'will leave your poor wife and son alone for half an hour. They need rest.' She carried a bundle of soiled linen out of the room.

Trevor smiled in relief at Lyn who looked pale and exhausted but deliriously happy.

She reached out with her free hand and squeezed his. 'I know you can't stay.'

'I wish I could.'

'Look on the bright side, when you can, you'll be able to spend the whole of the leave you've booked getting to know your son.'

'I'll ask Dan to arrange for you – both of you and anyone in your family who wants to go – to be taken down to my brother's farm in Cornwall. You don't have to stay in the main house with him and his family. You can move into one of the holiday cottages he lets out. There's always a local down there looking for casual work, who'll be prepared to cook and clean for you.'

'And you?'

'There are a few more loose ends to tie up on this case,' he answered evasively.

She gazed into his eyes, but left her finger in the palm of their baby's hand. 'I know you Trevor. Whatever this job is, it's not going well.'

'I'd be lying to you if I said it was,' he replied.

'Are you in danger?'

'No,' he replied quickly. Too quickly, he realised when he saw the look she gave him.

'You're a lousy liar, Trevor Joseph.'

'And you worry too much. I'll be fine. I have

Peter to look after me.'

'I would say he's more of a liability than a minder.'

'As I've said before, I prefer you as a room mate. You're quieter, tidier and much more loving.' He looked down at the baby. He was having trouble believing that he was really theirs. 'He is beautiful.'

'We made him well, didn't we?'

Like Lyn, Trevor was finding it difficult to look at anything in the room, other than the tiny miracle of life with his surprisingly full head of dark hair. His and Lyn's son. His son!

'Our first priority is to keep him safe.'

'Not at a high cost to you – or us as a family. You owe it to both of us to keep yourself safe, Trevor.'

'Which I will do all the better if I don't have to worry about you two,' Trevor said firmly.

Lyn knew when she was beaten. 'You'll come and get us when whatever you are working on is over?'

'The moment the case is wrapped, I'll drive down to Cornwall and take the two of you home. I promise.'

'How much longer … stupid question. You don't know, do you?'

'No,' he answered. 'No, I don't.

The midwife walked in. Her arms full of clean bed linen and towels. 'You still here, Mr Joseph?'

'No. I'm a hologram.'

'Very witty.' She dropped the linen on to a chair.

'Do you have to leave, right this minute?' Lyn pleaded.

'No, I'll stay around and see both of you settled before I go back.'

She kissed the baby again. 'He needs a name.'

Trevor gently stroked the baby's head 'We talked a lot but never made any decisions. What would you like to call him?'

'I thought Miriam would go well with Joseph.'

'He won't thank you for that when he's older.'

'No, he probably won't.'

'I'd say definitely, not probably,' the midwife observed briskly.

'My father's name was Martin.' Trevor wasn't sure why he'd mentioned it. He'd never had any thoughts of naming his son after the father who'd died before he'd reached his teens.

'Marty.' Lyn looked down at the baby and repeated it. 'Marty. Yes we both like that. Thank you, Daddy.'

'I suggested it because I thought we could use it as a middle name,' Trevor said in surprise.

'The middle name is no problem, that's Trevor.'

'Poor little man, he deserves better,' Trevor commiserated.

The midwife looked over Trevor's shoulder at the baby. 'I ordered you out, Mr Joseph.'

'So you did.' Trevor kissed Lyn again, then touched his fingers to his lips and dropped the 'kiss' on the baby's head. 'See you in a little while, Mrs Joseph and son.'

'Marty,' Lyn called after him.

Trevor walked out. The last thing he heard was the midwife, saying,

'Men! What do they know about women or

babies?'

Lyn's reply made him smile. 'Oh, I don't know. I think some of them know a lot more than we give them credit for.'

CHAPTER THIRTEEN

Dan was sitting in solitary splendour in the waiting room outside the entrance to the maternity ward. He was holding a folded newspaper and a pen and was apparently engrossed in a crossword but he looked up expectantly when Trevor joined him.

'A boy, a beautiful boy with his mother's dark hair and dark blue eyes.'

Dan was tempted to say that when the father's hair wasn't shaved it was dark too, but Trevor looked too happy for him to want to contradict him. Even in small ways.

Trevor sat beside him. 'You'll take them to my brother's farm in Cornwall and arrange security.'

'If that's what you want.'

'It is.' Trevor sank his head in his hands. He tried not to close his eyes because, every time he did, he saw the look on Bill's face when he told them Maria Sanchez and Michael Sullivan had been shot in the back of the head.

'You've done enough on this one, Trevor. We'll alert the locals. They can pull Chris and Sarah out this afternoon. This operation has proved too costly in terms of lives. And, I'm not counting Lee and his wife – not yet.'

Trevor had never been so tempted to walk away from a case. But then he thought of Alfred, and Alfred's wife and children. Maria and Michael – not that he knew them, but it took a particularly dedicated officer to volunteer for undercover work. And Lee … Jake Phillips … Alec Hodges … and the other young people who had died after taking Black Daffodil. But most of all he thought about his son. He wasn't even an hour old and already he knew that Bill had been right when he'd said,

'What kind of a world do you think your baby is going to come into if this crap hits the streets big time? No one will be safe. Not you. Not me. Not the young mother shopping in the supermarket alongside the chemist buying new supplies. And don't forget the crazed junkie who doesn't know what he's doing and doesn't care as long as he gets his next fix.'

'You gave Peter and me another twenty-four hours, Dan.'

'That was before you became a father.' Dan shook his head. 'You can't set the whole world to rights, Trevor.'

'I can take a shot at it.' Trevor dropped his hands and sat up.

'You think Darrow's behind Black Daffodil, don't you?' Dan asked.

'I don't know. It's an option to consider.'

'All right, twenty-four hours, but keep reminding Peter what you're looking for, will you. He's a bit too much of a maverick for my liking.'

'I'll try, but you know Peter.'

Dan nodded. 'Unfortunately, I do.'

'Where is he?' Trevor looked around.

'Quarrelling with Daisy. She's refused to go into a safe house or accept protection from us. As a mere girlfriend, as opposed to wife, she insists she doesn't need it. I'd say Peter's met his match there.'

'It's good to see someone putting Peter in his

place. But I'm not sure about leaving Daisy without any protection.'

'This hospital is plastered with CCTV cameras. I'll put one of our men in to help out with monitoring them and he can follow her home at the end of the day to make sure she gets there.'

'Stick a tap on her work and home phones,' Trevor advised.

'If you're thinking about Lee's wife, we've warned Daisy.'

'That doesn't mean she'll remember the warning if she gets a caller telling her Peter has been injured.'

'I'll see it's done. And, talk of the devil,' Dan left his chair when Peter and Daisy walked into the waiting room.

'Daddy!' Daisy hugged Trevor. 'I phoned down and your wife and son are ready to receive visitors.'

'Thought of a name yet?' Peter passed Dan and Trevor cigars. 'To be consumed later outside the hospital.' He handed Daisy one when she frowned at him.

'Yes.' Trevor pocketed the cigar.

Peter pushed his tongue into his cheek. 'Peter Daniel Joseph?'

'Martin Trevor Joseph, we'd like you and Dan to be godfathers, if you want to be. It goes without saying that Daisy is godmother.'

'Hasn't the mother any say in choosing the godparents?' Daisy asked.

'She did. We discussed it months ago.'

'I put a bottle of champagne in the ward fridge when I came in. Let's visit and crack it open, fellow

195

godparents.' Daisy slipped her arm around Peter's waist and looked at Dan. 'Thinking of all the football matches you're going to take him to when he's out of nappies?'

'More likely the strip clubs as soon as he's old enough,' Peter said.

'It's not too late for us to change our mind about one of the godfathers,' Trevor opened the door and led the way into the ward.

The following morning Trevor woke wondering if the day before had been a dream. He knocked on Peter's door, showered, dressed and ordered ham, eggs, toast, orange juice and coffee from room service. They ate on Peter's balcony after sweeping it for bugs.

'There are too many coincidences for Baby Darrow not to be mixed up in Black Daffodil,' Peter persisted. 'That party in the penthouse was expensive. A live band, working girls, free samples of drugs and booze …'

'As Darrow's given his son a penthouse I think we can safely assume he's given him an income to go with the lifestyle. You saw that taped interview. "Expense isn't a consideration when I entertain friends or host a business event".' Trevor filled Peter's coffee cup as well as his own.

'I still say …'

'There's no way we can go into the witness box with what we've got. "My Lord, Eric Darrow's a multi-millionaire and you can't make that kind of money legally – not when you pay taxes. He looks shifty. He allows people to deal drugs, torture and murder in his casino and we think he owns brothels. We have no proof of any of this, but we recommend he be sent down for life".'

'You're right; he's too slippery to end up in court, the evil sod.' Peter bit into a piece of toast as though he was punishing it. 'I'm fed up with scum getting away with murder because they've enough money to pay exorbitant fees to bloody clever lawyers. Give me five minutes alone with Eric Darrow. I'll strangle the man – slowly and painfully. Every time I think of Alfred. And what Lee has already gone through and his missus could be going through …'

'Like Michael and Maria, it has to be down to a leak from our side,' Trevor said soberly.

'You think it's a coincidence that Alfred was killed in the casino and Lee was maimed there?' Peter challenged him.

'It's possible.' Trevor knew he was irritating Peter by playing devil's advocate but Peter's major professional fault was trusting instinct before evidence.

'I don't buy it. Darrow knew about our operation …'

'How?'

'Because he owns bent coppers.'

'I'd agree with you if you'd said local bent coppers. But they didn't know about us. You heard Dan. He staked all our lives on the people he helped pick for this case.'

'Then it has to be someone who's liaising with Dan,' Peter fell silent for a moment, 'One of the make-over guys – like Ferdi. Or someone who falsified records to build our undercover stories …'

'You think someone working on the sidelines sold us out?' Trevor broke in.

'It has to be.'

'Because you don't want it to be one of us?'

'The only ones not undercover and risking their necks on a daily basis are Bill and Dan,' Peter pointed out logically. 'Do you seriously suspect one of them? Or Andrew, or Chris or Sarah or Tony …'

'Logic tells me I should suspect everyone.'

'Including me?' Peter questioned seriously.

It was Trevor who broke the tension building between them. 'This is getting us nowhere. Without anything to go on we could argue about who it could be for hours.'

'We need to find Kelly.'

'You're sure she knows something?'

'She was at that party, she was upset about what happened to Jake Phillips,' Peter insisted. 'I should have been more careful. If Eric Darrow owns that parlour, and one of his hired thugs was listening in when we were talking, anything could have happened to her.'

'She could have simply run.'

'That's what Dan said. You don't believe that any more than I do.'

'We can hardly go looking for her, not without treading on the toes of the locals.' Trevor wiped his hands in his napkin. 'I'll telephone Lucy later and ask her to make a house call here. She might know Kelly's whereabouts.'

'And she might not. You want to visit Chris and Sarah?'

'Given your obsession with him, we could try talking to Darrow senior first, but only if you promise to behave. You heard Dan – Chris and Sarah are under surveillance. They'll survive for another hour or two, without us.'

'Do you think we'll succeed in rattling Darrow's cage?'

'If you cool it, we might strike lucky,' Trevor said with more hope than expectation.

'If we do, we'd better stay at a safe ducking distance lest the shit that falls out lands on our heads.'

A casino ablaze with lights at night and a casino during the cold grey light of day – not that light ever reached the interior of most windowless casinos – was the difference between a living, breathing body and a corpse. The outward appearance might be the same, but noise and people were needed to lift a gaming den from dead, tawdry vulgarity to a semblance of glamour. Trevor had always found the cold smell of alcohol nauseating in the morning. And the paraphernalia that went with organised gambling – the baize-covered tables, roulette wheels and electronic flickering gaming machines looked like so many cheap toys in a room devoid of people.

Peter had used the 'we have important business with Mr Darrow' ploy to get past the body-builders on the door. To Trevor's amazement it had worked. When they reached the centre of the casino, he discovered why.

Eric Darrow was waiting for them on the walkway in front of the lift. In exactly the same position he had adopted twelve hours earlier.

'Good morning, Inspector Trevor Joseph, Sergeant Peter Collins. You have been promoted since I last saw you.'

Trevor returned his stare.

'You didn't really think that your amateurish disguise and drug-dealer cover would fool me, did you, Inspector? But I give you full marks for inventing one that enabled you and the sergeant to stay in a decent hotel. The high life must be a welcome change from your penny-pinching existence.' Eric leaned on the railing and looked down on them, using basic psychology to place them in an inferior position.

Trevor reined in his temper, but he could see Peter clenching his fists, which was a bad sign. He couldn't allow Eric Darrow to keep the upper hand or believe that he had the monopoly on information. 'Is your son Damian here, Mr Darrow?'

'No.'

'Do you know where he is?'

'I presume at college or on my yacht, *Lucky Star*. As your people have thrown him out of his home, it was the only accommodation he could find at short notice.'

'His flat is a crime scene,' Trevor reminded him. 'Someone attempted to murder Jake Phillips on the premises. We also have cause to suspect that that Alec Hodges was assaulted there. Your son would have been offered alternative accommodation.'

'Highly unsuitable accommodation' Eric Darrow answered. 'Unlike you, Inspector Joseph, my son is not used to roughing it. It is most inconvenient for him, having to live on a boat. Especially as *Lucky Star* has been chartered for fishing trips most weekends. There are only two weeks left of this term and he hoped to be able to work on a film he intends to showcase next year. He has everything he needs in his study in his penthouse, and only scratch facilities on the yacht.'

'He will be able to return to his flat as soon as the forensic teams have finished their work.'

'I don't know what they expect to find. The world and their friend trampled through Damian's penthouse on the night of the party, Inspector. My son entertained over a hundred people that night.'

'A fact we are well aware of, Mr Darrow.'

'Sometimes I think we are living in a police state. Damian's penthouse is bought and paid for. And being locked out of it is not only the only inconvenience. Damian has obligations as a landlord. He had to cancel lucrative charters on his own yacht, *Lucky Me* so Lloyd Jones could move on board.'

'They need a yacht each?' Peter questioned.

'Boys that age need their privacy.'

'The law allows the police to confiscate the profits of crime. I trust your son bought his penthouse and yacht with legal funds. Or did you buy them for him, Mr Darrow?' Peter played with the roulette wheel.

'They were paid for by his trust fund,' Eric Darrow said conversationally. 'I had my solicitor set it up the day Damian was born. It is important to look after your children financially. Wouldn't you agree, Inspector Joseph?'

201

Trevor felt as though an iron band had closed over his heart.

'I congratulate you, as one father to another. Boy wasn't it?' Eric Darrow continued. 'I like to keep up with the doings of old acquaintances, especially ones like you and Sergeant Collins. But much as I enjoy talking to you, Inspector, I am a busy man. Have you come here to discuss something in particular?'

'Black Daffodil.' Peter monitored Darrow's reaction.

'A new flower? I can't see the people of Wales abandoning the yellow daffodil as their emblem.'

'I'm not talking flowers.' Peter stepped up on to the walkway, putting himself on the same level as Darrow, which, given that he was considerably taller, was to his advantage.

'I misheard you. I thought you mentioned a daffodil.' Eric Darrow held his ground although Peter continued walking towards him.

'I did.' Peter didn't explain further. 'What do you know about Lee Chan?'

'Lee Chan?' Eric Darrow managed to look as though he'd never heard the name.

'The man whose arm was found in the car park of this casino last night.'

'Oh yes,' Darrow spoke softly. 'The individual your people believe fell foul of his friends and was mutilated in one of my back rooms – although I very much doubt any mutilation was carried out on these premises.'

'How do you explain the blood spots found in the room?' Peter challenged.

'A paper cut on the edge of a new pack of cards – a nose bleed – a torn fingernail. There are a hundred or more possible explanations. As I told your colleagues in the early hours, I never heard the name Lee Chan before they mentioned it. The Chinese are what is known in the trade as "excellent return customers" but they demand – and get – absolute discretion. When I rent them a room it is on the understanding that they will not be disturbed and their personal details will not be passed on to a third party – no matter who they are.'

'Are there any other ethnic groups that you give carte blanche to mutilate and murder on your premises?' Peter enquired.

Trevor was watching Eric Darrow just as closely as Peter. He saw the muscles tighten in Eric Darrow's jaw, but when Darrow spoke his voice didn't betray any emotion.

'As I said, I refuse to believe murder or mutilation was carried out on these premises and I will continue to do so until I am faced with definitive proof.'

'You're not disturbed by the death that occurred here last night or the arm that was found in the car park?' Trevor hoped to provoke a response.

'I am a businessman, Inspector. An optimist who expects everyone to be as civilised as myself. Unfortunately I find myself constantly disappointed, especially with your colleagues. Damian isn't the only one you have inconvenienced. The room the Chinese rented last night, along with the bathroom the drug addict Alfred Harding was found in, have also been designated crime scenes. I believe this has been done to penalise me – and at considerable cost. I can't re-open the club until I am given access to the areas your forensic teams are working in. And, after they leave, like Damian I will have to call in professional cleaners. The chemicals your people use are most unpleasant. They leave a nasty, gritty residue along with a foul stench. I warned your superiors that my son and I will have to invoice them for our losses. Between us, it will come to a substantial sum. I had hoped the prospect might galvanise your forensic teams to complete their inquiries sooner, rather than later. But my warning has had no effect. Nothing does, when it comes to the question of the police wasting taxpayers' money.'

'Like your son's flat, this casino is a crime scene. We are investigating one – possibly two murders – that occurred on these premises.'

'Are you certain it was murder, Inspector? A severed arm doesn't indicate murder. And I discovered that the man found in the bathroom had a syringe in his arm.'

Form the smirk on Darrow's face, Trevor was certain he knew that Alfred was an undercover officer.

'We don't discuss case details with civilians.'

'As you people insist crimes have been committed on my premises, I'd say I was an interested party, rather than a mere civilian.' Darrow eyed Peter who was standing too close to him for comfort.

'An interested party who can't guarantee the safety of customers who visit his "business"

204

premises,' Peter snapped. Trevor realised that he was close to losing his temper.

'How can I guarantee people's safety, Sergeant Collins, when this city, indeed the whole country has fallen into anarchy? The inevitable result of an ineffective police force. A force whose officers book into five-star hotels and live the high life while allowing criminals to roam the streets and enter respectable establishments such as this one, unhindered.'

'You admit you have criminals among your customers?' Peter questioned.

'If what you tell me about the arm you found in the car park is true, I would have to concede that I do.'

Tired of listening to Peter and Darrow fencing and wary of where it might lead, Trevor joined Peter on the walkway. 'For the last time, Mr Darrow, have you heard of Black Daffodil?'

'For the last time, Inspector Joseph, no I have not. But tell me, have you been seconded to the local force? Or are you operating out of your jurisdiction?'

'Some operations cross boundaries.' Trevor didn't know why he'd said that much. He sensed Darrow knew exactly what he did, where he worked, what he was doing in Cardiff – and – his blood ran cold at the thought of Lyn and his baby – where he lived.

'I wasn't aware that you could operate outside of your area, but still,' Darrow shrugged. 'what do I know about the law? Have you any other questions, Inspector, Sergeant?'

'Just one.'

Trevor looked mutely at Peter pleading with him not to push Darrow too far.

'How much commission do you charge the dealers for setting up shop in your premises?'

'Dealers – commission? I don't understand the question, Sergeant. The only dealers in this club are the ones I employ to run the gaming tables. And they are not paid commission. They are paid a weekly wage, plus a bonus at the end of the year which is based on a share of the club's annual profits.'

Peter stepped closer to Darrow. 'You might not understand me, Mr Darrow. But I understand you. I know who you are, and what you do. And I'm coming after you.'

Darrow's pale blue eyes glittered, cold and menacing. 'Is that a threat, Sergeant Collins?'

'No,' Peter stepped back and joined Trevor at the door. 'It's a statement. We *will* be seeing you again. Very soon, Mr Darrow, good morning.'

CHAPTER FOURTEEN

You shouldn't have pushed Darrow so hard,' Trevor went to the car and held out his hand for the keys.

'Why not?' Peter patted his pockets.

'If he makes an official complaint …'

'People like him are always making official complaints,' Peter found the keys and held them up. 'It's what they do.'

'To influential acquaintances, who only know the public front of the man who provides them with lavish nights out and supports charity fund-raisers. And, when asked, these influential acquaintances bring pressure to bear on "upstairs" who demand that poor souls like Bill and Dan take their complaints seriously and waste valuable time investigating them. All of which detracts time, energy and manpower from cases that warrant attention.'

Peter grinned. 'We succeeded in rattling Darrow's cage though, didn't we?'

'No,' Trevor contradicted.

'That's only your opinion. You work your way, I work mine.'

'Which is no bloody good when we're supposed to be working together. I'm driving.'

Peter knew when to concede to Trevor. He waited until Trevor opened the car and climbed into the passenger seat. 'Chris and Sarah next?'

'After the estate agent's. There might be something going down we should know about.'

'Andrew would have phoned us.'

'Change the Sim card.' Trevor gave Peter his phone and wallet.

'Is there any point when Darrow knows more about us than we do?' Peter opened Trevor's wallet.

'Old habits die hard.'

Peter dialled Andrew's direct number. 'You only want to find out if Lyn's safe?'

'That too,' Trevor agreed.

'You going to tell on me for baiting Darrow?' For all his flippancy Trevor knew Peter wasn't joking.

'I don't need to. Bill and Dan know what you're like.'

Peter nodded as Dan – not Andrew – answered the call.

Trevor drove out onto the main road that skirted the Bay and linked the newer glamorous, luxurious – and outrageously expensive – developments with the older, run-down social housing at the opposite end. He glanced at Peter, who was holding the phone to his ear but not saying anything beyond 'yes' and 'no'. After less than a minute Peter ended the call.

'Dan is in the office. He wants us to call in.' Peter proceeded to switch the cards.

'Did he say anything about our other halves?'

'You heard my side of the conversation. I didn't ask. But they were both fine last night.'

Trevor pictured his baby in Lyn's arms and smiled.

'You're one lucky bastard.'

'So are you. Not that you're married yet. And, if you take your time over setting a date I might be able to talk some sense into her.'

'Don't you dare try.'

'God alone knows what she sees in you,' Trevor drew up at traffic lights.

'A debonair, handsome, brilliant man. I also have other attributes you are unaware of, that modesty won't permit me to mention because they will make you feel inadequate. You know something,' Peter mused. 'I can't wait to start living the family life.'

Trevor thought of what was waiting for him at the end of the case. 'I never thought I'd hear you say that.'

'That's enough of winding me up.'

'I'm not.' Trevor looked out of the window at the shining waterfront development of expensive restaurants and boutiques. Well-dressed women strolled in the sunshine carrying bags printed with designer logos. Couples, families and groups of friends sat gossiping at café tables. It occurred to him that the lifestyle was artificial; he thought of the way his brother and his family lived on the farm in Cornwall.

He suddenly realised he wanted his children to grow up the way he had: in the country, among hard working people with simple tastes and values. People who'd rejected the 'advantages' of modern cities and a consumer society built around over-priced 'must have' rarely used objects. Whose socialising was not conducted in bars and restaurants; whose conversations were not centred on which restaurant to patronise and where to spend their all-inclusive holidays, which could be taken in Mexico or Marbella, Turkey or Tunisia – it wouldn't make any difference because all the places had the same layout, provided the same international buffet meals and drinks and sold the same Chinese-manufactured souvenirs in the resort shops.

'Look at all those different-shaped coffee cups.'

'Why?' Trevor reluctantly left the idyllic rural cottage he was renovating in his mind's eye.

'When I was a kid, coffee was coffee, and tea was tea. You drank one or the other. You could put milk and sugar in it, or not. Now, there's no such thing as coffee and tea. Instead you have menu boards of drinks. Tell me, how many people know what a Frapuccino, Cappuccino or Mocha is? Can anyone tell the difference between Brazilian, Guatemalan and Kenyan roast coffee beans? And what the hell is a mixed fruit tea when it's at home?'

'I have no idea,' Trevor wondered where Peter's train of thought was going.

'It's like drugs. In the old days there was LSD, pot and heroin and that was it. Life was simple. Now everyone wants choice. Choice complicates life. Some idiot has to go and invent a bloody drug that kills people in more ways than one. Take a dodgy Black Daffodil – you're dead. Cross someone who wants the formula – you're dead. Send in undercover police officers to stop the bloody trade before it gets a grip and puts too many smiles on undertakers' faces and the officers are murdered in cold blood.'

'You want to go back to the old days?'

'I'd like to go back to a time when half of the population didn't reach for habit forming pills or potions to give them a thrill and the other half didn't make themselves obscenely wealthy on the misery of the stupid bastards dull enough to get hooked.'

'Philosophical Peter is more than I can take. Let's see what Andrew and Dan have to tell us.' Trevor drove on, parked the car, turned off the ignition and stepped outside. He had an uneasy feeling that Dan had been holding something back when he'd spoken to Peter on the phone.

Dan always insisted on breaking bad news face to face. He hoped it wasn't about Chan – or any of the other undercover operatives. After yesterday he refused to consider the worst scenario – that it might be closer to home.

Trevor opened the door of the estate agent's and the bright, breezy clerk smiled.

'Mr Brown, Mr Horton isn't here.' She leaned towards Trevor. 'Dentist's appointment,' she whispered as though she were passing on highly confidential information. 'The area manager is here. He's with a colleague but he asked me to send you and Mr Ashton right in. May I offer my congratulations on your acquisition of one of the prime penthouses on the Bay, sir?'

'You may.' Trevor allowed Peter to walk in ahead of him. Dan was sitting behind the desk. Bill was in a visitor's chair.

'Thanks for coming in.' Dan motioned Trevor to close the door behind him.

'You two look as though you've been to a funeral ...' Peter fell silent when he realised that given events he was being tactless, even for him.

'Lee?' Trevor asked.

'Lee's left leg was delivered to the local police station yesterday afternoon,' Dan informed them. 'It arrived by parcel post. They're trying to track the parcel but as there were no stamps on it they think it was slipped into the van when the postman was busy in one of the local offices. Pathologist has examined it. Lee was alive when it was amputated.'

'So much for the Triads waiting for one amputation to heal before inflicting another.' Trevor sat down to steady himself.

'If we don't find him soon ...' Dan didn't finish the sentence.

'Lee's wife?' Trevor asked.

Dan shook his head. 'No sign. Andrew's missing.'

'What!' Peter exclaimed.

'When he didn't turn up here this morning I went to the flat that's been rented for him. Everything was neat, tidy and in its place. Breakfast dishes piled next to the sink, laundry in the basket in the bathroom, his wallet and keys had gone.'

'I went round later with the locals,' Bill continued. 'Nothing had been touched since Dan was there. There were only two sets of prints in the place – Andrew's and Dan's. We checked the CCTV in the area. Andrew left the apartment block at half past eight, in good time to get here for nine. We have pictures of him walking out of the foyer and along the street. He turned a corner by a coffee house, walked behind a line of stationary traffic held up at traffic lights and disappeared off screen.'

'Faulty or tampered tape?' Peter suggested.

'We're not ruling out anything at this stage,' Dan

said. 'The last camera that caught him captures an image every fifteen seconds. We looked at the CCTV in the coffee house. He didn't go in there. The locals have sent the numbers of the cars that were held up at the lights to the DVLA.'

'He was all right yesterday?' Trevor asked.

'Arrived mid morning, which wasn't surprising given the time he left the police station the night before. I phoned him at midday. He was upset about Chan, Alfred and the others.'

'As we all are,' Peter observed.

'Chris and Sarah?' Trevor asked.

'Are waiting for you to pull them out. I would have done it this morning, but another team are working on the estate on an unrelated case and they asked us not to raise our profile there.'

'How unrelated?' Peter sat up, interested.

'Arson and murder. A luxury flat was targeted on the Bay a month ago. A young woman was killed by the blast.'

'What's the connection to the estate?' Trevor took the peppermint Dan offered him.

'A suspect caught going into the luxury flat on CCTV before the blast. Locals believe their target is hiding in the adjoining block to the one Chris and Sarah are in.'

'We'd do the locals a favour if we flush him out,' Peter said laconically.

'Her,' Dan corrected him.

'Equality in all things, even crime.' Peter quipped.

'Thanks to that run-in you had with the thugs, the remaining dealers up there believe you and Peter are

Mister Bigs, so you can go in and pull out Chris and Sarah without raising suspicion. Follow their van to this address.' Dan handed Trevor a slip of paper.

Trevor read it. 'Safe house?'

'Transit stop to safe house. We'll keep them holed up for a few weeks. None of us are prepared to take any more risks with the remaining officers on this case. The operation is finished. It's a disaster for policing but, for those who have lost their lives, it's a tragedy. Bill and I are finding this one hard to live with. We both feel guilty as hell for sending you out there.'

'We're grown-ups, Dan. We knew what we were letting ourselves in for,' Trevor consoled him.

'Did you?' Dan demanded softly. 'Did you really?'

'It goes with the territory.' Peter perched on the edge of the desk. 'Stop being so hard on yourselves. Think of it this way, if you could turn the clock back, would either of you do anything differently?'

'I'd track down and string up the bloody leak – whoever he or she is,' Bill muttered darkly.

'If you find him or her, I'll do it for you,' Peter volunteered. 'Any sign of Kelly?'

'No,' Dan answered.

'As Dan said, everyone has been pulled off the case, but Alexander bribed one of the smaller fry. The Russian bid has been accepted. The formula for Black Daffodil will be handed one week from today.'

'In the casino?' Trevor asked.

'Presumably. All Alexander could get out of his nark was "the lucky place", which in a casino could be any table.'

'Darrow has to be in on it,' Peter crowed. 'And you had a go at me for rattling him,' he said to Trevor.

'You've seen Darrow?' Bill's voice hardened.

Trevor briefed Dan and Bill on their visit to Darrow in the casino that morning and Darrow's knowledge of their undercover personas. But he played down Peter's belligerence and goading.

'It doesn't mean necessarily follow that Darrow knows about the exchange because it's been set up in the casino. If Darrow had the formula he'd be manufacturing Black Daffodil and raking in the profits for himself. There's no way a man like him would turn down the chance of making a fortune that size that's there for the taking.' Dan spoke with the authority of someone who'd been stalking his quarry for a long time.

'He likes to pretend he's a legitimate business man,' Trevor reminded him. 'And the casino is a convenient place to do business. Look at the gangs that operate in and around there. The Triads had a regular booking for a back room. And just about every other gang on the Bay meet there.'

'The exchange?' Peter asked. 'Are the Russians paying cash?'

'Word is diamonds,' Bill answered.

'Small portable wealth. Clever,' Trevor commented.

'Now what?' Peter asked Dan.

'You bring in Sarah and Chris. And we return to our station.'

'And if the Russians go after Alexander, or the

Albanians, Justin?' Peter asked.

'They're already in safe houses.'

'And Andrew and Lee and Lee's wife?'

'We leave it to the locals to try and find them.'
Dan was obviously not happy at the prospect.

'That I don't like,' Peter said.

'Neither do we,' Bill agreed, 'but when it comes
to missing people, even on this case, we have no
jurisdiction.'

'And Trevor and me?' Peter asked.

'Debriefing in our home station tonight before
you hole up somewhere safe.'

'I don't like it, Dan,' Peter complained.

'What choice do we have? The operation is
blown …'

'It is blown. And do you know what I think?'
Peter didn't wait for an answer. 'I think that those of
us who have survived it will never be safe again.
Not while the leak remains within the force waiting
to sell any one of us to the highest bidder. This case
may be blown – but what about the next – and the
next? We need to find whoever's behind this and we
need to find him or her fast. And sit on the bugger
until he tells us exactly where Andrew, Lee and
Lee's wife are.'

'Carrying on is not an option, Peter,' Dan said
firmly.

'Trevor and I have to collect Sarah and Chris.
That will give us thinking time.'

'We'll meet you at the address we've given you.'
Dan turned his back on them and walked to the
window.

'Let's hope that at least one, and preferably

more, of our missing personnel will turn up in the next few hours.' Peter opened the door and walked out of the office.

Kelly wound the handles of the plastic bag she was holding so tightly around her hand that they cut off the circulation; but she didn't notice, even when her fingers turned white and numb. She glanced over her shoulder as the taxi drove closer to the tower blocks that had been home territory, until she'd been old enough to move away.

'Drop me here.' She leaned forward uneasily when they were within five minutes walk of the first block.

'You sure, love? It's no trouble to drive you to whichever one you want to go to.'

'Stop here!' She pulled out her purse, handed him a ten-pound note, opened the door and ran.

'Hey,' he shouted after her. 'Don't you want your change?'

'Keep it.'

'Ta.' He smiled at the thought of the extra four quid she'd given him, pressed the central locking and drove away. Normally he demanded money up front to drive to the area but the girl looked as though a puff of wind would blow her away. And she was on edge. He'd never had anyone quite as nervous in the back of his cab before. He wondered if she was a dealer the coppers had sussed. It was obvious she was running from someone. But then, whatever she was, or wasn't, it was none of his business.

* * *

Feeling as though eyes were watching her from every window and balcony in the surrounding blocks, Kelly headed for one particular building. She knew exactly where she was going. She even pictured the interior of the flat. It was shabby, grubby with the unkempt look so many old people's homes acquire when they lose interest in their surroundings – and life.

Amber had kept two keys back when they had handed the others over to the council six months ago after their gran's funeral.

'Most of the blocks are half empty. No one wants to move into the flats so the Housing Association won't bother to clear it or do it up. It'll be a bolt-hole if ever we need one, Kelly.'

Neither of them had thought they'd ever need the place. Not then.

Kelly entered the foyer, and tried to ignore the latrine stench that was common to all the buildings. Strange, when she'd lived on the estate it hadn't bothered her. She hadn't even noticed it until she'd started making the odd trip back to see old friends after she moved to the Bay.

She walked past the lift without checking to see if it was working, ran up nine flights of stairs and walked down a corridor to a door at the furthest end from the hallway. She looked over her shoulder, unlocked the door and slipped inside.

Trevor opened the door and climbed into the driver's seat when they reached the car. Peter didn't even try to argue. They drove out of the plush end of the Bay into the narrower meaner streets of the

1960s estate where people dressed differently. Not more cheaply, Trevor decided, when a girl walked past in a floor-length, fur-trimmed leather coat that must have been stifling considering the temperature. But in clothes that seemed to have been chosen for their vulgarity.

The jewellery was shinier and larger. Women of all ages, shapes and sizes showed flesh that would have been more alluring if it had been covered. Men who looked as though they were, in police jargon, 'carrying concealed weapons' swaggered as they walked. Children stood at the sides of the road and watched the world pass by with what Peter described as 'in your face' expressions.

'I can't believe upstairs are willing to drop this operation after all the man-hours that have gone into it.' Peter reached for his cigars.

For all the joking, Trevor realised they really were his partner's dummies. 'It's the expenditure in lives Dan is thinking about.'

'Dan seems certain the locals didn't know anything about our operation – only the outside team who loaned Bill the office – and those of us who went in on Bill and Dan's orders.'

'You still think the leak came from the outside team?'

'I prefer to think that, rather than consider the possibility that it came from one of us. Maria and Michael, Lee and Alfred are out …'

'Unless one of them *was* the leak and they were wasted as soon as they were of no further use to whoever wanted to shut down our operation.' Trevor assumed the role of devil's advocate again.

'You always have to come up with something that is not only diametrically opposed to what I say, but bloody plausible,' Peter grumbled.

'Are we agreed the leak shopped the operatives to the gangs they infiltrated?'

'Alfred, Maria, Michael – and Lee were all targeted by their 'new friends' as Lee's wife probably was. They were killed or kidnapped as a warning to anyone else with thoughts of trying to infiltrate the 'in crowd'. But Andrew?' Peter questioned. 'Why take Andrew? He hasn't joined any criminal fraternity, yet he's disappeared.'

'Andrew knew everything there was to know about the operation, including all our identities. His office was the clearing house for information. If there's a leak, Andrew would have been pinpointed as the officer who knew the most. I think he's been taken by whoever's behind the sale of the formula of Black Daffodil, because they see Andrew and what little remains of this operation as an obstacle. They're afraid we'll frighten off the Russians and track them down as the vendor.' Trevor closed the car window against a blast of rap music emanating from an arcade.

'And Darrow?' Peter asked.

'Let's get back to Black Daffodil. The first time it's noticed is when it surfaces in Jake Phillips's and Alec Hodges' bloodstream after a party in Darrow's penthouse.'

'And the next time is when it kills and sends people crazy on a no go estate geographically if not socially close to Darrow's penthouse,' Peter murmured. 'We know that Kelly and Lucy were at that party …'

'Blast! I meant to telephone Lucy to arrange a private visit.'

'As the case is closed, there's no point. But we can carry on brainstorming.'

'The next time we hear of Black Daffodil the formula's being sold to the highest bidder.' Trevor turned out of the older suburbs and entered the wasteland dominated by the tower blocks. 'The profit potential is unlimited, which is why the Russians and Albanians are prepared to pay millions for the formula. Probably the manufacturer of Black Daffodil, or a representative, was at that party giving out free samples. Perhaps they even wanted to test the drug and sold or gave it to Alec Hodges.'

'That person has to be one of the Darrows,' Peter persisted.

'You're beginning to sound like a stuck CD.'

'Both Darrows are evil sods.'

'As I keep saying I can't see either of them getting mixed up in something as blatantly illegal as this.'

'I can think of fifty million reasons.' Peter bit back.

'The manufacturer's an amateur,' Trevor declared.

'What makes you say that?'

'If it was one of the major players there'd be no need for an auction. They'd sell it alongside their existing merchandise and rake in the profits for themselves.'

'An amateur wouldn't have the wherewithal to organise an auction among the big time dealers.'

'Not without help,' Trevor admitted.

'And that's where the Darrows come in,' Peter smiled, feeling vindicated.

'I concede Eric Darrow is shady. He wouldn't stop, and probably hasn't stopped, at murder. But I think he'd steer clear of big-time drug dealing that will attract the attention of the major players who enjoy slitting their rivals' throats.'

'Which is why he's selling the formula to the Russians.' Peter clung to his theory like a limpet to a rock.

'He's got it too pleasant on the outside to risk being put away for the rest of his natural.'

'If not Eric then it's Damian. He was the one who hosted the party.'

Trevor considered the idea. 'It's possible Damian wants to stand on his own two feet and say "look Daddy, I've done all this by myself".'

'It wasn't an amateur who informed the gangs about Lee, Alfred and the others. And it wasn't an amateur that set up the auction,' Peter said.

'That's why I think a career criminal is involved. Supposing the manufacturer offered Black Daffodil to someone who saw its potential but didn't have the infrastructure to manufacture and distribute it. And that someone set up the auction – but at that point we moved in and he found out about us …'

'Through the leak?'

'Yes.'

'The organiser of the auction has access to a leak.'

'Stay with me. The amateur manufacturer and professional criminal organiser – two separate people, possibly two separate groups, spotted us moving in. We knew a number of new people moving in at once was a risk, but Dan and Bill took it because of the lethal nature of Black Daffodil. We could have been unmasked because we were recognised from previous cases. The seller also knew if we cottoned on to them the deal would never be made and they could kiss goodbye to millions. That's when the professional criminal looked for someone on the inside who was prepared to sell us out. Taking the knowledge he paid for, he tipped off the gangs knowing they would take out the undercover officers. He guessed that every available officer would be detailed to investigate the murders of the police officers ...'

'Which were carried out by the gangs, not by the seller or manufacturer of Black Daffodil?'

'Exactly.'

'And the seller of Black Daffodil could carry on making plans to sell the formula without hindrance from us.' Peter stuck his cigar between his lips. 'If Andrew is still alive, whoever has him could be torturing him as the Triads are Lee.'

'Yes,' Trevor said shortly.

'The chances are that, even if Darrow was the only one who knew about us before Andrew disappeared, Andrew has fingered us by now. And Chris and Sarah.'

'We'd be fools to think otherwise.' Trevor slowed the car when he saw glass on the road. A sign they were close to the tower blocks.

'How long do you think Andrew will hold out without telling whoever has him all he knows?'

'That depends on what they do to him.'

'He never struck me as the heroic sort.' Peter looked out of his side window.

'None of us are, under torture.'

'So, we are walking dead,' Peter said with an incongruous cheerfulness.

'If whoever is in charge of the auction thinks we know who they are, or are in a position to stop the auction, yes.'

Peter returned his cigar to the box. 'If I was the leak, and I worked inside the force, I'd be shit scared.'

'You'd be wise to be. Because we police can be nasty when it comes to turncoats. And you,' Trevor glanced at Peter, 'have proved that you can be nastier than most.'

'Upstairs,' Peter murmured slowly. 'It has to be someone upstairs. Or Alexander or Justin.'

'Only because you don't know them, as well as you know me, Chris, Sarah, Dan and Bill.'

'You're dead right.'

Trevor pictured his colleagues. People he'd worked with for years. He couldn't bear to think that one of them was capable of selling him out, or any fellow officer. Not even for a share of fifty million pounds.

CHAPTER FIFTEEN

Trevor drew up outside the tower block and switched off the ignition. A dozen kids who should have been in school were raiding a bottle bank in the car park and hurling the contents against the wall.

'That explains the broken glass.' Trevor left the car, waited until Peter had closed his door and locked it.

'Hey you,' Peter shouted to one of the kids.

He received a chorus of 'Fuck off's and raised fingers in reply.

'Want a tenner?' Peter held up two five-pound notes.

'You'll get flattened in the rush,' Trevor warned as another half a dozen kids appeared from nowhere and charged towards them together with the ones they had seen playing 'smash the bottles'.

Peter looked at the kids ranged in front of him. 'I'm going in there.' He pointed to the tower block. 'You see anyone mess with this car, you come and get me.'

'You calling on the druggies, mister?'

Peter looked at Trevor who shrugged.

He held up one of the five-pound notes. 'Who gets the money?'

'She does.' Fortunately they all pointed to the same girl. She looked about ten although she had five studs in both ears, one in her nose, one in her eyebrow, another in her lip and when she opened her mouth, Peter saw one in her tongue.

'You said ten.' She snatched the note from

Peter's fingers.

'Five now, five when I come out – if the car is still in one piece.'

'It's deal.'

'"You calling on the druggies, then, mister?"' Peter mimicked a child's voice as he and Trevor walked towards the block.

'I'd forgotten how communal communal living is on these estates,' Trevor said.

'Forget the cup of sugar. Now, it's can I borrow half a gram of weed or Charlie.' Peter raced up the stairs, taking them two at a time. When he reached Chris and Sarah's door he banged on it and Tiger barked. He put his eyed to the spy hole. 'It's me,' he shouted.

The door opened. Chris ran out, almost knocking Peter over.

'Hey!' Peter complained.

Chris was down the stairs before Peter had time to remonstrate further.

Peter stepped inside, glanced through the window and raced after Chris.

Trevor joined Sarah and looked across at the neighbouring block. Two figures swathed in black, their heads and faces hidden by balaclavas, which, apart from eye-slits, covered their entire skulls, were standing in front of an open window on the tenth floor. One was holding a girl by her wrists, the other her neck. They were feeding her though the window. Desperate, she kicked, thrashed and fought to stay inside the room.

Her long blonde hair fluttered in the breeze as her head was forced outside. Soon, there was more of her outside the window than inside the room.

Trevor reached instinctively into his pocket for his Glock, although he knew it was useless at that distance.

Sarah moved beside him. 'There's no way Chris and Peter will get there in time,' she whispered, unable to tear her eyes away from the scene.

Trevor looked down. Chris and Peter were racing over the car park towards the building. The girl's attackers saw them. They moved in unison and gave one final push. Trevor watched in horror as she tumbled out of the window. She floated slowly downwards for what seemed like an eternity although it could only have been a few seconds. Afterwards, he was never sure whether he had heard the sickening crunch of her bones smashing on the glass strewn concrete, or imagined it.

'Stay here, lock the door.' He thrust the Glock into his pocket.

Sarah was already dialling her cell phone.

'The police as well as the ambulance.' Trevor ran out.

The children Peter had spoken to were circling around the victim, pushing and jostling, hoping to get a better view of the girl although Trevor sensed a few were hanging back. When he drew closer, he realised why. The girl had landed face upwards. Her long blonde hair, splayed out like a halo behind her head, was splattered with blood and tissue. Her face was bruised, her eyes open. Surprisingly blue irises shone out from swollen discoloured sockets, reminding him of the glass eyes in china dolls.

'She's dead, i'n she, mister?'

Trevor turned to the small boy. He couldn't lie to him. 'Yes.'

'Can I touch her, mister? I never touched a dead body.'

'No.' Trevor overcame his initial revulsion at the question when he glanced at the rest of the children. They were staring at the girl in much the same way he assumed they would a television screen. He hoped the horrific reality of the girl's death would be treated in the same way; as something to be seen and forgotten as soon as something else came along to distract them.

'All of you stand back,' he ordered.

'She needs an ambulance,' the girl Peter had given the money to declared.

'No point. Her brains have come out of her head. Just like my cat when she got run over. She's dead.' Another boy pointed to a split in the girl's skull.

'Move back. Now!' Trevor waited until the children had shuffled back a few feet before studying the victim. Her thin, pinched face looked vaguely familiar. She was dressed in cut-off blue jeans and a shoestring, strapped red top. He looked for, and found bruise and needle marks in the crook of her elbow. He slipped off his jacket and hesitated. His initial instinct was to cover her face so the children could no longer see it, but the police forensic team wouldn't appreciate his sense of propriety. They needed to examine murder victims exactly as they lay with the attendant DNA of victim and murderer intact.

The police officer in him won over the

gentleman. He kept a grip on his jacket and looked up. The window was still open, swinging wide in the breeze. Peter looked down at him. He shook his head at Peter. He wasn't sure why. It was obvious no one could have survived a fall from that height. Peter pointed to something behind him. He turned and saw the flashing lights of an ambulance hurtling up the thoroughfare. Peter pointed to the ambulance and to the room behind. He nodded to show he'd understood before speaking to the children.

'Clear off, kids,' he said quietly, making an effort not to sound threatening. 'Haven't you homes to go to?'

'The other mister promised us another fiver if we looked after your car.'

'Then go and look after it. Stand around it to make sure no one touches it.'

'Will you or the other mister give us the money?'

'The other mister, but only if you go to the car.' Trevor watched the children move away, before looking back at the girl the ground. The sight of any murder victim was distressing, but someone so young, who should have had the best years of her life in front of her, tore at his heartstrings.

He had seen from the way she had fought her attackers how much she had wanted to live. Death was an inevitable part of his job but not death seen in the company of children who shouldn't be exposed to it.

Siren blasting, the ambulance screeched to a halt. Two paramedics jumped out and ran towards him.

'One of you is needed up there.' Trevor pointed to where Peter was still leaning out of the window.

'I'll go.'

The remaining paramedic knelt next to the girl. 'What happened?'

'She was thrown from that window.'

The paramedic looked up. 'Ten floors! She was thrown down ten floors?'

'Yes,' Trevor confirmed.

'Then it's murder. She's way past any help I can give her. You sent for the police?'

'They've been called.'

'Did you see who threw her?'

'Yes. Two of my ...' Trevor only just stopped himself from saying 'colleagues', 'friends went after them.'

'Them?'

'I saw two people.'

The paramedic peered at the needle marks in the dead girl's arm, but was too much of a professional to touch the corpse. 'Poor thing. Hope your friends don't get the same treatment if they find the bastards who did this.'

'They can take care of themselves,' Trevor assured her.

'The police will want to talk to you.'

'Will you stay with her until they come?'

'Where you going?'

'To help my friends. There may be more than the two we saw pushing her out of the window.'

'I have to stay here. This is a crime scene. Someone has to make sure it's not tampered with.'

'I know,' Trevor said dryly.

'I'll tell the police what you told me.'

'Do that,' Trevor entered the building. The lift

doors were open, the panel that held the buttons smashed. Electrical wires dangled loosely from it. He quickened his pace and raced up the stairs counting off floors as he went. He reached for his mobile and hit the speed dial number for Andrew's office.

Dan answered on the second ring. He updated him in between gasps for breath as he continued to charge up the stairs. After extracting a promise from Dan that he'd deal with the local police and take the heat away from him, Peter and Chris, he switched off the phone and stopped on the tenth floor landing.

He took a moment to regain his breath while making a mental note to exercise more. And not just to accommodate the demands of the job. He might be in his mid thirties but he wanted to enjoy fatherhood and that included being able to kick a football around the park with his son.

Keeping a firm grip on his gun, he opened the door to the corridor, and walked cautiously forward. Graffiti-smeared walls studded with graffiti-covered doors lined both sides of the passageway. There were no windows. The only light came from a small glazed panel set high above the door that opened on to the landing behind him. He found a light switch and hit it. Nothing happened.

It was then he noticed every single lamp and light bulb in the corridor had been smashed. He stood still, held his breath and heard a low murmur of conversation coming from an open door at the far end. He visualised the outside of the building and realised that it was the apartment the girl had been thrown from.

He could hear no other sounds – no music – no conversation – nothing. He wondered if the inhabitants of the other flats were lying low because they didn't want to get involved in anything that might be 'trouble'. Or if the flats were empty? There were doorbells and nameplates on every door but they could have been left by the last tenants.

He continued to walk towards the end flat. The door was open. He stepped towards it.

Peter and Chris whirled around and pointed their guns at him.

The paramedic was bending over a girl on the floor. She was motionless but he could see a pulse flickering in her scrawny neck.

'It's Kelly.' Peter said. 'She was out cold when we got here.'

'She has a lump on her head but it doesn't look as though anything's broken.' The paramedic straightened up. 'We'll take her into hospital just to be sure.'

Chris was looking out of the window. 'The police have arrived.'

'Want a hand to carry her down?' Peter asked the paramedic.

'I have to wait for a stretcher.'

'Stretcher my arse. She weighs less than a bag of sugar,' Peter said dismissively.

'Health and safety regulations …'

'Are made up by bloody civil servants who drive from their smug semis to their smug offices where they sit on their backsides all day dreaming up regulations that hamstring common sense. Can I or can't I pick her up?'

Trevor's phone rang. He stepped away from the argument and out into the corridor. Dan's voice echoed, strained and tinny down the line.

'Daisy Sherringham has disappeared. We think she's been kidnapped. I'll see the locals leave you and Peter alone. I'll be with you as soon as I can.'

Every inch of Daisy's body ached, especially her head. All the other pains in her body seemed to emanate from it. She was lying on the floor of a back of a car, trussed like a chicken in an old-fashioned butcher's shop. Her hands and feet were fastened by plastic ties that skinned her wrists and ankles. The ties had been looped together, forcing her arms and legs high behind her back, placing an intolerable strain on her knees and elbows. Her lips were plastered shut with tape. Rough sacking covered her head. Coarse and abrasive, it stank of oil and rancid grease. A pile of suffocating, heavy blankets – she knew they were blankets because she had seen them when she had looked in the car – had been piled on top of her.

She didn't want to breathe because each breath she took was laden with exhaust fumes. She knew the car was moving because she could hear the engine and her body throbbed every time the wheels jolted over a pothole.

She forced herself to think slowly and logically in an effort to stem her rising panic. She needed to plan an escape. All kidnappers made mistakes – didn't they? All she had to do was be ready to take advantage of it when it came.

She had fallen for the oldest trick in the book.

Peter would laugh and shake his head at her in mock despair when she told him about it – if she ever had the opportunity.

She recalled her blunt refusal to go to a safe house. Her insistence on being allowed to continue working unhindered. She replayed yesterday's conversation with Peter in her mind.

'Look here, Daisy ...'

'Look here, Peter. I'm your girlfriend not your doormat. I have my job, you have yours.'

'But ...'

'But nothing. There is no way that I am going to allow any mess that you have got yourself into ...'

'Mess?'

'Yes, mess ...'

That morning had been like any other. She had left her bed, showered, dressed, driven to work and parked in the bay that was reserved for her. Her ego received a boost every time she looked at her name on the plaque fixed to the wall behind it. *Dr Daisy Sherringham.*

She recalled wondering if she should change her name to Dr Daisy Collins when she and Peter married. She had been weighing up the pros – having the same name as Peter, against the cons – would people still connect her with all the research papers she had published under the name Sherringham – when she had walked past a car illegally parked at the end of the run of bays at the drop off point for A & E.

An ambulance was next to it, close to the back door, obstructing it from fully opening and now, with hindsight, she realised also blocking the car from the view of anyone walking in or out of A & E.

A man she'd barely noticed, other than that he was young and nondescript, had stopped her. He'd asked her to help him lift a sick child from the back of his car. She had squeezed in front of the door, looked inside and seen a mound of blankets, but no child. The next thing she knew – and felt – was a hand clamping over her mouth.

A knife waved before her eyes. A massive bladed hunting knife. Her lips were taped shut. She had been forced face down onto the floor of the car and jammed in the well in front of the back seats. Her ankles and wrists were fastened …

She tried to move … if only she could breathe properly and stretch her cramped legs and arms. Her head ached so much … her mouth hurt … She thought of Peter again. Pictured his face as she relived the conversation they'd had in the restaurant just before he'd left to go undercover.

'I won't be able to see you for a while.'

She recalled the effort it had cost her to sound light and carefree.

'No ties, no commitment, that's what we agreed from the outset.'

Unlike her, he hadn't bothered to keep the irritation from his voice.

'Aren't you going to ask why?'

'That's your business, not mine.'

'It's work.'

'Fine.'

'It shouldn't be bloody fine, Daisy.'

'It is and keep your voice down.'

'Don't you care?'

'I'm busy – you're busy – we knew that when we started spending time together.'

'Time together. Bloody hell, Daisy, is that all we're doing "spending time together".'

Now when she was trussed up in the back of a car by a maniac and being taken to God only knew where, possibly to be killed, it was so obvious. Peter's proposal shouldn't have come as a surprise. He loved her. Loved her to distraction. But, being the man he was; obsessed by his tough, steely-eyed, hard-nosed image, he was too afraid of rejection to tell her how he felt. And she had been too afraid of it ending between them to see that he found it difficult to voice his feelings.

She promised herself that if she got out of this alive, she would never – never be afraid to tell him – or anyone else – that she loved them ever again.

If?

Was he going to kill her? She began to shake uncontrollably. Not at the thought of death – because, whatever else – one thing that she was certain of was that pain did not exist after death. But at the thought of dying without ever seeing Peter again. Or being able to tell him exactly how much she cared for him.

CHAPTER SIXTEEN

Trevor had never attempted to analyse the relationship that existed between him and Peter. The fact that, under pressure, they thought alike had saved both their lives on several occasions. Before he had even pressed the button on his cell phone to end the call from Dan, Peter eyed him quizzically.

'What?'

'Tell you in a minute.' Trevor knew he was acting like a coward but he needed a moment to work out the best way to pass on the news. He walked over to where Kelly was lying on the floor and realised why the dead girl had looked familiar. She was an older, more haggard version of the photograph of Kelly that he had seen in the brochure.

'Chris called Sarah,' Peter said. 'She's coming over as soon as the locals are down there.'

Trevor didn't need Peter to elaborate. Given that the brutes who'd thrown the defenceless girl out of the window were still free and somewhere in the vicinity, Sarah needed someone to cover her back. 'The girl that was thrown looked like Kelly.'

Kelly's eyes flickered at the mention of her name. 'Marissa ...?' she mumbled. She opened her eyes wider. Disorientated, she tried – and failed – to focus on the medic who was standing over her.

Peter kneeled on the floor beside her. 'Was Marissa with you here, in this room, Kelly?'

She opened her eyes wider and looked around. 'Gran's flat?'

'Was Marissa here, with you?' Peter repeated patiently.

Kelly saw the open window and screamed, 'Marissa!'

'Kelly, who is Marissa?' Trevor asked.

'Marissa!' Kelly's cry was agonising. A bestial, animal cry that shook even Peter's equanimity.

'She was fighting them. I tried to help …'

'We know, love,' Peter assured her. 'Is Marissa your friend?'

'My sister. Where is she? Tell me? Where is she …' Kelly reached out and knotted her skeletal fingers into Peter's shirt.

The paramedic opened his bag. 'I need to put in a line.'

Kelly saw the syringe and panicked. 'No! No needles!' Her voice grew shrill. 'I'm not a junkie …'

'I know you're not, love, but we need to get a line into you,' the paramedic tried to reassure her. 'You need fluid and you may need medication later …'

'No needles! No needles!' she shrieked.

The paramedic set the syringe aside. 'All right, no needles –' he eyed Peter. 'For the moment,' he added.

'You have to calm down, love.' Peter gripped Kelly's hand.

'You won't leave me, will you?' she begged.

'You've been hurt, Kelly. You need help. Medical help. You'll have to go into hospital,' Peter warned.

'No! I saw them. They saw me. They know who

238

I am. They'll find me.'

'Who saw you?' Trevor drew closer.

'They had masks on.'

'We saw, love, but whoever they are they won't find you in hospital.' Peter squeezed her hand lightly.

'Yes, they will and then they'll kill me too.' Kelly whimpered. 'You can't leave me. They'll come looking for me ...'

'You'll be taken care of, love, I promise you.' Peter straightened his back. 'You must have an idea who they are.'

Kelly pushed her knuckles into her mouth. 'I don't know.'

'Did they speak? Did you recognise their voices?' Trevor pressed her.

Kelly tried to sit up, shook her head and retched.

'Concussion,' the paramedic diagnosed, turning Kelly's head to the side to keep her airways clear.

'Look after her, Chris. Make a note of everything she says.' Trevor drew Peter into the outside corridor and lowered his voice. 'That was Dan on the phone.' He took a deep breath. The only way to give Peter Dan's news was to come straight out with it. But now the moment had arrived, he simply couldn't bring himself to do it.

'And?'

Trevor braced himself. 'Daisy's disappeared.'

The colour drained from Peter's face. 'When – how long ago –'

'Dan didn't say. He's on his way and he said he'd fix it so the locals won't drag us into this mess.'

'Where was Daisy last seen?' Peter's voice was distant, mechanical.

'I don't know.'

'Did it happen this morning?'

'I told you everything Dan said.'

'What exactly did he say?' Peter demanded. 'Word for word.'

'He said to tell you that Daisy has disappeared.'

'His exact words.'

Trevor searched his memory. '"Daisy Sherringham has disappeared. We think she's been kidnapped. I'll see that the locals are kept at bay. I'll be with you as soon as I can."'

'Dan wouldn't have mentioned "kidnapped" without proof. He's coming here?'

'That's what he said.'

Peter thumped the wall with his fist.

'Did you or Chris see who threw Marissa out of the window?' Trevor asked.

'Not without their masks. They saw us coming and scarpered. We heard them running up the stairs as we got here. I left Kelly with Chris and went after them. They weren't on the roof and the corridors on the two top floors were empty. But they could have been hiding behind any of the doors. I knew Sarah would be watching the building so I came back down to see how Kelly was.' Peter stopped talking when they heard sirens.

Trevor returned to the living room and looked through the window. 'The locals have arrived. So have Dan and Bill.'

'I'll go down and see him.'

'No need. The paramedic is pointing this window

240

out to Dan now. He'll be here in a few minutes.'

Chris's voice fell, loud into the room. 'You'll like Sarah, Kelly. She'll stay with you …' Chris was trying valiantly to soothe the girl but Trevor could see that Kelly was hysterical.

'No! I'm not going anywhere … and not to any hospital …'

'You can't stay here,' Chris insisted. 'The police will need to search this place for evidence …'

'No!' Kelly screamed even louder. 'I'm staying with him.' She turned to Peter. 'He'll look after me.'

'Kelly …' Chris persisted in trying.

'I don't know you. I don't trust you. I only trust him.'

Peter walked over to Kelly. 'Look, love, you can't allow whoever killed Marissa and attacked you to get away with murder. They have to pay for what they did.'

'Don't you understand?' she pleaded. 'They have got away with it. If I talk to the coppers, they'll never leave me alone. They'll come after me.'

'People in prison can't come after you,' Peter insisted.

'The coppers won't put them in prison. They're too clever. You've no idea what they're like. Or what it's like to live round here. All anyone's got is their reputation. Once that's gone you're as good as dead. If I grass them up to the coppers I may as well buy my coffin because I'd never be safe again. Never! Marissa thought she'd be safe here and she wasn't. They may be coming after me right now. Right this minute. I'll be stuffed out of that window like … Marissa.' The horrors Kelly had witnessed finally took their toll. She buried her head in her hands and broke down.

Bright red stars punctuated the darkness that surrounded Daisy. The car had stopped moving. She wasn't sure when. Lost in darkness, time no longer held any meaning. She could have been left, for a minute – an hour – a day. The blankets that covered her had closed out all light. She listened hard but only heard a silence that buzzed, like insects in her ears.

A door opened. Arms slid beneath her body. She was dragged a short distance and bundled, still covered by blankets, head first into a confined space. A slam above her head paralysed her with fear.

Had she been closed into a coffin?

The air stank of petrol – were they going to burn her … footsteps echoed fading in the distance. Then, the insects began buzzing again.

'We will find her.' Trevor said it to reassure himself and Peter. He only wished that he knew where to start looking.

Peter looked across the room at Kelly. 'If anyone does to Daisy what they did to Kelly's sister or Lee, I'll track the bastards down and turn them into chopped liver.'

The threat was all the more deadly for being spoken without Peter's usual venom.

'Dan will know more,' Trevor said with more hope than conviction.

'If they've already killed her, I hope they did it

quickly. Not like Lee. Bit by sodding bit.' Peter remained unbelievably cool. 'We have to find out who took her. Then start looking for them. I won't let her disappear, Trevor. Not the way Lee's wife and Lee have.'

Dan walked into the flat. Sarah followed and went to Kelly, freeing Chris to join the others. They congregated in the doorway. Far enough inside the room to reassure Kelly, and not far enough to compromise any forensic evidence.

'The locals have sealed off the area. They're now sealing off this block; we'll get the bastard who did this.'

'Bastards,' Peter corrected. 'Chris and I chased two of them.'

Dan nodded towards Kelly. 'Get a name.'

'No,' Peter could barely contain his irritation, 'she's adamant she won't give evidence. She's terrified that if she does they'll kill her the way they killed her sister.'

Dan looked around at the stained carpet and overturned furniture. 'We need to get the lab boys up here. Fortunately, we have all your DNAs on record, so we don't need to take new swabs.'

Sarah joined them.

'No go?' Dan guessed.

'She's refusing to go to hospital. I told her she needs medical attention and promised we'd take her to a safe house afterwards, but she wants to stay with Peter.'

'The last thing I need is a kid to baby-sit.' Peter looked expectantly at Dan. 'Daisy?'

'I ordered an officer to follow her and keep his

eyes open. He followed her home from the hospital yesterday. When he went off shift I detailed someone to stay outside her flat all night. The original officer took over again at seven this morning. He drove behind Daisy to the hospital car park at eight. She has her own parking space, he didn't. It took him a couple of minutes to find one. We have Daisy on CCTV parking her car, walking past A & E …'

'Which she'd have to do to get to the burns unit.' Peter spoke as if he were walking alongside her.

'Then she vanished.'

Peter folded her arm across his chest. 'I don't understand.'

'Neither do we. There were cars parked in the loading bay, and an ambulance at the end. We have footage of her walking towards the ambulance, then nothing.'

'It's Andrew all over again,' Trevor observed.

'Time?' Peter demanded.

'Eight thirty-eight. The cameras are set at one minute fifteen second intervals. She disappeared in less than one and a quarter minutes.'

'You checked inside the ambulance?'

'It was locked because the driver was taking a break, but it was the first vehicle we searched. We sealed off the hospital within ten minutes, and searched all the ambulances and cars in the area. We checked the CCTV footage by the gate, so far all we've picked up on is a Ford with false number-plates. We're trying to track it on motorway.

'This was e-mailed to Andrew's computer in the estate agent's office one hour after Daisy went missing. I asked them to forward it to me on my cell phone. We put a track on it. It looks as though it was sent from an internet café in Morocco but, according to the Tech boys, false trails can be laid by a hacker. They seem confident that they can track it back to its rightful place of origin but it will take time, and that's something we don't have.' Dan handed Peter his mobile phone. Trevor looked over Peter's shoulder.

If you want to see Andrew Jones and Daisy Sherringham alive, close down the operation immediately. We are watching you. Non-compliance will result in two more corpses in the Bay.

A uniformed constable put his head around the door.

'Inspector asked me to inform you, sir, that we've finished locking down the building and, we're about to begin sweeping it. The paramedic is on his way up and so are the forensic team.'

'Thank the senior officer for keeping me informed,' Dan replied in his slow Welsh lilt.

'Yes, sir.' The constable glanced at Peter, Trevor and Chris before running back down the stairs.

'There goes our cover,' Peter muttered.

'That went when Darrow found out who we were. Probably even before we booked into the hotel,' Trevor said dryly.

Peter read the e-mail again before handing Dan back his cell phone and quoted, "'*If you want to see Andrew Jones and Daisy Sherringham alive, close down the operation immediately. We are watching you. Non-compliance will result in two more corpses in the Bay.*" Who are the "we" who are watching and do you think they really are watching us? Or bluffing?'

Dan looked at him quizzically and Trevor realised that he wasn't the only one who thought that Peter was reacting to Daisy's kidnapping too coolly and calmly.

'If we knew the answer to those questions we would be arresting them,' Dan replied.

Peter retreated towards the corridor to make room for the second paramedic to enter the flat. Kelly saw him move away and screamed hysterically.

'Don't leave me, please ...'

'I won't be far,' Peter reassured her with remarkable patience considering the strain he was under. 'Let the paramedic do his job and look at you, Kelly.'

White-suited officers walked through the doors that led from the staircase.

Dan nodded to the forensic teams. 'A crime scene is not a good place to hold an impromptu conference.'

Trevor glanced around for a quiet place where they could talk. 'If the staircase is empty we can go out there.'

'It won't be quiet for long once the locals have locked down the building ready for searching.' Peter observed.

Trevor flattened himself against the wall as two officers carried a bulky equipment box past him.

'It will do for the moment. The landing is big enough and we only need a corner.' Dan led the way.

'I'll tell Kelly I'll be outside the door then I'll join you.' Peter walked back into the flat.

Dan looked at Trevor. 'What's going on between Peter and that girl?'

'A sudden and over-developed bout of paternal instinct.' Trevor followed Dan on to the graffiti-ornamented concrete landing. 'It is obvious that whoever's behind the sale of Black Daffodil tipped off the respective gangs about the undercover officers. Do you think they've taken Daisy and Andrew because they couldn't get anyone else to do it for them?'

'Probably.' Dan pulled a pack of peppermints from his pocket. 'You saying that because you're hoping that whoever's holding Daisy and Andrew aren't capable of cold-blooded murder?'

'Yes,' Trevor replied honestly. 'Think of the situation from their point of view. Why would they risk being banged up in prison for years when they can get someone else to do their dirty work and leave the murders to the gangs' hit-men? The Black Daffodil vendors will remain squeaky clean, divorced from the crimes they instigated. And the people they wanted dead, will be just as dead.'

'They'll only remain squeaky clean if they let Daisy and Andrew live – and didn't push that poor girl out of the window.'

'How could she possibly be mixed up in this? She was a junkie – I saw the marks on her arm …'

'Remember me telling you about the arson case the locals are investigating?'

'The one on the Bay. They thought the arsonist was holed up here.'

'Not any longer. The suspected arsonist was Marissa Smith. And she is lying dead on the concrete car park.'

'Then Kelly Smith …'

'Was at Damian Darrow's party. And that arson attack – was on another sister's flat. Amber Smith.'

'I don't see …'

'Neither do I – yet.'

Dan glanced up when Peter joined them. 'Trevor's updating me on your thoughts. As Daisy is the one involved how do you want to play it?'

Peter hesitated but only for a split second. 'First we go back over the interviews of everyone who was at the party in Damian Darrow's penthouse.'

'If "they" really are watching us, they'll know we are still working on the case. That is a risk to Daisy and Andrew,' Trevor leaned against the wall.

'Not if we three go over the transcripts in secret,' Peter said.

'We'd still have to pull the interview files. And whoever is watching us – and given what happened to Alfred and the others, I think someone is – they have to be on the inside.' Trevor was speaking his thoughts aloud, more than to the others.

'Any ideas?' Dan asked. 'Me – one of you two – Bill …'

'Throw your net wider, Dan. It could be anyone from upstairs, or the undercover boys who drew up our backgrounds, the office staff who rented our cars and booked us into the hotels. You might have kept it from the locals, but you couldn't have kept it from everyone.' Peter reached for the inevitable pack of cigars.

'He's right,' Trevor said. 'And given that e-mail we have no choice but to close the operation immediately, finally and publicly.'

'It's done. I telephoned Bill from the car when I was being driven here. He was passing orders down the line as we spoke.'

Peter showed the first signs of irritation. 'You could have told us …'

'I wanted your take on the situation. But, as Bill said, too many lives have been lost on this operation for us to want to risk more. And, you're not the only one who values Daisy Sherringham. She's a very special lady. The world needs people like her. Although I can't understand what she sees in you.'

For once Peter wasn't flippant in his reply to Dan. 'Neither can I. I just count my blessings every time I look at her. We need to find her. And quick!'

CHAPTER SEVENTEEN

Dan looked up the stairs as three constables from the local force escorted a dozen protesting residents downwards.

'It's security, madam. Dangerous criminals have barricaded themselves into one of the flats on your floor. We are not prepared to take any risks when it comes to public safety. I'm sorry for the inconvenience ...' the constable faltered in the face of the fury of a young girl Trevor recognised.

'The lift's not bloody working – is it ever – and my Auntie Dolly is sick. She needs rest, peace and quiet, not a fucking route march up and down these stairs.' The girl was wearing too much make-up, not enough clothes and an abundance of gold jewellery. Along with another girl, she was helping a plump elderly woman who was wheezing asthmatically and could barely stand, let alone walk down the stairs.

Peter glanced at the woman and turned back to the girls. 'I know you two, don't I?'

'I do.' Trevor stepped forward. 'Hello, Lucy. Making a house call?'

'Here – in this place? Don't make me bloody laugh.'

'You clients?' Ally stared at Peter and tongued her lips.

'You're Ally.' He remembered her name from the brochure in the massage parlour.

'You *are* a client.' Ally stepped down a stair, hitched up her skirt to show off her legs and bent forward until one of her breasts popped out of her low cut top.

Peter shook his head. 'Friend of Kelly's.'

'So why are you and Lucy here?' Convinced Kelly knew her attackers, and disturbed by her assertion that she wouldn't give evidence against whoever had killed Marissa, Trevor was hoping to find witnesses who might help them put the people responsible behind bars.

'Not a job, that's for sure.' Lucy propped the old lady against the banister on the landing as if she was a broomstick. 'No one who lives here could afford me or Ally. We're high class.'

'Odd that you two and Kelly decided to visit here on the same day.'

'No, it's not. Kelly and I grew up on this estate.'

'You too?' Trevor asked Ally.

'It's my afternoon off so I offered to keep Lucy company. Auntie Dolly enjoys visitors. The more the merrier she says. Don't you?' She wrapped her arm around the old woman and hugged her. The old woman glowered at her.

'Is Auntie Dolly your real aunt?' Trevor recognised the symptoms of dementia. He doubted the elderly lady knew Lucy or was aware of where she was.

'If you must know, she's a friend,' Lucy gave Trevor a hard look. 'She used to give us fifty pence to do her shopping when we were kids.'

'Likes to ask questions, doesn't he?' Ally commented.

'Coppers do. And you are a copper?'

It wasn't a question but Trevor responded. 'I am.'

Lucy looked over Trevor's shoulder at the number painted high on the wall. 'Kelly's gran's old flat was on this floor. Is Kelly here?'

Trevor didn't answer her. 'Do you two know Kelly well?'

'Course we do. As you well know, we all work in the same bloody parlour.' Lucy watched white-suited officers emerge from the flat into the corridor. 'What's going on? People have been running up and down all over the place, disturbing Auntie. And all the coppers would tell us is that someone fell out of the window on the other side of the building.'

'Kelly and her sister Marissa were attacked,' Trevor gazed directly into Lucy's eyes.

'Attacked, what bastard …?'

'That we don't know. Can you help us?'

'Who? Me and Ally?'

'You are here.' Trevor reminded her.

'As I said, Auntie Dolly's flat is on the other side of the building. Are Kelly and Marissa all right? – not that Marissa is ever all right,' Lucy added. 'She's a dope fiend.'

'Dope fiend?' Trevor repeated.

'She used to sell both her sisters for a fix once she got too scabby to sell herself. Amber was twelve the first time she did it. She couldn't wait that long with Kelly. Poor kid was ten. Amber was bright, she could have gone far. She even got a place in university but Marissa leaned on her for money, so she became a working girl.'

'So Marissa wasn't your friend but Amber was and Kelly is.' Trevor leaned back against the wall.

'Amber and me started working in the parlour

252

together. Not that she was there that long. Six months and she struck out on her own. Did well too, rented her own flat before she burned to death in that fire. As for Kelly, someone had to look out for the kid. Amber was too busy and Marissa never did, that's for sure,' Lucy looked over Trevor's shoulder. 'There's a lot of men wearing white suits down there.'

'There are,' Trevor agreed.

'All for someone who fell out of a window.'

'They were thrown.' Like Trevor, Peter was monitoring Lucy's replies to Trevor's questions very carefully.

'From the tenth floor?' Lucy's eyes rounded. 'You sure whoever it was didn't fall?

'Quite sure,' Peter echoed. 'There are witnesses.'

'Well, I didn't see anything and, even if I did, I'm no grass. And, if I'm asked, I'll deny I ever spoke to you.'

'Not even when it comes to murder and an assault on one of your friends?' Trevor asked.

'What friend?'

'Marissa's dead.'

'I told you, Marissa was no friend of mine. And Kelly's all right.' Lucy hesitated. 'Isn't she?'

'Not really.' Trevor didn't elaborate. He watched Peter take a cigar from his pocket. Peter hadn't said a word but he knew he was suspicious as him. 'Off the record, do you know anything else about Marissa?' He tried to make the question sound casual.

'When Marissa had money, she dealt as well as shot up. So if she was pushed, I suppose it could

253

have been by an unhappy customer, or one who didn't have the money to pay. Or a revenge attack by a relative. Half the poor sods around here who are hooked on drugs, got hooked by her.' Lucy patted the hand of the old woman. 'Auntie Dolly's ill. She can't go on. Not all the way downstairs. She's confused as it is.' She lowered her voice. 'Dementia.'

'Constable,' Trevor called a young rookie. 'Help Mrs …'

'Jenkins,' Ally supplied.

'Back to her flat.'

'We think the pair that threw the girl out of the window have holed up in one of the flats on her floor, sir. The Super's sent for the armed response team.'

'Use your initiative. Take her to a flat on another floor. But take a good look around first to make sure there's no one hiding in any of the cupboards or under the bed. Stay with her and make her a cup of tea until we've finished talking to her nieces.' Trevor gave the order but he was aware that he had absolutely no authority over the constable.

'What do you mean "finished talking?"' Lucy demanded suspiciously. 'We have finished.'

'Not quite,' Peter took Lucy by the elbow, and propelled her into the corridor. 'I think the Inspector would like a word with you about Marissa Smith.'

Lucy's voice pitched high. 'I don't know anything.'

'Neither do I,' Ally echoed.

Trevor stood back for a moment. He watched the constable signal up the stairs. Another uniformed officer came down. Together they helped the old woman up on to the next floor. He looked back at Peter who was shepherding both girls towards Dan. He hesitated for a moment before following the constables.

The forensic team, dressed like so many snowmen in their white paper suits and caps, were hard at work on their hands and knees, taking samples from the worn carpet in the living room of Kelly's grandmother's old flat. Kelly had been moved into the empty living room of the flat next door in a wheelchair that the second paramedic had brought up.

'Kelly ... oh my God! Your face is all bruised and swollen ...' Lucy ran towards her. Dan blocked her path.

'Best not to talk to her for the moment. Let the paramedics do their job.'

'She needs a friend.' Lucy sidestepped past Dan and stood in the doorway.

'She needs to go to hospital,' Dan said.

'Kelly, you want me to go to the hospital with you, don't you?' Lucy said. 'It'll help to have a friend with you.'

'She has someone with her at the moment.' Peter indicated Sarah who was standing beside the chair, holding Kelly's hand.

'I know all Kelly's friends. She's not one of them,' Lucy countered.

'She's a police officer,' Dan informed her.

'Kelly needs a *real* friend, not a copper with her.' Lucy insisted. 'Kelly, tell him, you want me to go with you.'

She looked at Kelly. White faced, Kelly looked back at her. After a few moments she nodded.

'See,' Lucy crowed. 'I look out for her …'

'Constable,' Dan hailed a uniformed officer who was standing at the end of the corridor. 'Watch these young ladies, would you, and see they don't disturb Miss Smith here.' He led Peter away from the girls.

'After talking to Kelly, I'm not sure if she knows who threw her sister out of the window. But what I do think is that we won't get anything out of her that we can put in front of a judge. You and Trevor have any luck with those two?'

'Trevor's working on it,' Peter hedged. He had seen Trevor follow the constables up the stairs.

Dan frowned. 'Where is Trevor?'

'Not far.'

Dan sighed. 'I can't even blame those girls for not helping us. Look at this place and this estate. They never stood a chance. And still don't. If the brutes who threw Marissa Smith out of the window don't get them, some other thug will. We can't police these places every minute of every day.'

'No we can't. But two of those kids are hardened prostitutes,' Peter reminded him. 'And I'm not talking about their age. Look into Lucy and Ally's eyes.'

'I see junkies,' Dan agreed, 'but you can't just write off people.'

'Watch me. And none of this bloody pontificating is getting us any closer to finding Daisy. We need to go to the casino and shake down Darrow.' Peter showed the first signs of his short fuse since he'd been told that Daisy had disappeared.

'Most of the local manpower is tied up here. I'll ring another force. It won't hurt to bring Damian Darrow in for questioning again under the auspices of the investigation of Jake Phillips's murder. And before you ask if you can sit in, the answer is no. Until Daisy Sherringham is safe and sound, you and Trevor are taking a holiday,' Dan ordered.

'The hell we are. Give me twenty-four hours.'

'To do what?' Dan asked suspiciously.

'Shake down Eric Darrow and get him to admit he's behind the sale of the formula of Black Daffodil.'

'And if he has nothing to do with it? He'll complain and if there is a leak coming from inside, they'll know that the operation hasn't been shut down. And then they could carry out their threat to kill Daisy. That, is a risk I am not prepared to take.'

'I can't sit back and do nothing while Daisy is missing,' Peter snapped.

'We're all agreed that "they" could be watching us. On that basis the best thing you and Trevor can do for Daisy and Andrew is drive to your hotel and pack as publicly as possible. Keep ringing down to reception for bell-boys, packing materials and demand to have your bills sent up. I'll put someone in the foyer to see if anyone is watching the activity.'

'And then?' Peter asked. 'And don't say drive back to our station.'

'Daisy could be close to home. It's where they snatched her. In my experience of similar cases they won't have taken her far.'

'I hope to God you're right and she is still alive,' Peter said fervently.

Daisy wasn't sure whether she'd been asleep or not when she heard footsteps again. A lock sprung above her head. She was lifted up, blankets and all, and stuffed into a tight, confined space. Something pressed down above her, pushing down her head and closing out what little air there was. She sensed movement and listened hard, trying to picture what was happening around her but the blankets muffled most of the sounds.

She thought she heard gulls again but couldn't be sure where the noise was coming from – perhaps it wasn't gulls at all but the squeak of wheels that need oiling beneath her. The movement stopped. The lid opened, she was lifted out but the sacking wasn't removed from her head. Something cold slipped beneath the plastic ties on her wrists and ankles, it jerked. The ties cut painfully into her skin then fell away.

More footsteps, then bolts being slammed home and keys being turned in locks.

She thought of Peter again. The cavalier way she had dismissed Dan's offer of security. How angry Peter had been until she had managed to talk him around to her way of thinking.

She knew he'd look for her. But would he find her here?

She had been stupid. Taking him and her life for granted. Assuming that they had all the time in the world.

And now – now they had no time left – no time at all.

Trevor stood in Dolly Jenkins's flat and watched the white-gloved and booted, uniformed officers methodically carry out their search.

He looked around. The wooden mantelpiece over a glassed-in gas fire was crammed with dust-coated, small china dogs. The fitted carpet was a swirling pattern of orange brown and green. The rug in front of the gas fire a muddy brown that might have once been beige.

The three-piece suite was covered with yellow cracked vinyl. The sideboard … he took a pair of thin rubber gloves from the box one of the officers had left on a chair, snapped them on and opened the doors. The cupboard was stacked high with photograph albums.

He removed them and piled them on the carpet. When the cupboard was empty he pulled out the bottom drawer of a bank of three set beside the cupboard.

He had to tug hard. It had been crammed full of envelopes. Unopened, most bore the logos of insurance and credit-card companies. Junk mail, all carefully stored. A veritable rain forest. In the second drawer, below yet another layer of mail he found boxed sets of dainty silver forks and spoons. The top drawer held a jumble of elastic bands, defunct and leaking biros, old spectacles, rusting scissors and batteries.

He sat back and looked at the photographs on top of the sideboard. A young couple, he dressed in

1950 Teddy-boy fashion, she in a ballerina length white length dress stood in a church doorway. There were several photographs of children, standard yearly school shots. Black-and-white ones from the fifties and sixties. Newer ones from the eighties in colour. His thoughts turned to his son. People – that was all anyone really had to show for a life.

'Sir?' A constable stood in the doorway that led to the inner hall. It hadn't taken him long to realise that the flat had the same layout as the one Chris and Sarah were staying in.

'What are we looking for, sir?'

'I wish I knew, Constable. Other than to say, we'll know it when we see it, I can't help you.'

Trevor looked around the living room one last time. There was a stack of newspapers, a coffee table loaded with dirty cups, plates and stale biscuits and crumbs. A bin full of sweet wrappings.

Only when he was sure there was nowhere else to look did he follow the constable into the largest bedroom. The bed was heaped high with clothes that had been lifted out of the wardrobe. He pulled them off one at a time and dropped them on to a rug on the floor, then stripped the bed layer by layer shaking each sheet and blanket out as he removed it. When he was down to the bare stained mattress, he called out to the constable who had asked what they were looking for.

'Grab hold of the other end of this and help me lift it off the bed, will you, please?'

The officer did as he was asked.

Trevor checked the sides of the divan base. They were solid – no drawers. He lifted one end of the bed and looked beneath it.

The constable crouched down alongside him. 'There are enough dust balls there to stuff a pillow, sir.'

'I'll take your word for it, Constable.' He turned back to the wardrobe.

The bottom was a jumble of clothes, some clean, most not. He lifted them out, one at a time. All of them were women's. At the very bottom he found a pile of handbags and stiletto-heeled shoes.

'These look as though they've come out of Noah's Ark, sir. Not even fit for a car boot sale.'

'The other bedroom?' Trevor went into the hall and looked inside.

'We've been through it with a toothcomb, sir,' the young officer assured Trevor. 'It's more or less the same as this one but with fewer clothes.

Trevor walked into it. The constable was right, but he noticed something that the constable hadn't mentioned. A tower of unopened boxes of cheap talcum powder and soaps. The standard gifts for an elderly relative. He was glad that Lyn had taken the trouble to get to know his mother and send her the USB pens she'd asked for to store her photographs on her computer. He hadn't even known that his mother had owned a computer. 'You've looked at the bed and the base?'

'Of course, sir.' The officer appeared to be offended by the question. 'We carried out this search by the book.'

Trevor went into the bathroom. The officer had taken the panel from the side of the bath. The lid had been removed from the cistern. A mess of toothbrushes, dried up bits of soap, mildewed flannels and tubes of dental cement had been piled into the bath.

Trevor knew the answer to his question before he asked it.

'Nothing sir.'

He went into the last room. The kitchen. The officers had emptied the cupboards on to the work surfaces.

'Most of the food is out of date, sir.'

Trevor tapped the backs of the cupboards and ran his fingers over the empty shelves. Under the sink he found a solitary bottle of bleach jammed behind the waste pipe that the officers had missed. He opened the electric cooker. The walls and shelves were coated in grease and he shut it again, quickly.

He opened the microwave and removed a box of corn plasters; another of sticking plasters, a blunt-ended scissors and a bottle of antiseptic.

'She must use it as her First-Aid box.'

'Obviously.' Trevor noticed the clothes dryer in the corner, it was empty. He returned to the sink and opened the door on the washing machine.

It was full. He pulled out two pairs of dry black jeans, two black polo-necked sweaters, four black trainers and two full-head black balaclavas.

'That, Constable, is what I was looking for. Bring me an evidence bag, will you, please?'

CHAPTER EIGHTEEN

The paramedics tucked blankets around Kelly and wheeled her out into the corridor past Dan and Peter.

'Her blood pressure is dropping and she's complaining of dizziness,' Sarah whispered.

'You'll stay with her?' Dan asked.

'Yes.'

Dan reached for his mobile phone. 'I'll send a couple of officers with you, in case you need help and order a twenty-four guard. Don't try anything heroic.'

'I won't, sir.' Sarah answered.

Kelly hauled herself out of the chair when they wheeled her past Peter. She grabbed his arm and held it in an iron grip he would never have suspected anyone as slight and frail as her of possessing.

'You can't leave me.'

'I have to work, love.'

'No!' Kelly dug her fingernails into his hand, drawing blood.

Dan was amazed. He knew Peter was going out of his mind with thoughts of what was happening to Daisy but he took the time to talk to the girl.

'I'll do all I can to help you. This is no life for you – your sisters are dead. You're lucky to be alive but for how long, if you carry on living the way you are now? How old are you anyway? The truth?' Peter dared Kelly to lie.

Kelly glared back at him. After a minute her

defiance crumbled. 'Fourteen.'

'I could help you find somewhere to live?'

'Like where?' she asked suspiciously.

'A foster home or school that will give you a chance to live a normal life. You're a bright kid, but you need to get right away from the parlour and the company you've been keeping.'

'I'll go anywhere with you.'

'Me? Not me, love. I work all hours of the day and night. I hardly ever see my home.'

'But I could keep it nice for you. Look after you. I can cook and clean …'

'Kelly, you're a kid. You should be out and about having fun with your mates not cleaning up after anyone.'

'But I like you. I trust you.' She sneaked a glance at Lucy. 'More than I trust anyone else in the world.'

'Then trust me enough to sort out a decent life for you that offers you a future. I'll visit you now and again but I won't make any false promises. You need more help than I can give you, love, specialist help. And, you can start getting it by going into hospital and getting those injuries seen to.'

'You will come and see me?' she pleaded.

'Yes. But now you have to go. Take her,' he ordered the paramedics.

They wheeled her down to the stairwell, picked up the chair and carried it downwards.

A cell phone rang. Although the ring tone wasn't the same as theirs, Dan and Peter reached for theirs. Ally glanced at hers and switched it off.

'Customer?' Peter asked.

'What if it is?' she challenged.

'The only thing you sell is sex in a parlour – that's illegal.'

'You should know, you were there – and buying,' Ally said angrily.

'Your boss is Damian Darrow,' Dan interposed conversationally.

'Only because he was handed the parlours on a plate by his daddy,' she sneered. 'He's never done a day's work in his life. He doesn't even know what work is. His father told Damian to manage the businesses but Damian treats them – and us girls – as his own bloody private harem. When he isn't getting us to give it to him for free, he's getting us to give it to his mates.' She suddenly realised what she'd said. 'But like Lucy said, if anyone asks, you didn't get any of that from me. I never talked to you.'

'You've spoken in front of witnesses.' Peter smiled coldly.

'You wouldn't say anything to Damian, would you?' She began to panic. 'It's more than my job is worth. There's a waiting list of girls wanting to come into the parlour ...'

'You stupid bloody cow,' Lucy turned viciously on Ally, punched and kicked her and pulled her hair.

'Ladies, please,' Dan stepped between them.

'Time to hand them over to the locals, sir.' Trevor appeared. He held up several clear plastic evidence bags. 'Nice of you to collect Ally's DNA for us, Lucy. I hope you remembered to take out the follicle as well. We'll be needing samples. But it'll be a formality. Four police officers saw you wearing these outfits when you threw Marissa Smith out of the window. Tell me, did you get the idea after throwing Jake Phillips from the balcony in Damian's penthouse? It worked better here. No balconies.'

Daisy moved slowly and sluggishly. Pins and needles sent mini-electric shocks through her arms and legs. As soon as she tried to put any weight on one of her limbs it crumpled beneath her. It took several minutes of fumbling before she managed to pull the sack from her head. She tore at the tape over her mouth. When she finally managed to pull it away, her mouth was sore, and she felt as though she had ripped off all the skin from her lips. She sat back on her heels and took in great gulps of air – freezing cold air.

She pulled the blanket closer around herself and covered her head again, but not her face with the sacking. She wished she'd put on something warmer than the linen slacks, sleeveless top and shirt she'd taken out of her wardrobe that morning. But the hospital was always over-heated and it was summer.

She hadn't dressed with kidnap in mind – she tried to smile at the thought and discovered that her facial muscles were stiff, numb and frozen. That was the sort of thing Peter might say.

She was in a very dark, very cold place. Given the sound of the gulls and a slight rocking movement she felt before she'd been dumped here, she could be on a boat. Near the sea in an urban area? She had heard traffic. She stared at her wrist. But it was hopeless. She couldn't see her hand in front of her face let alone her watch.

She was lying on freezing cold metal. Steeling herself she lifted the blanket from her shoulders and extended her arms. First one way then another. She only encountered freezing air. Wrapping herself back in the blanket she moved to the right until she felt something – something cold and solid. She ran her hands over it and touched cold hair.

Heart thundering, she moved her fingers downwards. She knew the feel of frozen, dead flesh from her days dissecting bodies as a medical student. She summoned her courage and shouted, 'Is anyone there?' only to jump, startled, when her voice echoed eerily back towards her.

Shivering she huddled back into the blanket. How long before she froze to death like the corpse alongside her? She held her finger in the air in an attempt to gauge the temperature. It felt below freezing. She tried to recall the statistics she'd studied in college, but already her mind was wandering.

All she could think of was warmth – survival – she had to see Peter again. She simply had to.

'Talk.' Peter was sitting on a kitchen chair he'd placed in front of Lucy and Ally who were standing against the wall of the living room in the flat the paramedics had taken Kelly into.

'Not without a lawyer,' Lucy snapped.

'You've watched too many American TV programmes. It's a solicitor in Britain.' He looked at Dan and Trevor. They'd emptied the girls' bags out onto the floor and were going through the contents.

Trevor opened a large envelope and tipped out the contents.

'Black Daffodil.' He showed them to Peter. Dan checked the numbers and messages on Lucy's phone.

Peter glanced at the pills. 'Too many for personal use. You a dealer, or a manufacturer, Lucy?'

'I'm saying nothing.' She clammed her mouth shut and made a zipping motion.

Trevor shook out Ally's make-up bag, picked up her phone and hit the voicemail button.

'You have one new message ...'

He listened, and listened again. There was no mistaking the caller's voice although he didn't identify himself.

"It's me. I need you and Lucy, now. We have to take the boat out to dump the rubbish. Meet me at the lucky place. It's half past one now. I'm waiting."

Trevor handed the phone to Dan, who listened before handing it to Peter.

'"The lucky place",' Trevor said quietly to Dan. 'Alexander said the deal was going down "in the lucky place".'

Peter listened to the message and looked at Ally. 'Tell me? Where's the lucky place?'

Lucy went wild again, and attacked Ally. 'Don't you say another bloody word,' she threatened in between blows.

Ally held up her arms to defend herself. 'It's no bloody secret, you silly cow. Everyone on the marina knows where it is. It's the stretch where the Darrows' berth their lucky yachts,' she shouted at Peter.

Dan hauled Lucy off Ally and held her fast. 'They have more than one?'

'The biggest, *Lucky Star* belongs to Damian's father. Damian's is *Lucky Me* and they own *Lucky Charm* which they rent out for fishing parties – not that I've seen any fishing whenever I've been out on it. There's huge freezers on board all of them, Damian says to store the catches but all I've ever seen in them is booze.'

'You know Lloyd Jones?' Trevor asked.

'All of us in the parlour do. He lives with Damian.'

'What's the rubbish he has to dump? Quickly,' Peter snapped.

'Say a word and I'll kill you,' Lucy hissed at Ally.

Dan pushed Ally towards the door.

'If there's any killing to be done, I'll do it,' Peter threatened, 'but I go in for torture and disfigurement first.'

'You wouldn't dare,' Lucy hissed. 'You're a copper …'

'All three of us are coppers who have seen our colleagues murdered, maimed, and had limbs removed by gang members over the last two days. And my girlfriend, who I love very much, is missing. Believe me, ladies, there's nothing I wouldn't do to save her pain.'

'Let me make your position clear,' Dan spoke more quickly than he had done in years. 'Both of you were seen murdering Marissa Smith. You have a large quantity of Black Daffodils in your bag, and you were at the party the night Jake Phillips and

Alex Hodges were forcibly injected with Black Daffodil and Jake Phillips was thrown from a balcony. You are both facing life sentences …'

'So there's nothing you can do to us?' Lucy tossed her head defiantly.

'There are prisons and there are prisons,' Trevor said. 'In some, prisoners have to share a cell. How would you like to share with Lucy, Ally …?'

'I'll tell you everything you want to know,' she shouted. 'Just keep me away from her …'

Peter left his chair. 'You can start by telling us where Daisy Sherringham and Andrew Jones are?'

Dan escorted Lucy, still kicking and screaming, out of the room and handed her over to a couple of constables.

'I've never heard of Daisy Sherringham. This was all Lucy's idea. Amber was making a fortune from Black Daffodil …'

'Amber Smith?' Peter stood facing her.

'Amber couldn't afford any Charlie one day and she started mixing things. She'd an A level in chemistry or something. Anyway she made a couple of batches and started selling them on the estate. Made enough to get out of the parlour. Lucy wanted a share, said with her help it would take off. The pills were cheap to make and Amber was selling them for a couple of quid. But Amber told her to sod off; she didn't want to get too big because she was afraid she'd get noticed. Lucy went to Lloyd. He'd do anything for her, and he knows all about special effects, explosions and things. Lucy and Cynara had a regular in the block Amber lived in. Lucy left

Cynara to it, broke into Amber's flat when she was out, stole the pills and formula and left a firebomb Lloyd had made on the door. Lucy said it was supposed to set fire to the flat so Amber wouldn't realise she'd been there and taken anything. I didn't believe her. And some of the pills she took were from a bad batch; so when she sold them on, people died.'

'Why kill Marissa? Trevor asked.

'Lucy didn't see her but she was in Amber's flat when Lucy broke in. Marissa hid. But after she saw Amber die, she phoned Lucy and tried to blackmail her.'

'Lucy and Lloyd have been trying to sell the rights to the drug?' Dan checked.

'Yes.'

'What about the police officers who were undercover and were killed … '

'I don't know anything about that. Lloyd saw to all of that. Him and his uncle. He called him Andy I don't know his other name.'

'I'm not waiting for a warrant. I'm going to those boats,' Peter examined his gun.

'Whatever and whenever it goes down, you two can't be a part of it,' Dan cautioned.

'Yes we can,' Trevor contradicted him.

'You saw that e-mail. If we're following the wrong lead and you're being watched by people Darrow's bought…'

'If we're being watched people will know we're in here.' Trevor looked up as a couple of rookies knocked the door. He turned to Peter. 'We need bigger ones.'

'Bigger what?' Dan was mystified.

'Bigger rookies,' Trevor said decisively. 'We need two constables, officer. Over six feet, thirty-six inch waist, thirty-four inside leg, forty-two chest, preferably with dark hair. Is there anyone like that upstairs?'

'Jack and Tim are the closest to that description,' his colleague answered.

'Tell them to come down here will you, and ask your Super if we can borrow you for a couple of hours. We're about to make a raid.'

'We don't have a warrant yet, Trevor,' Dan cautioned.

'We have suspicion of people trafficking. Remember that Jamaican girl Alfred met in the casino who gave him a sob story – what was her name …'

'Freda,' Peter answered off the top of his head. 'We have reason to believe that she is being held against her will on a boat. If we wait for a warrant, we risk her being moved on and, then we'll be too late.'

Dan sighed. 'You two will be the death of me.'

'But you love us, Inspector Evans,' Peter said. 'You love us – really.'

It had been a long time since Peter and Trevor had worn uniform and, although the sizes were approximate to their own, they were tight.

'Too many five-star steaks and five-star good living,' Dan commented when he saw the buttons straining on both tunics.

'Just in case there is anyone else involved, which I doubt, our alter egos,' Trevor eyed the two constables, who were dressed in their suits, 'stay visibly here with you, walking in front of the windows. Meanwhile, two constables …'

'Trev and Pete,' Peter interrupted.

'Walk out of the door with our uniformed friends and drive to the lucky place and search the yachts for illegal immigrants.'

'You're dealing with Darrow, make sure there's no film of either of you breaking and entering any of those boats,' Dan warned. 'I'll have back-up standing by,' Dan took his cell phone from his pocket and hit speed dial.

Ten minutes later Peter and Trevor left the tower block. They pulled their hats down low over their eyes and followed the two constables to the squad car. They climbed in the back.

'The marina, sir?' the one who'd taken the car keys asked.

'Not, sir, Trev and Pete, we're the same rank as you. And yes, straight to the marina.'

'How do you want to play it?' Trevor asked Peter when they'd parked as close as they could get to the Darrows' yachts.

Peter tapped the driver on the shoulder. 'Names not numbers?'

'I'm Jason, he's Neil.'

'Right, Jason, you and Trev start with *Lucky Star*. You are acting on "information received" relative to people trafficking.'

'Still think the Darrows are involved?' Trevor asked Peter.

'I do. You?'

'No, but we'll soon find out. Neil and I will take a look at Lloyd Jones's new home, *Lucky Me*.' Trevor ran his hand along his shin to check his Glock was in place before he climbed out of the car. He looked at Peter and saw that he was doing the same.

Trevor and Jason walked up the gangplank to Lucky Star. A man walked down to meet them.

'Can I help you, officers?'

Trevor did the talking. 'We've had a complaint.'

'What kind of a complaint.'

'The kind that gives us the right to search the premises.'

'I'm sorry, my orders are to allow no one on board. Mr Darrow …'

'We don't need to see him.'

'I can't allow you to …'

'We have received a report that people are being held on this premises boat ~~their~~ against will. We are duty bound to investigate such reports immediately.'

'I have to telephone the owner.' The man dialled his mobile. Trevor could hear it ringing the other end. A standard voicemail message cut in. Had Dan already arranged for the Darrows to be picked up? He pushed past and walked on deck.

'You take the rooms on the right, I'll take the rooms on the left,' Trevor ordered Jason. If you see any young women enquire if they are being held against their will.'

274

'You can't do that.' The man ran up to Trevor.

'Stay on deck. Otherwise I may be forced to arrest you for obstructing an officer during the course of his duties,' Trevor ordered.

After he and Jason searched the cabins, they searched the engine room, heads and galley. Remembering that Ally had mentioned a walk-in freezer, he opened the door. It was stacked high with crates of vodka and frozen food.

'Hold the door, Jason.'

'Yes ... Trev.'

Trevor stepped inside and shivered. Move the crates and it was big enough to hold a couple of people. He only hoped Daisy hadn't ended up in here. And Andrew? What did he hope for Andrew?

That Ally had been lying?

He knew she hadn't been.

CHAPTER NINETEEN

Trevor was returning to the deck when his phone rang.

'We've cuffed Lloyd Jones to the wheel. I might have found something.'

'I'm there.' Trevor switched off the phone and turned to Jason. 'I'm joining Peter. Handcuff our friend to the wheel. Stay with him.' Trevor looked at the deck of *Lucky Me*. It didn't seem so far. He almost jumped it before thinking of his age – and his son.

As Trevor approached the cabin of *Lucky Me*, Peter held out an earring. 'I found it in here.' He pushed an empty water barrel towards Trevor. 'Daisy wears earrings.'

'But you don't know if that's hers because you never notice them,' Trevor suggested.

'They're earrings, not suspects. Daisy always looks great to me.'

Trevor took a closer look at the piece of jewellery. 'It's Daisy's.'

'How do you know?' Peter asked suspiciously.

'It's hand-made, the beads are antique. I was with Lyn when she bought two pairs at an antique fair. One pair for herself and one for Daisy. She gave them to Daisy on her last birthday. That's what you do when you marry. You notice what your wife wears.'

Peter looked down into the barrel. 'If they dumped her in there – she must have been bloody terrified. If they threw her overboard …'

'They wouldn't have while they were berthed. You've searched the boat?'

'Yes.'

'The galley?'

'Yes.'

'The freezer?'

'I looked inside.'

Trevor ran into the galley and pulled down the lever that locked the freezer. Like *Lucky Star* there were crates of vodka, and frozen food. He stepped inside and peered behind the crates.

Just like on Andrew's, frost had formed on Daisy's eyebrows and lashes. Their skins were paler than porcelain. But the frost on Andrew's face was thicker than on Daisy's.

'Call an ambulance!'

Peter stepped behind him. 'Oh Christ.' He fell to his knees.

'There's a pulse. Faint but there,' Trevor moved his fingers from Daisy's neck. 'I can't take her out. You have to be careful with hypothermia. Bring victims round too quickly and they won't survive. The ambulance crew will know what to do.'

Peter and Trevor followed the paramedics off the boat. Dan and Bill were waiting for them on the dockside.

'Daisy?' Dan asked.

'Touch and go, but she's a fighter.' Like Peter, Trevor didn't want to believe she could die.

'Andrew?' Bill asked.

'Dead and I'm not sorry,' Peter snapped. 'It takes a dirty worm to turn on his own kind.' His eyes were dark.

Jason and Neil were escorting Lloyd Jones and Darrow's man into the back of a police van.

'I didn't hurt my uncle or the woman,' Lloyd shouted at the uniformed officers. 'I couldn't. That's why I put them in the freezer. I had no choice.'

Bill walked over to him. 'Go on.'

'I had to take her to make you call off the investigation. My uncle planned it but he changed his mind. He was going to tell you everything. All Lucy wanted to do was stop your investigation long enough to sell the formula. We were going to take the money and go abroad. Start a new life together. Lucy had it all planned. We were going to the Med …'

'You saying that Andrew Jones was going to tell us that he had leaked the identities of undercover police officers to the criminal gangs they'd infiltrated?'

'Yes. He told me he didn't think they'd kill them. Just stop working with them. When they were murdered, he panicked. Lucy and I couldn't let him go to you just because he got cold feet …'

'Bad choice of words, boy.' Bill returned to where Dan, Trevor and Peter were standing.

Trevor remembered how upset Andrew had been when he'd heard about Alfred, Lee and the others. It all made sense – now. 'The Darrows?' Trevor asked Dan.

'Looks like they had nothing to do with it. But that won't stop us impounding their yachts – for a while.'

* * *

It was quiet in the hospital waiting room. Still in uniform, the buttons of their tunics undone, Trevor and Peter sat side by side, listening to the doctor's footsteps echo down the corridor.

'She's going to make it.' Peter repeated the doctor's words as if he couldn't believe them.

Trevor looked up as Bill entered.

'Did I hear you say what I thought you said?' Bill asked.

Peter rose to his feet. He couldn't trust himself to speak so he nodded.

Trevor patted his pockets and found the key he was looking for.

'You win some, you lose some,' Bill said quietly.

'Don't expect me to cry over Andrew Jones. No copper should sell out another, not even for a share of fifty million quid,' Peter said bitterly.

'I wasn't talking about Andrew. Jake Phillips's – or rather Evans's – life-support system has just been switched off. Dan's with his mother now.'

Peter blinked hard. 'Tell Dan I'm sorry. Really sorry.'

If Bill hadn't known Peter better, he might have thought Peter was fighting back tears. 'Jake was the first one Andrew shopped. When Lloyd contacted Andrew with Lucy's "get rich quick on Black Daffodil scheme", Andrew ran a check on undercover officers working in the area.'

'How?' Trevor demanded. 'Andrew wouldn't have had clearance.'

'According to Lloyd, who couldn't get the full story out quick enough after we told him there might be a chance he'd get a lighter sentence if he came clean and co-operated, Andrew tricked the monitoring office. Rang them and said a call had come into our station from an officer in trouble. The stupid bloody clerk asked Andrew for his number so he could check it out. When he found out it was from a station, he rang Andrew back and told him there was only one undercover officer working on the Bay and gave him Jake's ID. Lloyd said that after he and Lucy approached Andrew, his uncle came up with the idea for the auction. But none of them made allowances for the contaminated pills in Amber's flat. Chances are Amber Smith knew they weren't right. But Marissa and Lucy didn't. Marissa saw Lucy break into Amber's flat and steal the pills and formula. Marissa hid, took the Black Daffodil Lucy had left and managed to get out after the blast killed her sister. Marissa sold the pills on the estate and Lucy dished them out at Damian Darrow's party. That's when we came in. Andrew must have been delighted when Dan offered him a chance to work undercover. But, Lloyd said Andrew changed his mind when Alfred, Michael and Maria were killed and Lee and his wife disappeared. He rang Lloyd and told him he was going to turn himself in. Lucy had other ideas. There was no way she was going to give up fifty million quid. She may look pretty but she was the brawn of the operation.'

'After being massaged by her, I can believe it.' Trevor recalled her muscle-roped legs and arms.

'Lloyd's insisting he was completely under her spell. He's trying to convince everyone that Lucy all but hypnotized him into helping her throw Jake off the balcony, and kidnap Daisy after teaching him the moves that enabled him to do it. According to Lloyd she kidnapped Andrew by herself. Enticed him into her car then killed him with a karate chop to the neck. I don't entirely buy Lloyd's "I was under Lucy's evil influence version" but we'll know how much truth there is in his story after Andrew's post-mortem.'

'And Ally?' Peter asked.

'In Ally's own words, she's Lucy's lover, accomplice and paid heavy,' Bill said. 'As you mentioned, Peter, equality in all things, even crime.'

'Lee and his wife?' Trevor asked.

'Two heads were found floating in the Bay this afternoon. Man and woman, both Chinese. The locals are looking into it and hoping to find more body parts, but you know the Triads. Anyone who talks will get the same treatment as Lee. The case will remain open.'

'And never closed.' Peter turned towards the ward.

'If Daisy's awake, give her my apologies for our screw-up,' Bill called after him.

'And my love.' Trevor left his chair.

'Where you off to?' Bill asked Trevor.

'To hire a taxi to take me to the estate to pick up the car. You'll make sure the gangs know the case is closed, that there's no Black Daffodil to fight over any more?'

'Already done. You'll be back in an hour or so to sort out the paperwork?' Bill checked.

'I'm going to Cornwall.'

'The paperwork ...'

'You do it so well.'

'Trevor, you can't take the Maserati to Cornwall, it costs a fortune to rent and you're in uniform …'

'I've split the seams. Put it down as expenses and buy the owner a new one.' Trevor held out his hand. 'Can I borrow thirty quid? I left my wallet in my suit. The taxi will cost at least ten and Peter paid a couple of kids to look after the car. We were away longer than we expected. They deserve a bonus.'